if the tongue

fits

Diane Brown

TANDEM PRESS

First published in 1999 by
TANDEM PRESS
2 Rugby Road
Birkenhead, Auckland 10
NEW ZEALAND

Copyright © 1999 Diane Brown

ISBN 1 877178 47 0

All rights reserved. No part of this publication may be reproduced, stored in a retrieval system or transmitted in any form or by any means, electronic, mechanical, photocopying, recording or otherwise without the prior written permission of the publishers.

The publishers gratefully acknowledge the assistance of Creative New Zealand in the production of this book.

The publishers also acknowledge the assistance of Buddle Findlay who sponsored Diane Brown to write this book as the 1997 Buddle Findlay Sargeson Fellow.

Grateful acknowledgement is made to WW Norton & Company Inc, New York for the Adrienne Rich poem 'Translations' from *Diving Into the Wreck*, 1973.

Cover design by Christine Hansen
Text design and production by M & F Whild Typesetting Services, Auckland
Printed in New Zealand by Publishing Press Limited

For all my women friends

Acknowledgements

This novel was begun in 1997 with the assistance of a Buddle Findlay Sargeson Fellowship and completed in 1998 with the assistance of a grant from Creative New Zealand.

My grateful thanks to Helen Benton and Bob Ross for their enthusiasm and support and to Jane Parkin for her editing skills and insight.

I also owe a great deal to all my friends, especially Elizabeth Allen and Wensley Willcox who offered valuable criticism and support and to Beverly Reynolds, Sue Fitchett, Judith White and Chris Young, who spent endless hours cheerfully discussing the issues raised in this novel.

part one

~ cocktail conversation ~

This art salesman at the bar, plying my friend Moppy with Tequila Sunrises, could become her lover. He is wearing a heavy gold chain around his neck. I entertain myself, pretending I am a woman of potential, weaving urban myths and personal history into matted anecdotes. Our friend, or perhaps more accurately Moppy's friend, Jill, has already left. Her husband requires her to be home by midnight. There is no one waiting for Moppy or me.

'Do you believe in arranged marriages?' I ask the salesman.

The wedding should have been perfect. The bride and groom beautifully matched. Perhaps it was the memory of the steak eaten at the stag do, perhaps it was the lack of breakfast, but whatever the reason the groom couldn't wait. Taking one look at his bride, he sank his teeth into her breast. The blood dripped over the bouquet of yellow roses; the guests carried on eating. They were Siberian tigers, but even so.

The salesman does not answer my question. He is waiting to dissect us with his own. 'What's wrong with you? Why have you never married?' he asks me. Turning to Moppy, he says, 'Why did your husband leave you? Why aren't you like her?' He is referring to Jill. She is his type. Slinky and quiet. 'She knows a good thing or two. How to hang on to her man.'

The rose outside my writing room is pale pink and has no relation at all to this conversation, except that I think of roses as I nod my head in a parody of consciousness. Moppy is wet with dew and slippery enough. She says, 'I needed a change of colour in the garden but my husband was always complaining that I was never in the same place twice. I gave him away to the first woman who walked past and went back to pruning the roses.'

'Do you know you must cut on an angle, above an outward-gazing eye?' I ask, knowing Moppy never prunes the tangled bush of old-fashioned roses in her garden which nevertheless rewards her every spring with an abundance of sweetly scented white blossoms.

~ licking is not a sign of love ~

Moppy is not yet reconciled to being single. She has had more than two decades of male attention. More than four if you count her father. She is an only daughter with three older brothers. Having a male always focused on her has been taken for granted. As reliable as roses. In a novel she reads of an eighty-one-year-old woman who never heard anyone say to her, 'I love you.' Such an absence has been foreign to Moppy, until recently.

Our generation is possibly the last to grow up believing that acquiring a man of your own means an end to the heavy work of decision-making and makes sense of all those forbidden itches 'down there'. Despite all the books on feminism there is still a gap between the theory and the solidity of a man sleeping next to you. Jill reckons Moppy wouldn't feel like this if she felt complete in herself, but Jill lives with a rich man in a very expensive house.

However you look at it, Moppy is not a woman to stay home alone on a Saturday night eating bean sprouts. Back in the '70s she would have dressed in her shortest mini and gone to the nearest pick-up bar. Tonight she casts a critical eye in her dressing-table mirror before she heads for the video shop. Holding her head to one side as if she is considering her man at home, she picks *Sleepless in Seattle*. Perfect for a sad drizzly night. Moppy has not yet realised you can go to church barefoot these days. No one notices. They are too consumed with their own images.

The heroine in *Sleepless in Seattle* falls in love with a voice on the radio, although she already has a respectable fiancé. Mind you, the fiancé is allergic to strawberries so there goes the possibility of picnics in the park. The hero is played by Tom Hanks. He has no known allergies. Meg Ryan is the heroine who gets to meet Tom in the Empire State Building, one minute before it closes. They walk out holding hands.

If I was there, I would shrug my shoulders, meaning, 'This sort of timing only happens in the movies.' As it happens I am at a man's flat. He is cooking dinner for me and serving it on a table dressed with candles and flowers, although one cannot assume this means he has seduction in mind. The flowers are carnations, not roses. He is an intellectual and ten years younger. 'Watch out for my cat's tail,' he says. 'Licking is not a sign of love.' His voice is soft, at odds with the words.

~ column casting ~

Moppy puts the video in the machine, turns off the light, then positions herself on the couch with chocolate and wine, sauvignon blanc in a blue glass from Mexico. She drapes her pale mauve hand-made rug over her legs. It's a little cold for January. She is wearing electric-blue silk pyjamas. You might imagine she has everything a woman could wish for. Except that the pyjamas are imitation silk, twenty dollars from Deka, and Moppy is alone. Her sons, Sam and Thomas, are at her ex-husband's for the weekend. Tim has moved in with a widow, Wendy, who has three children. They call themselves The Brady Bunch 2.

Moppy instantly identifies with Meg Ryan. The seductive power of the voice on the radio tightens her groin. If it's all right for Meg Ryan, is it all right for her? She opens the newspaper and starts scanning the long list of possibilities. It's only nine o'clock and the video is finished. To convince herself she is merely curious, she tries the erotic poetry line first. A woman's syrupy voice talks about a man doing the deed then withdrawing. It would be more erotic if the voice didn't try so hard, thinks Moppy.

Under the 'Men Seeking Women' column are about fifty messages. Most looking for someone younger, slimmer but not brighter than themselves. As a matter of principle Moppy ignores any seeking the slim and any mentioning sports. She is especially proud of her passionate hatred of sports. Anyone who mentions a love of the theatre or arts gets a tick. She selects six and keys in the numbers. Most of the voices are hesitant, as if reluctant to give too much away: 'Leave your number if you like my voice.' Some contain a slight innuendo: 'I'm a big boy, you know what I mean.' One or two seem more generous – a faint trace of gold beneath the everyday conversation – but it is difficult to avoid the nuance of shame on both sides. The suspicion that each possesses some secret defect which may or may not be discovered before it is too late. Why else would one be advertising or replying?

'I'm looking for a strong woman,' says Keith. 'One who knows what she wants and doesn't need a man to tell her what to do.' Moppy draws a double ring around his ad. She dials the number, listens to the prompts, starts, 'It's Moppy here,' then realises she should use the name on her birth certificate. She hangs up and starts again, hoping she'll be able to afford the phone bill. She gets the giggles. It takes three goes to get it right or near enough. 'Hi. My name is Margaret. I haven't done this before so I'm not sure what to say. I'm looking for a man who is not afraid to be tender, not the usual rugby, racing and beer type.' She leaves her phone number. As she puts the phone down, she remembers she forgot to say she is an artist with a liking for movies and cooking. Italian in particular.

Putting the rubbish out later, Moppy discovers a small piece of driftwood at the back door. It's bleached white, almost a mermaid shape, Moppy concludes, running her hand over the tail. There's also a piece of blue paper underneath it. A poem of sorts:

> *this sea is alive with eels*
> *their thin black bodies*
> *casting mermaids*
> *neat on the rocks*

In the lounge of her old extended bach she has fixed a large piece of netting against one wall. Collaborative art, she calls it. Anyone can hang found pieces on it. She got the idea from a film. It saves on wallpaper. Moppy hangs the driftwood at the top, then stands back to admire. She pins the poem up too, wishing that the writer had given more thought to the paper and to the formation of the letters. Still, she takes things as they come, as her due, and she likes the way the hanging adjusts to each new addition.

~ he offers flowers and a trip to Paris ~

If Saturday nights are lonely, Sundays are worse. Reading the paper can't be made to last the whole day, and Moppy has noticed a faint irritation in the voices of married friends she rings. Doesn't she know how lucky she is not having the kids on the weekend? Thank goodness for the likes of Jill who actually enjoys shopping in the flea market.

The crowds are soothing for Moppy. Many look poorer than herself, and imagination is free. 'We could be anywhere,' Moppy says, 'Paris, Rome, or Spain.' But every week Asia is becoming more prevalent in the faces, the smells, the vegetables. In the middle an old man plays a saw with a violin bow to the accompaniment of a tape. The music is melancholic, of another age, but the man is smiling.

'What do you think of these?' Jill asks, holding up a small gilt-painted angel. 'I think I might buy three for my bathroom wall. They're only ten dollars each.'

'Fine,' says Moppy. These days she sometimes wishes she was back in West Auckland where poverty is more acceptable. Her part-time job in Just Art Books, occasional art tutoring and Tim's maintenance give her enough for essentials but not enough for angels.

'No,' says Jill. 'Robert would have a fit. He'd say they were too kitsch.'

'So what does he say about your op shop bargains?'

Though Jill's blonde hair is sleek and well cut she is wearing her flea market outfit, a long voile sun-dress made in India. Robert hates it.

'I haven't told him. I always pretend any new clothes are just that, brand new.'

'You're crazy. If I had your money I'd be buying designer clothes.'

'If Robert had his way I'd look like a Remuera wife. And have to act like one.'

'Flowers for a beautiful lady,' a stall holder calls out. He is holding a bunch of white Christmas lilies. 'Only three dollars.'

'Why not?' says Moppy, though she knows the lilies drop pollen and stain rimu tables. 'He reminds me of this Israeli boyfriend I had in England. He was a bit of a shark but incredibly sexy.' She sighs. Speaks a little louder. 'Such a long time since anyone sent me flowers. It's time I found a lover.'

'Have me, I'm single,' the flower seller says.

Moppy laughs. 'Only if you promise to take me to Paris for the weekend.'

'For you, beautiful lady, anything.'

A small girl comes running up.

'Daddy, Daddy, look,' she says, 'Mummy bought me an ice cream.'

Daddy has the good grace to look ashamed. 'Forgive me, madam,' he says, bowing low. 'A minor lapse of memory.'

Moppy does forgive him, for he has made her laugh and sometimes she wonders if she will ever giggle uncontrollably again.

~ like lovers after the act ~

The cat-owning intellectual did not make me laugh. He wanted to know if I still dreamt and was I happy? I told him I had given up all possibility of love at first sight. I keep my eyes shut in populated rooms and on crowded buses. Focus on the internal colour and running words. Unlike Moppy, I was always shy in dance-floor conversations.

I'd forgotten the details of intimate dinners but I had come armed with a poem. 'Not a love poem,' I said. I did not want to scare him and I was uncertain of the meaning of his hugs. Simply an act of friendship, he said. He was sexually attracted to me, he added, but he was not sure I was the woman for him. His hands couldn't encircle my wrist and he'd have trouble carrying me over the threshold.

Nevertheless we lay on the couch, like lovers after the act, he said, stroking my hair, imparting the lightest possible touch of desire. My tongue was stumbling over the hard shapes. He wanted a woman to bear his child. Preferably a fellow academic.

My womb has been removed. A flat useless barnacle-encrusted piece. It was never plump, overflowing with all the usual things a woman keeps in her handbag.

~ unwelcome childlessness and attention ~

'Do you regret not having children?' Moppy asks Jill as they are walking to Navona's laden down with vegetables. She's asked me the same question, not realising that children and the lack of belong often in some secret compartment of the heart, never talked of but always present in their absence. Jill closes the door on her private bereavement by displaying a dislike of all children.

'Don't be stupid.'

'You're so cynical. Look at the baby over there.' He is wearing matching multi-coloured felt hat and slippers and sitting in a three-wheeled buggy. The kind that parents who have the time and energy for running own. 'Isn't he gorgeous? Reminds me of Sam.'

'Yeah,' Jill says, 'but does he look so cute at four in the morning? Anyway,

I've got two part-timers. That's enough. I know when I'm well off.'

'Do you?' asks Moppy.

Before he married Jill, Robert had a vasectomy. He told her after the marriage.

'Won't need these any more, darling,' he said, throwing her pills out of the hotel window. 'This is my present for you. Just the two of us from now on.'

Jill told Moppy it was a mutual decision. Robert told Moppy differently one drunken night shortly after Tim had left. He'd called in on her with two bottles of a 'good French'. The wine and Moppy's loneliness conspired. By the time she sobered up it was too late.

'Don't worry, you won't get pregnant,' Robert said. 'Best thing ever for a man. They're not meant to be monogamous. Jill was bloody angry when I told her. She threw a glass of champagne in my face. She's forgiven me of course. Always does. Loves me to death.'

Moppy has persuaded herself she must have exaggerated the episode with Robert. Unlike Paula Jones she can't remember the exact size and shape of his penis. Perhaps presidents are different.

'Robert still working hard?' asks Moppy.

'Of course. Someone's got to support our extravagant lifestyle, he always says. But I've got stroppy now and have insisted he comes home early the night his kids are there. If they're not, it's usually after midnight. It's not much different than being single.'

'Well you're welcome any time to join the ranks of the disaffected wives,' says Moppy. 'It's not as if you've got kids holding you down.'

But they do. Twins Emma and Georgia affect a constant hatred. They stand in the hall with angelic faces, hiding pins behind their backs. As Jill walks past, their hands dart out. Snakes' tongues. Anonymously, they ring her up from their mother's place and blow raspberries down the phone. Knowing Jill is a gourmet cook, nauseous at the sight of sausages and tomato sauce, they refuse to eat anything that has the slightest hint of sophistication. Their trump card: tinned spaghetti sucked noisily through the gaps in their teeth.

'I know, but really we do get on most of the time. You know the good-enough relationship. And I like being married. The security of it.'

'Personally I don't think it's worth it. Despite the loneliness and my panic attacks, I never regret Tim leaving.'

'I don't know. Overseas trips every year. There are advantages. And I'm not getting younger. No one whistles at me any more.'

'No one whistles at anyone any more. It's sexual harassment.'

'I don't believe in it,' says Jill.

Moppy raises her eyes.

Robert's a prime practitioner. Even Jill's ears have picked up the odd whisper. He's known to have hands that linger a little too long on the shoulders of the pretty, when they come to his office distressed. There's no end of problems for a handsome and empathetic man like Robert to solve.

'There'll come a time,' says Moppy, 'when women will stop falling for it. When his stomach starts hanging over.'

'I don't know. Born a charmer, always a charmer. It runs in the family. His father's had four wives and I don't know how many mistresses. Anyway, you're just jealous. You could do with a rich man of your own. Then you'd have time for art.'

'Ha. What rich man would choose an artist? Trouble-makers and messy.'

'That's true. Robert would never allow you to hang a net on his wall.'

'Don't worry, he'll never get an invitation. Anyway, I don't have the poker face required for mistresses.'

~ Italians are experts on salads and love ~

In the spring Moppy always buys basil at the flea market. Later she might invite me around to eat tomato and mozzarella cheese salad, though it's a fatal combination. Chopping basil with a large chef's knife releases spicy memories. The two of us licking gelatos in the Piazza Navona. Watching beautiful young men watching us. A naked man stepping from behind a tree. The midnight air in Rome is responsible for many illusions.

A large crowd gathered around a woman sketching a portrait. All for the price of a bowl of spaghetti. The lips are the wrong shape but the artist has captured Moppy's eyes. It is late, and the eyes are weary and wary. Back in the suburbs, in Torbay, Moppy runs her fingers down her face on the wall. Her lips are covered in dust but are still parted in anticipation. She remembers the waiter taking down the details. His eye unfastening her blouse. The stranger on the bus cupping his palm over her breast.

The magazine literary editor asks me to write about sex. I tell her that is not my speciality; cookbooks are more in my line. I can still taste in my mouth a meal I ate in Rome fifteen years ago. Antipasta, risotto, calamari, insalata, zabaglione, gorgonzola, even the powdery liquid of the digestive between courses. As for the man who took me, the taste of his tongue has not been filed away for future reference.

Actually I lie about the cookbooks. Cooking is not my favourite occupation. It doesn't seem worth it for one person. The truth is I eat anything and everything, whatever comes my way. It's the same with writing. I like the idea of randomness, of using what is in front of you rather than planning. In this regard Moppy and I are quite similar. She's kinaesthetic, touching everything she gets her hands on. Observe the way she holds a wine glass. Her fingers stroking it up and down, sensuously. I'm more verbal, on paper at least, but we share the collector mentality. In the fourth form the three of us read *The Collector* by John Fowles. Jill couldn't finish it, but Moppy and I were equally appalled and thrilled. Is this how I justify stealing her story?

Cafe Navona in Takapuna is not Michelangelo country. The heat is humid rather than dry but the name is reminiscent. Jill was surprised when I rang up to invite her to coffee without Moppy, but she turned up all the same. After all I'm a name she can drop in her book club. 'I went to school with Barbara Ballard. We're still friends, but she's changed, got awfully big, since those days. She's very funny, you know. A bit of a recluse but we have a laugh.'

~ a collector of men ~

When she gets back from the flea market the red light is flashing on Moppy's answering machine. It's a legacy of Tim's but a lifesaver for Moppy. Ever since childhood she has been terrified of missing out on anything. She blames this anxiety on the experience of never being picked to play basketball. On account of being called butterfingers.

'Hullo Margaret,' the voice says, 'Keith here. You have a lovely voice. I'm definitely the one you're looking for.'

Moppy is not so sure. She doesn't like men who assume. It's the thought of spending her next free Saturday night alone that motivates her fingers into returning his call. She talks in fast nervous mode.

'I teach art sometimes at night school and I work three hours a morning in Just Art Books and I've got two kids, Sam's just turned eleven and Thomas is nine. When I get time I like to collect.'

'Really. What do you collect?'

'Men.' She laughs.

Keith says nothing.

'Just kidding,' she says. 'I'm into driftwood and shells. I like making sculptures. Kind of weird and witchlike.' She laughs again.

Keith says, 'I like the idea of a witch. Have you long dark hair?'

A bolt of lightning suddenly appears in the room.

'Of course, but auburn not black. It's curly and out of control.'

The punctuation of thunder adds to Keith's excitement.

'You're a powerful woman,' he says, 'I can tell.'

She's disappointed when he reveals he is a real estate salesman. She doesn't believe they have anything in common. Keith is insistent they meet. She agrees to a coffee in Shore City on Thursday after work. At heart, Moppy is still an only daughter, anxious to please. Men in particular.

'How will I know you?' she asks.

'Easy,' he says, 'I'll recognise you. You've already told me you've got long dark hair and are no doubt beautiful, and besides I'll be carrying flowers.'

Moppy giggles.

She is beautiful, but if Moppy ever knew it she has long since forgotten, just as she has forgotten the time when Tim constantly yearned to caress her skin. Possibly a throw-back to Spanish blood, a palmist once told her. 'Only the Spanish have such hairless olive skin.' Usually, she doesn't believe the compliments regarding her dark blue eyes, curly auburn hair and long slim legs, but after the palmist she did take up Spanish dancing and was a hit at parties. She had a red flounced skirt. But that was before the children and her expanded waist. The skirt has been forgotten. It's in the dress-up box under Thomas's bed, its hem ripped.

Navona's is busy as usual. Moppy and Jill like the tables outside, the slice of sea between buildings, and the lemon cream-cheese muffins.

'I'll save a table,' says Moppy, 'and look after the bags.'

'Cappuccino?'

'Please.'

'This man Keith,' asks Jill, 'did he say what he does?'

'I don't know,' says Moppy. 'All I've got to go on was the recorded sound of his voice and I liked it. You can tell a lot from a voice.' She scoops up the froth and sips it.

'Remains to be seen,' says Jill, 'but if you do meet him, for God's sake go somewhere public and don't tell him where you live or what your surname is.'

'Oh don't be so suspicious. Not every man is a rapist.'

~ hawks and roses in the shopping mall ~

Keith carries a bunch of red roses and is scrubbed up well in that real estate way. Short well-cut curly grey hair, the kind she likes, a trimmed moustache, the kind she doesn't, navy blue jacket and grey trousers. Words come easy out of his mouth.

'All my dreams come true,' he says, looking at Moppy as if she is the cottage at the end of a rose-lined pathway. They sit down amongst the afternoon shoppers, tired mothers mostly and a few unemployed trying to make a coffee last an hour.

'So what are you looking for?' he asks.

'I'd like a house on the cliff, four bedrooms and a spa bath in my ensuite please, and I don't want to pay more than a hundred thousand.'

'In a man?'

'I'm looking for intelligence, devotion and a sense of humour.' Which she doubts he has.

'I bet you don't let a man push you around.'

'I have my own opinions. And I'd never put up with violence.'

'Good. Good. I think we could do business together. You and me could go places. You know what I mean? And what about me? Do I suit you?'

'How do you know what you want till you find it? But I know what I don't want. I don't want a husband. I keep losing them. They're like umbrellas – handy on a rainy day, but once the sun comes out you leave them somewhere and, before you know it, someone else has picked them up.'

She's practised this. It works.

'You're the woman for me, all right.'

Moppy looks into his light blue eyes which are strangely opaque. It's not reciprocal. He hasn't looked under the house yet. For all he knows there could be dry rot.

'But you don't know me,' she says. 'I have sharp fingernails.'

'Great,' Keith says, 'the sharper the better.'

'Have you done this before?' asks Moppy.

'Yeah,' says Keith. 'I talked to this woman over the phone. She was really spunky. Sent me a poem about hawks. I was fascinated but she never turned up for our meeting. Never mind, it was meant. Everything comes to those who wait. It's what I keep telling my clients. Now, when can we see each other again?'

'I'm not sure. It depends on my ex. When he's having the kids next.'

Back at home Moppy throws out Keith's roses, cut too soon and already drooping. In her blue Mexican jug she arranges the crimson hydrangeas she found on her doorstep, along with another poem.

a nimble fingered
salesman
spreads a bolt
of crimson water-silk
over the sea

and I think of you

Moppy jumps when the phone rings. She does not answer but stands next to it, listening.

'Hullo Queen Margaret. It is your loyal subject Keith here, wanting to arrange an assignation with humiliation, sharp nails lashing my skin, caustic tongue whipping the heart within.'

Jill screams when Moppy gives her report. 'Oh my God. What a weirdo. You didn't tell him where you lived, did you?'

'No.'

'Well you're not going to answer, are you?'

'No. Give me some credit. Mind you, at least he's original. He may have been joking. Or he may have some sexual problems.'

'Sexual problems!' Jill screams again.

'I must get a book on this sort of thing,' Moppy says. 'Perhaps I could make a living at it.'

'Don't you dare,' says Jill.

'No, I'm only joking. I can't imagine me standing with a whip. I can't even slap the kids.'

Who knows why Moppy does not tell Jill about the flowers and the poems. Surely she doesn't think they come from Robert?

~ amongst critics and murderers ~

Like Moppy I have two jobs, one teaching English as a second language, the other in a prison, supposedly teaching writing. More often we discuss love and other pressing issues. Often I wonder how my pupils will make it back in the other world where nothing is so enclosed, where a magpie or a hawk can suddenly swoop down on you.

The intellectual borrowed my car for a journey to another city. He came back, elated. When I picked up my car, I could smell the woman of his dreams, a musky blend that made me sneeze. He insisted on telling me the details. She possessed a Pre-Raphaelite face, a PhD and a car of her own. Even the parsley in her garden was thick and lush. And though he was a paid-up member of the Sceptics' Society he believed his mother's dictum that only the fertile can grow parsley. 'There's none in your garden is there?' he asked. He thought it wise not to send me an invitation to his wedding.

And there was Moppy blithely stepping into the shopping mall like she had never heard of magpies or hawks or that anyone who confessed to liking witches was to be avoided. If she had discussed Keith with me I might have said stay away.

After an unanticipated lonely winter I too resorted to the newspaper columns, putting my own ad in. *Rubensesque woman, would like to lie on your couch and entertain you with wit and wisdom.* The response was large enough to keep me busy for weeks. I flirted with the applicants, who sat uneasily laughing on the edge of their seats. None possessed the ability to entertain me. None rang me back. Perhaps I was too much of a good thing. Over the phone this man Keith told me he loved my caustic tongue. He sounded very excited, but by this time I had realised the necessity for cunning. From my lair, behind the fountain, I took one look at his face, grey round the edges, and decided he was not fresh enough.

My favourite pupil, Mati, laughed like a drain when I read my snide anti-intellectual poem.

'I wouldn't want to come across you in the middle of a burglary,' he said. 'I'm sure you could murder someone with your pen.'

And he should know.

~ having it out with a mallet ~

Moppy escapes the thought of Keith by taking Sam and Thomas camping for a week in the summer holidays. It's a ritual event but this is the first year that Tim hasn't come. Moppy is relieved that she won't have to put up with the usual comments about Tim's snoring and unrelenting negativity from her old still-coupled friends, Jill and Robert, Amanda and Ross, Grant and Mary, but she is also worried. So worried she invites me for a few days. With two cars we can avoid the need for a trailer, and Moppy thinks my arms will have no trouble slamming in pegs.

I agree, purely for the opportunity of lying awake in the tent giggling with Moppy like we used to when we went camping with her parents, Iris and Jack. Particularly the year our breasts began developing. Pulling up our tops to compare. Being chased around the campsite by a group of spotty boys.

The women aren't there when we arrive a couple of days after the others. They have taken themselves off to the local craft shops for a bit of retail therapy. The men are in charge of the kids and keeping the beer cold. They watch with amusement while Moppy and I try to sort out the poles.

'Just think,' I say when Moppy looks as if she's going to cry. 'We can snort and fart all night and I've brought a box of chocolates.'

Moppy gives me a half smile and hands me a bottle of suncream. 'Do you mind?' she says.

I don't, but I get the impression she prefers the fingers of men.

'Want a hand?' Robert calls when we finally figure out the tent construction.

'Yes,' says Moppy, taking no notice of my frowning.

'Told you, you couldn't live without us,' says Robert.

'So why didn't you leave us a bit of shade?' I ask. Their tents all face towards each other and are under the trees.

'We thought you girls would like some privacy, just in case you manage to get lucky on a dark night.'

'I shouldn't think so,' I say. 'Seems to me there's only social retards around here.'

Ross saunters up. He's another lawyer but he's a little more civilised than Robert. He's been swimming and looks genuinely pleased to see us. I'd forgotten he always had a soft spot for Moppy.

'I'm here if you need me,' he says, 'for sunscreen or peg-bashing or if Robert gets too obnoxious.'

'So what do you think about this place?' Moppy asks when we're tucked up at night, me on the airbed and Moppy on the stretcher.

I can't deny it's beautiful. The wildness, the beach, the bush walks, and at night the clear sky and the stars we don't get to see in the city. I guess when I go home I'll write some poems, but I don't say any of this to Moppy. Although we once were both frustrated office workers in government departments and then discovered freedom and Europe together, in the past twelve years or so our lives have taken different directions – in her case children and husband, in mine, retreat and writing.

'I don't understand why you persist in camping with them,' I say. 'It seems to me that you have nothing in common any more, if you ever did. Honestly, that bitch Amanda, the way she said, "How's your sex life Moppy? Are you getting any yet?" And then the way that they all muck in together for meals and exclude you. Is it me?'

'No, they've always been like that. Mind you, I think that's my role. The outsider. Even when Tim used to come they were like that. He never fitted in either. It's like I threaten their perfect marriages. Not because I might pinch their husband but because I reveal the awful possibility. The truth of things.'

'Like that Japanese pupil I had who told me she was born in a bad luck year. She reckoned that outsiders and scapegoats provide the salt for the steadiness of human relations. A teaspoon of salt for a sweeter taste. I wrote a poem about her.'

'Yeah, I remember it. But maybe it's not their fault. I'm just not interested in houses or making money. I come for the kids. Sam and Thomas really love camping. And all the kids get on well. Sam knows I get upset sometimes. He's very perceptive really. He said to me, "You wouldn't want to be like them anyway." I guess he means smug.'

'I'm surprised Jill and Robert haven't got a beach house at Pauanui.'

'Yeah, but Jill has a desire to confound the stereotypes. Besides, Georgia and Emma aren't so bad with the other kids around, and she likes the company. I think she's quite lonely.'

'Is she?'

I keep my knowledge to myself. I don't think Moppy would like the idea of me meeting Jill alone. It springs back to school days. She's always been the mediator.

'She's a reverse snob.' I say. 'Fancy shopping in op shops. Robert must be earning $300,000 a year. Just like when she was at school and reckoned her father was a milkman instead of a doctor.'

'No, she shops in an op shop because it's a way of keeping some sort of control. Asserting her individuality. The house is all Robert's taste. Completely minimalist.'

'Maybe you're right. I can never figure her out.'

'I think she's scared of you.'

'Scared?'

'Of your independence from men. Boy, the way you spoke to Robert. "Social retard." He was shocked.'

That's it, we're off, giggling. Half an hour later Robert comes over to tell us to shut up. We laugh even more then.

'Would you like to join us?' I ask.

'Not bloody likely,' he says.

~ walking the ecology trail ~

In the morning, the sky is overcast. A good day for a walk, we decide. Only the women and children go. The men prefer running. Ross shrugs his shoulders. I get the feeling he'd rather join us. We walk through farmland, up past another bay and a frog pond. We are headed for the nikau palm grove, Moppy tells me. A favourite place.

The other three women are way ahead. They go to the gym for at least a couple of months before Christmas. Though Moppy is a lot skinnier than I, she is not all that much fitter.

'This year,' she says, puffing.

Eight kids plus a couple of hangers-on from other families are a little ahead.

'How much longer?' asks Georgia. 'I'm getting hungry.'

'Ssh,' says Moppy as we approach the bush. 'See how quiet you can be. Listen to the birds.'

Surprisingly enough, the kids obey. As we get closer I see why. There's an uneasy feeling here; the bush is dark, almost primeval. A huge puriri tree hollowed and rotten at the base lies on one side.

'This is how New Zealand was once,' whispers Moppy. 'Until the farmers came.'

'Bastards. I'd shoot them if I was allowed a gun,' says Sam.

I raise my eyebrows at Moppy. She has tears in her eyes.

'I always cry when I come here,' she says, 'I don't know why. I'm not sure whether I'm happy or sad.'

'Maybe there are spirits here.'

The kids reach the creek. Amanda's son Nigel has a big stick and is poking the water.

'I'm going to get an eel and chase you with it, Emma,' he yells. He hasn't forgiven her for telling everyone about his bedwetting.

'You dare,' Emma squeals.

The moment is past.

'I didn't realise Sam was so sensitive towards ecology,' I say to Moppy.

'I did,' she says. 'Everyone thinks Thomas is the sensitive one, but I've always thought Sam has the aesthetic sense. Just because he's a boy most of the time.'

'Look, Mum,' Sam says. 'A frog.'

We all stop. There, perching on a branch, above the creek. Sam picks up a stone and throws it.

'Sam, what are you doing?'

'Trying to knock it off.'

After our camping special, spaghetti bolognaise, Moppy and I sit on the bank watching the stars.

'Look, a falling star,' Moppy says.

I miss it.

'Tell me what you wished for.'

'Someone slightly off track and kind to frogs.'

'What about Ted?' Ted was my tutor at varsity and is Moppy's neighbour. He talks to Sam but not to Moppy.

'Weird Ted. What made you say that?'

'He's a poet of course, and lonely. I'm sure he's the one sending you poems.'

'But he's a bit of a recluse. And he stutters.'

'Precisely. He has a chronic problem with shyness. But once he gets to know someone he gets over it. And he's really bright. They don't hand out fellowships to just anybody, you know. Anyway you should have more sympathy for stutterers. Remember that woman in the shop telling us off for laughing at Dennis.' Dennis is Moppy's closest brother, in age and in spirit. He stuttered badly as a child.

'But Ted's old and kind of wizened.'

'He's not that old. Fifty-five maybe.'

'Too old for me. I'd prefer a younger man. I've thought it might be Sean.'

'You're assuming, of course, that it is a man.'

'I'd die if it was a woman. Oh God, it's not you having me on, is it?'

'Don't be fucking silly. And what makes you think of Sean? Driving all the way from Ponsonby to deliver. Anyway he sees you most days at the shop, doesn't he? If he wanted to make a pass, he could.'

'Well maybe it's because he's technically my boss or he's shy. After all, we've been friends for years. I've always felt he fancies me.'

'What man doesn't?'

'I prefer to think of them coming from someone different. A stranger from afar kind of thing. I guess it's the romantic in me. But what about you, Barb? Do you want a man?'

'Me? No, I've given up. It's hard to find someone who wants a large woman of equal intelligence. Men seem intimidated by me. The only thing I regret is the lack of a source of poems. You know, the penis as muse.'

'That's a good one.'

'I heard this guy talking on the radio about his muse. It got me thinking.'

~ the penis as muse ~

On the radio the male poet describes his muse as a lover. Lamenting the fact he is too busy concentrating on the prosaic world of work to listen. Her words lying unloved and barren on the kitchen floor. I wonder why no muse has ever appeared, unbidden before me, in a burst of shimmering light.

Why my friend Moppy depends on pillow talk, silky tongues occupying the void. Why we women show gratitude for a late night tête-à-tête with the wagging tale of a love poem or a painting. Pavlov's dog all over again. And absence reducing us to silence. Why my mouth always refuses to turn tricks for itself.

She lights a candle, anoints her skin with sweet lover words. Long syllables stroking her breasts. Her tongue stretching over the text, her fingers playing a fluent rhythm. Learning to be self-articulate.

And incidentally making the penis redundant.

~ treading air ~

If only it worked like that, Moppy said.

She never was the sort of child who learnt from mistakes. Scarred knees testify to the number of times she took a flying leap off the back porch steps trying to get airborne. There was nothing to it. Treading air instead of water.

Foreign man, 44, interested in culture, dancing and politics. Looking for intelligent, non-smoking, affectionate woman. Kids OK.

His voice is slow, formal and foreign. 'I'm shy and quiet but I do have a sense of humour.'

Moppy's is young, with a trace of amusement. 'Hello Vincent. I'm

Margaret. I'm forty-two. I'm interested in art and conversation. I like going to the theatre and to foreign movies, and I keep up with politics though politicians leave me cold.' She refrains from saying, I'd never fuck one again. It's true but it was a long time ago and he was Australian. 'I have two children, boys, but they spend most weekends with their father. I haven't danced for years but I'd like to.' An understatement.

Vincent rings at 6.30 on a Tuesday night. Moppy is trying to stir-fry chicken and vegetables, listen to Vincent's quiet voice and tune out Thomas who is demanding dinner.

Vincent patiently suggests she rings back later. 'At your convenience.'

Thomas is safely in bed and Sam is watching TV when she rings back, shutting her bedroom door as she does so.

'It's all right about the children, I like children,' says Vincent. 'I have a daughter myself.'

'How old?'

He hesitates. 'She must be twenty now.'

'Must be?'

'I've never met her.'

'Why's that?'

'It's a long story. I will tell you if we get to know one another better.'

Perhaps he's a paedophile. You can never tell, especially with smooth talkers. Moppy can't place his accent except he sounds educated, his voice plummy and careful.

'Where are you from?' she asks.

'Pakistan originally.'

Shades of Imran Khan. Long white gowns. Soft folds around limbs.

'How long have you been here?'

'Two years now. Before then I worked in England for ten years. I'm a civil engineer. I work for Ross and Ross.'

At least he's not a real estate salesman, thinks Moppy, but still she considers engineers to be precursors to computer nerds. The ones at varsity had a penchant for practical jokes: 'Kick Me' signs on the back of unsuspecting mates.

'Not a cricketer then?'

'Not all of us are.'

'I suppose you like practical jokes?'

'I am too shy,' he says, 'but I don't mind listening to jokes. I like women who are funny.'

'I can't promise,' says Moppy, 'but I like to think of myself as entertaining.'

'I would like very much to take you out for dinner,' says Vincent.

'But what if we're boring?' asks Moppy.

'In that case we will concentrate on the food.'

~ can you supply chaos? ~

'I think Robert and I will come along,' Jill says, 'sit in the corner and observe. Might be interesting.'

'Don't you dare, I'll be nervous enough as it is.'

'Nervous? Why should you be nervous? It's not as if you're a virgin. What are you going to wear?'

'Nothing too flash. My black short skirt, I think. And my new rust blouse.'

Jill sighs down the phone. 'It's not fair, you've got beautiful skin and sensational legs.'

'And a fat waist. Lucky for me long tops are in these days.'

And lucky to be in her late teens when minis came in. Strolling down Queen Street on Friday nights in a 'wide belt' and platform shoes, collecting admiration and boyfriends. Jill's shorter, stumpier legs were built for pioneering work on farms, not for minis or hot pants. Fancy dress parties suit her. With her blonde hair piled high she's stunning in low-cut bust and crinoline. But it's always Moppy who receives the over-the-top compliments. Jill cannot understand her popularity. Is it the way Moppy looks at men, straight in the eye? It doesn't make sense. Why is she ringing men in the paper?

Simple. Available and articulate men are very rarely discovered on the back doorstep.

By his own account Vincent is available but not easily articulate. Sitting across the table from her, he waits for Moppy to fill in the gaps.

'Sorry I'm late. The babysitter was late, then Thomas wanted a ruler and of course I couldn't find one. I'm not the most tidy person in the world. In fact I'm messy.' She laughs and takes a deep breath.

Vincent stands up, shakes her hand. He is about five foot ten. His hair is thick and curly, his face broad. Not quite as sexy as Imran but Moppy considers him handsome. Certainly an attractive body to wake up to. He is wearing gold-rimmed glasses, pressed jeans, a navy moss-knit jumper with a pale blue denim shirt underneath. An ironed look, as if he has just unfolded himself from the linen cupboard. There is no trace of excess living hanging over his jeans.

'I am too organised,' says Vincent. 'I find myself attracted to the idea of a little chaos.' His face is serious, smooth, almost shiny. A bronze glowing. Moppy wants to reach over and eat him.

'We should be well suited then,' she says, 'I have an infinite amount of chaos.'

She proceeds to tell Vincent stories of her life, her children, her two marriages, the lovers in between, including the politician just to show she has an interest there, her jobs, her stalled artistic ambitions. She's aware she's giving too much away, her voice brittle and self-deprecating. But she's the one drinking the wine while Vincent listens carefully. She can hear the cracks. Fears that if he holds her voice up to the light he will see right through her. He smiles as if he doesn't quite believe.

The boy approaching them at the table has a good line. He bends over, earnestly explaining that the profits from the sale of long-stemmed roses go to sick children in foreign countries. Perhaps the very land that the man comes from.

There is no doubt that Vincent will buy. The only question is what colour will she choose?

'Yellow. Yellow is my favourite colour. I am a morning person and red roses are dangerous,' she says, wondering if she should wrap her foot around his leg.

'I should have said. I'm going on holiday next Saturday. To Melbourne. I have family there. My brother and his children. I'll be away one week but I would very much like to take you out when I get back.'

Why not? He might have read the *Karma Sutra*. Indian, Moppy knows, but what's the difference.

'Okay,' Moppy says, and is surprised when Vincent kisses her quickly on the cheek at the restaurant door.

'Good,' says Vincent, 'I think you are very good at, how do you say it, taking me out of myself. You are a very cheerful person, I think.'

'Thank you. By the way, my real name is Margaret but everyone calls me Moppy.'

'It suits you. Your hair. My real name is Vikram but I've been Vincent for so long now.'

On the motorway she feels as if every car but hers is inhabited by lovers. This awareness, a consequence perhaps of so many years of occupation. Though she keeps a full fridge, Moppy knows there is nothing in hers to satisfy appetite. And yet, a bunch of silverbeet lies on the concrete steps, the stems wrapped in newspaper like flowers.

> *forgive me*
> *for intruding*
> *but I just wanted to say*
> *this silverbeet*
> *this poor man's spinach*
> *is so green and*
> *so good*

Shades of William Carlos Williams.

It's not true that spinach contains more iron than other vegetables, thinks Moppy before putting the silverbeet in the fridge and ringing up the 0900 number again, purely to roll her tongue over Vincent's vowels. Tomorrow she'll make a silverbeet and cottage cheese pie using fillo pastry. She'll also try to balance on Sam's stilts. The hedge is too high to peer over. Has Ted got silverbeet growing in his garden?

~ a reunion of broken parts ~

By the time Moppy has eaten the silverbeet pie she has put Ted's garden to the back of her mind. Considering how hopeless she was at algebra, that's not surprising. A reunion of broken parts is one definition. The science of restoration another. Moppy could never see the point. A poem and silverbeet equals a poem and silverbeet. No solution is required.

Algebra was one of my strongest subjects. Poetry is a similar art. Taking disparate things and uniting them. Also the art of revelation.

Moppy does the same thing with her art pieces, combining different media – string, junk, paper, photographs, shells, whatever – but she is not required to come to any resolution. Currently she is casting around for the next project. Her speciality is photography. She considers herself to be too restless for the stillness required. And her basement darkroom is damp underfoot.

~ ready and waiting for revelation ~

When Vincent rings on his return from Melbourne, she has no trouble finding the way to Newmarket, to his apartment.

She looks around the bland room. The prints are soft watercolours: a river scene and trees in a park. The curtains are pink chintz, the lounge suite burgundy brocade.

'It was a motel once,' Vincent says, handing her a duty-free plastic bag. A post-Christmas present. Inside are two bottles of Australian dry red, well chosen though Vincent does not drink. A reformed alcoholic or Muslim? There is also a T-shirt, an aboriginal design on a black background, and a wall calendar.

'I thought about you every day,' Vincent says.

Not counting Robert, and she doesn't, Moppy calculates it is at least eighteen months since she had sex. Until he discovered a reason for leaving in the shape of Wendy, Tim had been sleeping in the room that is now Sam's. For a year before that they had slept in the same bed, which was carefully divided by an invisible line. Occasionally Moppy would step over the line with her foot to see if she could provoke some sort of reaction. Tim always pretended to be asleep. She never considered what she would do if he responded.

Ripe, thinks Moppy. I'm so ripe I'm about to drop. But she kisses Vincent briefly on the mouth and takes her succulence home to lie in the dark conjuring up a scene from Anais Nin's *Delta of Venus*. Fingers stroking the lips of her vulva until she dissolves into a world where her body has no bones.

~ turning funny ~

'His birthday's on Valentine's Day so I'm going to invite him around for dinner, then see what happens,' Moppy says.

'Do you think that's a good idea?' asks Jill. 'You ought to be careful. You don't know where he's been.'

'Well he looks pretty clean to me. In fact his apartment puts my house to shame. I'm sure he never cooks, the kitchen was spotless.'

Jill bangs her cup on Moppy's cluttered bench. 'That's not what I mean. I'm talking about AIDS, you dumb woman. Anyway, I think you're taking a big risk. What have you got in common?'

'The fact that we're both single and lonely. And he likes me. He thinks I'm witty.'

After Vincent has battled his way through the overgrown garden, he is indeed horrified by the state of Moppy's kitchen.

'Could I please clean up a little?' he asks, not waiting for her answer, placing letters, recipe books, pens and pencils into tidy piles, the cups into the dishwasher. How will she ever find anything in the morning? Perhaps he has an ulterior motive. Has read the survey revealing that women are turned on by men who do housework.

Vincent is not taking advantage. He ties a tea towel tightly around his waist. Moppy considers him incongruous in yellow rubber gloves.

He is a little dubious about the wall hanging.

'I can't quite see it in the Tate,' he says. 'Are you serious about art?'

'At Elam, they considered me to be very talented,' she says in her best clipped voice, 'but it's difficult with kids and no money, and that's the point of this work. It's egalitarian.'

'I see.'

She has planned the dinner for days, searching through recipe books for the right combination, avoiding Indian. Spicy pumpkin soup, chicken breasts, peppers, beans and tomatoes in saffron sauce on couscous and, for afters, a fresh fruit salad. She laments the fact that Vincent can't eat her special chocolate mousse on account of migraines. Maybe it's meant to be.

After all, chocolate releases endorphins to the brain and obviates the need for sex.

With every mouthful Vincent takes a minute pause.

'It's all right, you know,' says Moppy. 'I may be untidy but I'm not dirty. I'm very careful with food. I've never given anyone food poisoning.'

'I'm sorry. I have a delicate stomach these days. I'm very careful.'

After dinner he gives her a heart-shaped box of chocolates. She gives him a tie, the most gaudy one she could find. Mickey Mouse and Donald Duck. She wants to shake him up, to disturb his equilibrium. She also gives him a card, a black and white thirties-style photo of two children. One is saying, 'I'll show you mine if you'll show me yours.' Innocent, of course.

Vincent laughs in an embarrassed way. 'Really you didn't need to buy anything. Being here is enough.'

There's a silence. Moppy changes discs. Puts on Miles Davis. 'Do you like jazz?'

'I'm not overly familiar but this is nice.'

'Were you a good girl at school?' he asks.

'Yeah. I was incredibly shy. Used to cry all the time. My big brother Dennis got sick of me. I disgraced myself one day, though. I asked the teacher if I could go to the toilet. She said no, so I stood in front of her and peed my pants. She was so mad, I had to mop it up myself. Looking back, I think of it as my first act of defiance.'

Vincent laughs and laughs.

'It's not that funny,' says Moppy.

'It is, it is,' says Vincent.

After prompting, he says, 'I went to boarding school in England. My parents were middle class and determined I should succeed. I was the eldest and the only son.'

'And are they proud of you?'

'No, my mother is disappointed. She would have liked me to go back home and marry a nice girl and have a family, but I don't fit there any more. I don't fit anywhere.'

'Not in New Zealand?'

'Maybe now.'

Moppy is disturbed. Vincent is looking at her with soft sloppy eyes.

~ the first seduction ~

They are not meant to last. Moppy has read the books, but she cannot bring herself to tell Vincent that this is a transitional relationship. All she wants right now is his body. She has drunk almost a whole bottle of wine. Vincent is sober, of course.

'I've got to go,' he says.

'Must you?' she asks, wrapping her arms around him. Tongue slipping under his teeth.

'Yes. It's late.'

'Please?'

'I'd rather wait. Next week. When we know each other better.'

'I suppose we could but…this is embarrassing…I'll have my period then. And I want you now.'

Vincent responds by turning her round. Leaning into her back, he caresses her stomach. She is wearing a thin summer dress. His hands move rhythmically lower.

'Don't stop,' she whispers, 'it's so nice.'

His hands haven't reached her clitoris and already she's feeling an intense warmth enveloping her.

Slow down.

She's thinking of the thirty-year-old virgin she once tried to seduce. A fellow pupil in an art class. An ex-priest who had succumbed to the temptation of paint but not yet of women. Moppy saw him as a challenge. She got him into her bedroom one night and stripped off all his clothes. He took one look and came. Mortified, he grabbed his clothes and ran to his car.

She is breathing heavily but she says nothing, allowing his soft hands to pluck her through her dress. Such sweet music. After she comes, shuddering but silent, she turns around, unbuckles his belt and leads him into her bedroom. The walls are painted deep blue. The curtains blue and white, the duvet cover white lace. It's Moppy's favourite room. She lights a candle, pulls Vincent down on her bed and unzips his jeans.

She likes the colour, copper as opposed to motley pink. And the size, moderate and curved a little. In her wild years between husbands she saw more penises than most, but she wouldn't consider herself an expert.

She lies on the bed, legs apart, and tries to look seductive. But Vincent has not forgotten his lessons in political correctness. 'I'll just slip one of these on,' he says, producing a condom from his jacket pocket.

'So you came prepared?'

'No. I'm just careful. I never thought we'd do it tonight.'

He buries his head under her dress. Kisses her stomach. Pulls off her pants, then her dress. Her lips are wet. Inviting. He enters slowly, a little at a time.

'Is that good?'

'Mmm.'

So slowly, she can feel the head stopping at the entrance, and the mouth of her womb opening, wanting to suck him in. He thrusts gently. Not asserting himself, but a partnership. When he asks if she is about to come she can say yes almost truthfully. He comes silently himself with a soft sigh.

It is the aftermath of lovemaking that Moppy has been missing. The relief. The tears. Trying not to let Vincent see. She had forgotten the way sex split her open. She is not sure she is ready to be so consumed.

'What are you looking for?' asks Vincent.

'Intimacy.'

'No, I meant what kind of arrangement?'

'Arrangement?'

'I want an exclusive relationship. How do you feel about that?'

'Do you always ask a woman this the first time you sleep with her?'

'No, but you are not just any woman.'

'Vincent,' she says, 'my marriage has only just broken up. I'm not ready for commitment.'

'Okay. Fun. We'll have fun.'

In the middle of the night he goes home. Moppy does not want Sam and Thomas waking to find him in the house. They had gone to bed by the time he arrived; still innocent, she thinks. She does not mind him going. Now that she has experienced occupation, she can enjoy again the luxury of stretching out over the whole bed.

She goes to the window to wave goodbye but she cannot see him. He has blended into the darkness and become invisible. His car is black and sleek. The neighbours do not stir.

~ when she awakens into speech ~

'Be careful with your heart,' I tell Moppy.

'It's not my heart I'm worried about,' she says. 'I've never had such a sweet lover.'

She twists her body before him, expecting some point of recognition. Smaller, darker, more foreign than imagined. He is not wearing armour or riding a white horse, but her lips are parched and he is hacking his way through. Confusion is easy. Seduced by the whiff of fairytale, he bends to her lips, releasing words from her womanly mother-tongue.

When I go to prison the usual gender roles are reversed. I am the one charged with releasing, though in the case of my prisoners I am not supposed to go too far. It is necessary that I leave them in there. Not altogether fluent. In order to compensate, I smuggle in muffins. Still warm as I take them out of the basket. Apricot with a melted chocolate button tucked in the top.

In the corridor, prisoners and guards walk up and down, glancing casually at the opposite sex, as if they are out for an evening stroll. Out in the real world Vincent is looking around the bedroom for someone kind enough to offer a translation as Moppy speaks fast, articulate, making up for one hundred barren weeks.

Muffins are easy, but when it comes to the real thing I am as dumb as anyone. The inmates bring me tea, thick and sweetened with their precious sugar rations. Like Moppy I haven't the heart to tell them I prefer it without.

~ how to make the most of the undesirable ~

Sam and Thomas are not averse to the idea of their mother having an exotic lover. Not if the lover can see how important they are to his continuing status. Their first serious encounter is at Victoria Park Market.

'Mum, Mum, would you buy me these sunglasses, I really need sunglasses,' says Sam. 'These are cool.'

'And expensive,' says Moppy. 'No.'

'Let me buy them,' says Vincent, whipping out his wallet before Moppy can stop him. He performs the same trick for Thomas, and buys him a watch.

'I've got no one else to spend money on,' he says. 'And you don't know how proud I am to be seen with you.' His hand is resting on her shoulder. Moppy finds the weight of it reassuring, though as they walk through the crowds she notices other people watching. Their faces weighing up the bloodlines.

They go to Kelly Tarlton's after lunch at McDonald's. Sam and Thomas poke their faces through the whale cutouts, smiling for the camera.

Moppy thinks Vincent would like to be their father but she prefers him as lover. His skin. She imagines him lying on her table, face down. His slim buttocks polished and golden.

Watching the boys play in the park, his hands circle her belly slowly. 'A mother's stomach,' he says. 'Every part of your body tells me something about you. I love watching you come, the way your head falls back and your mouth opens.'

'Vincent, how come you never married? Isn't it unusual in Pakistan?'

'True. But you forget, I've hardly lived in Pakistan. And in England I never met any girls I wanted to marry.'

'But you have a daughter?'

'Yes. I have. I am very proud of her.'

'But you said you'd never met her?'

'She's still my daughter.'

Later on in the week, when the children are at Tim's, Moppy visits Vincent. He hands her a gold picture frame. In it a photo of a girl about five, very pretty with long dark hair.

'Isn't she beautiful? Her mother was English, a student, only twenty-two. When I learnt she was pregnant I asked her to marry me, though I knew my parents would be angry. But she said no. She married an old boyfriend. Her husband's name is on the birth certificate, though anyone can see she's half-caste. Her mother has always refused to let me see her, though I have sent money. It is a great sadness in my life.'

'How did you get the photo?'

'From an old friend who felt sorry for me. I hope my daughter might seek me one day.'

'How old is she?'

'She will be twenty-one in June.'

'And where does she live?'

'I don't know. My friend wrote and told me she had moved with her mother and father to New Zealand. That's why I came here. In case she tried to find me. I have sent letters to the last address I've got in England. They haven't been returned. It's hopeless but I am sure if she wants to find me she will. I have all her presents saved up. One for every birthday and Christmas. They are under the bed.'

He hops off and pulls out a large brown vinyl suitcase. Moppy sees everything is wrapped and labelled: Katie Christmas 1996, Katie Birthday 1992. She feels like crying.

'It's too sad. But why didn't you fight? You must have some rights.'

'Perhaps…I thought it better for my daughter if she had peace. If she had been a boy it would have been different.'

'Why?'

'A boy needs his father. His real father.'

~ family matters ~

Moppy can't imagine not knowing her mother. She rings Iris most days. Iris doesn't ring Moppy if she can help it. She believes in non-interference. If only Iris didn't have such a gloomy outlook on life, thinks Moppy. Still, what else can you expect from growing up in the Depression? Iris wants Moppy to find herself another husband as quickly as possible. Preferably someone stable with a house of his own and a good job so she won't have to worry.

'I am happy, Mum,' Moppy says, sounding like the TV ad. 'I'm going out with a very nice man. An engineer, so he can afford to take me to dinner.'

'How did you meet him?'

'Some friends of mine. You don't know them.'

Iris has a suspicious mind. She knows when Moppy is leaving out vital information.

'Where does he come from? What's his name?'

Vincent is acceptable. A nice name. But Pakistan is not.

Her mother screams. 'You have broken my heart. God knows what your father will say.'

Moppy slams down the phone. As a child her parents were always exhorting her to be more tolerant. 'Not everyone has your talent and looks,' they said. Her mother made comments about the Maori man down the road. 'He's a lazy sod. Drinks too much and I think he beats her. I wouldn't put up with it myself. Mind you, what choice has she got with all those kids.' It wasn't just race, though. Iris made the same comments about her own brother-in-law.

Moppy had never had a Maori boyfriend. She's shocked to find it an issue now. She rings her favourite brother, Dennis.

'Sweetie,' he says. 'It's not fair. First new man you like. Is he good-looking?'

'Yeah, and he's a snag. Too nice for me probably.'

'I blame talkback radio,' Dennis says. 'It's all those voices Mum and Dad listen to every night. *A man's not safe in his own country any more. We should send them back where they come from.* It's terrible, all the prejudice. But give them time, they'll come round.'

After a silent few days Iris phones. She dives straight into the previous conversation as if she has been momentarily interrupted.

'All he's after is marriage and a visa. Once he's got that, he'll drop you like a hot potato. He probably wants your house too.'

Moppy takes a minute to tune in. Like arriving at a movie ten minutes late, it puts her at a disadvantage.

'For God's sake, Mum. What are you talking about? He already has permanent residence, a good job and more money than me. Anyway, I don't want to get married again, and what makes you think he might not like me, just for me? Some people do.'

'I'm just saying, dear. It's my job. I worry about you.'

'So you say. But I'm a big girl now and I can get on with my own life.'

'You're still my daughter, Margaret. No matter how old you are.'

Coming back from the supermarket with the kids, she almost stands on three small gourds, yellow, green and orange.

'Are these yours, Sam?' she asks.

'No,' he says, 'they're cool though. We can hang them on the wall.'

'I wonder who left them?'

'Weird Ted probably,' Sam says. 'He's left peppers too. Yuck. I hate peppers.'

Moppy looks around for a piece of paper. She notices one of the green peppers has been cut. She lifts off the top.

misshapen tokens
but beauty
all the same

'Sam, does Ted grow peppers and silverbeet?'

'Dunno. Haven't been over for ages. Brad says he might do things to me.'

'Like what?'

Moppy is not too keen on Sam's friend Brad. In particular, the way Brad's mouth twists itself into a sneer when he walks into their stucco cottage. Brad lives in a new large townhouse with a swimming pool and impenetrable gates.

'You know, bad touching.'

'And what do you think?'

'Na. Ted's cool. Weird but.' Sam runs off inside. *The Simpsons* are on and he doesn't want to miss a trick.

Ted's old fibrolite two-roomed bach can't be seen from the road. His hedge is six foot high and he doesn't mow the front lawn. Out the back he maintains a large vegetable garden. Moppy rescued Sam from there once when he was a toddler. He'd wriggled his way through. She'd overheard Ted talking to him. Moppy apologised for Sam and Ted said, 'It's ooooo kay.' On the rare occasions Moppy sees Ted in the street, he usually blushes and half waves. Moppy can't tell whether he's waving her away or being friendly. According to Sam, Ted doesn't stutter when it's just the two of them.

~ a boy needs his father ~

On Friday Moppy is running late for her job at Just Art Books in Ponsonby when the phone rings.

'Shit,' she says as she splashes water over her burnt-orange blouse. A bargain in the sales. She picks the phone up, knowing it will make her even later.

'Is that Moppy?'

'Yes.'

'It's Angela. David's mother. Is Sam supposed to be at school?'

'Of course.' Stupid woman. 'Why?'

'I've just seen him and Brad Duncan down at the creek, hiding. I thought you'd like to know.'

'Not really,' says Moppy, knowing it's exactly the wrong thing to say to Angela, who takes mothering very seriously indeed.

'If I was you I'd go straight down there and march him off to school by the ear.'

'Yeah. Have you rung Brad's mother?'

'I tried but she's not at home. She's a busy woman.'

'Playing tennis no doubt whereas I'm late for work.'

'It's a matter of priorities, Moppy.'

'Yes, Angela. I'll go down there and sort them out. Don't you worry.'

Moppy rings Sean. 'Not to worry, darling' he tells her. He'll open up the shop. She can always work on Saturday.

When she gets to the beach she can understand why Sam's skived off. It's a beautiful day in March. Some of the trees are starting to turn, and underneath the heat there is a faint nip in the air. Sam hates being inside and subject to authority, but Moppy knows she can't convey her sympathies. She's supposed to reinforce the school message – a point Tim makes often. 'The two of you are a bad combination,' he says, 'too much alike for your own good.'

Sam is nowhere to be found. Perhaps they are hiding somewhere. Moppy walks a little around the rocks. Only older people with dogs and mothers with toddlers are to be seen.

Back at home there are no messages on the answer phone. Moppy rings Tim, who reacts as expected. 'That boy knows he can get away with anything. I'm going to ring the school and tell them he is playing truant. They'll fix him if you won't.'

'He's your child too,' says Moppy.

'Yes but you're the one he lives with. With the influence. And I hear you're hanging around with an Indian. Sam's probably upset and that's why he's run off.'

Moppy bites her tongue. 'Actually he's a Pakistani. Anyway, what am I going to do about Sam? I'm supposed to be at work.'

'I pay you enough money to stay home and look after my children and not work.'

'No you don't, not the way Sam eats. Anyway it's none of your business.'

'It is if it impacts on my children, and obviously it does. I expect you to be there for emergencies.'

Moppy slams down the phone. It rings. She picks it up in case it's Sam. It's Tim.

'Don't hang up on me.'

'It's my phone. And there's no point in talking. I'll let you know when he turns up.'

Moppy finds waiting one of the most difficult things in the world. She'd never make a spy. Action is easier. She walks back to the beach. On the way home she decides to try Ted's place. Reaching the door is a bit difficult. The path is completely overgrown with kikuyu. There's no reply when she knocks, and Moppy can discern no movement through the thick glass panes. She goes home and leafs through the sketch book she keeps beside her bed for the visual ideas that seem to come only in the middle of the night. She's too aware of the missing Sam to settle down to work. She starts cleaning the oven, a job long overdue, and one requiring muscle power.

Running up the back steps, Thomas as usual starts talking before he gets in the door, about the too-easy maths test, about the story he wrote. 'I don't know where Sam is, Mum,' he says when Moppy asks. 'I'm only his brother.'

At 3.30 Sam strolls in, throwing down his bag and opening the fridge door as if nothing has happened. Moppy adopts an unnaturally calm voice.

'Did you have a good day at school, Sam?'

'It was okay.'

'What did you do?'

Sam hesitates a little. 'Usual stuff.'

'Like what?'

'I dunno.'

'I bet you don't, because you weren't there.'

'How'd ya know?'

'I was told you were down at the creek this morning.'

'Who told you?'

'It doesn't matter. Is it true? I'll be even madder if you lie.'

'Yeah, it's true. But school sucks.'

'Maybe so, but you have to go. As it is Dad's rung the school, so I expect you'll be in big trouble tomorrow.'

'Why did you tell him, Mum?'

'I had to, I was worried about you all day. I didn't even go to work. Now I'll have to work on Saturday and I wanted to go to Piha to see Dennis and Don.'

Sam bursts into tears.

'I'm sorry, Mum. I'll try to be good from now on.' He pulls out some shells from his pocket. 'Look, I got these for you.' He hands her some transparent oyster shells. 'This one's really pretty.' It's bright orange.

'That's terrible,' Vincent says when she phones him. 'He's heading down the wrong track. Why don't you put him in a private school? I could help you with the fees.'

'There's no need to overreact. He's just a typical boy, Vincent. Anyway I don't like private schools.' She refrains from adding, 'and you're not his father.'

~ the complications of fathers ~

I was still overseas when Moppy met Tim. He'll make a good father, she told me over the phone, not realising he'd soon be transferring his razor-sharp skills on the macro economy to her household management. I had hoped things might be different in the next generation, she wrote two years later. But the moment I stopped work the balance of power in our relationship shifted. Favouring Tim of course. The thing that is most difficult to accept, she added, is that Tim has no patience with Sam. He's educated and ought to know better, and he has no excuse like our fathers.

She blames the Second World War for both of our fathers' difficulties. All those men coming back to produce the next generation while still harbouring unadmitted nightmares. 'You ought to get counselling,' Moppy once told Jack. He shouted at her. 'I don't need a trick cyclist. You're the one that can't keep a husband.' Not that he ever liked Tim. 'I can't help it if my daughter keeps marrying idiots,' he said to me when I came back from Europe.

Moppy has a point, though. I don't believe my father was indulging in drinking bouts on a regular basis before he went away with his mates, fellow apprentices, for their big OE. A bit of a lark at the time. Coming home alone. The only survivor. And what did it do to the women? My mother first met my father on the day he was leaving. Her fiancé was one of his mates. Perhaps my father watched my mother gaily waving from the dock and wished she belonged to him. On his return five years later he called around to see my mother and added to the bare facts of her fiancé's death. They clung to each other. Grief rather than love.

So my parents are in it together despite their separate beds. My father disagrees with my sense of the truth. He is threatened by my being a poet. The revelation of family secrets. Drunkenness and death and who knows what else remains buried in the subconscious. If I must write, I should invent new characters who bear no resemblance to anyone alive, he says, having clearly forgotten our last conversation. The one in which he told me I lacked the imagination to be a novelist.

the family urges silence

in this American
book celebrating poets, a quote

'revelation is their reason
for being'

no apology
considered necessary

it's almost enough
to silence the critics

such a sweet sound
next time they tell me

to remain close lipped
I'll start singing

and who cares
how loud

~ a socialist relationship ~

'Tell me the funny story about peeing again.'
   'No. Don't be silly.'
   'Please.'
   Moppy tells the story for the fourth time. Soon he'll be asking me to give him a golden shower, she thinks, but Vincent is too fastidious. He likes kissing her clitoris but only with her cotton panties as an intermediary. 'If you like,' he says, 'I could get some glad wrap and put it over your vulva, then I could stick my tongue into you.' The absence of stickiness is making Moppy feel removed. Clinical.
   Her favourite cake, Sour Cream Coconut, emerges from the newly cleaned oven smelling faintly of caustic soda.
   'Why don't you ever cook for me, Vincent?'
   'I think we should have a socialist relationship,' Vincent replies.
   'What do you mean?'
   'Each of us contributes whatever we can. You like to cook and I like to be cooked for. I reciprocate by taking you out to restaurants and paying.'
   'But,' says Moppy, 'occasionally I would like you to cook for me. Going out to dinner is not the same thing, you know. Cooking for someone is an act of love.'

Ignoring Moppy's breaking of the law, they are walking to the beach, hand in hand, leaving Sam and Thomas at home alone. Vincent is getting used to staying the night. Moppy finds she gets a good night's sleep with him beside her. Since Tim left she has spent too many hours lying awake, knowing if her car breaks down or the roof caves in, the responsibility is entirely hers.

Tim is coming the other way. Face set in stone. Moppy notices there is something different about him, apart from his obvious anger.

'Hi. What have you done to yourself?'

'I've shaved my beard off. Where the hell are the kids?' Tim's shoulders have drooped in the way that frightens her. He stands very close to her face.

'The kids are at home and quite safe, watching a video. They didn't want to come. This is Vincent, by the way.'

'I'll speak to you later.'

He marches off in the direction of Moppy's house.

'Oh,' says Vincent, 'I really thought he was going to hit me, or you.' He's shaken. Definitely not Imran Khan.

'He wouldn't with you there.' She starts crying. 'I'll have to pay for this.'

'What do you mean?'

'He's always threatening me in one way or another. Trying to control me. But it's nothing visible, nothing as clear cut as a black eye.'

At home they discover Sam and Thomas have been fighting. Sam has locked Thomas out of the house. Thomas is banging on the french doors and screaming. Sam is inside pulling faces.

'Who wants corn fritters for lunch?' Moppy asks, trying to put everything right.

Tim's voice hisses over the phone. 'I don't pay you to gallivant around the neighbourhood with your boyfriend. If you can't look after the kids to my requirements, I'll take you to court and get custody.' He hangs up before Moppy can get a word in.

'I hope he won't do anything physical,' says Vincent. 'He hasn't got a gun, has he?'

'No, but he does have a Samurai sword.' Moppy laughs mockingly.

Fear does not prevent Vincent arriving in the dark on a weeknight. He has become addicted to the weight of Moppy's body. One night they are rolling naked on the floor. Vincent is about to enter Moppy when they hear a shrieking outside. By the next day she has transformed the story into a comedy.

~ a fine tale to tell ~

Moppy waits until Jill and I sit down at Navona's.

'There we were,' she says, 'naked and getting really close on the sheepskin rug, when all of a sudden we hear this hideous noise outside. I thought it was Tim, bursting in with his ceremonial sword. Vincent tried to hide under the bed but I told him he had to protect me. He's going,

"Where's my pants?" I handed him a towel. He ran outside. The neighbours on the other side of the street were peering out the window and the kids came in wondering what the noise was. Sam was brandishing his baseball bat. Vincent comes running back in yelling, "Keys, keys, where're my keys?" Turns out it was just his car alarm. Stupid things anyway. It completely put me off sex. Poor Vincent looked so pathetic, running around, panicking.'

'You are horrible,' I say.

'He reckoned someone must have tried to get in it.'

'God, perhaps it was Tim hiding in the bushes,' Jill says.

'Yeah, I thought of that. Or Ted. Or Sean. You know once I was going out with two guys at the same time.'

'What's this got to do with anything?' I ask, not terribly sure I want to know.

'Patience. It was when you were in England. Anyway, I was having sex with one of them. The window was open and just as I was about to come I heard this noise. A sad low moan outside. Incredibly creepy.'

'It was probably a dog,' Jill says.

'You never did have much imagination. But the guy who I think was outside never rang me again. He was really nice too.'

I sometimes think Moppy should be the writer, but who's running this show? If Moppy was, she wouldn't let me speak at all. 'Give him to me for the weekend. I'll soon get rid of him,' said the famous American novelist to the famous New Zealand novelist. She was complaining of the character who refused to be murdered. I must admit to being a bit squeamish in that regard myself, though I deal with real-life murderers twice a week and have perceived there is nothing substantially different in the way they enter a room.

Nor in the way they enter a dream, as I discovered last night. Mati was stroking my face and telling me I was beautiful. I was reluctant to wake up. I don't normally notice such things, but Mati is definitely handsome. Thick curly hair and the most wonderful smile. Unusual, such a smile in prison. He is also very intelligent, though he refuses to believe that rhyme is redundant and adjectives an unwelcome intrusion.

~ talking of unwelcome intrusion ~

Anzac Day is a big event in Moppy's family. A day to congregate and an implied understanding that this is a moment of forgiveness. In the past Moppy and her father have had words. Over politics, feminism and men. On Moppy's side the deepest unspoken hurt has arisen from Jack's jealousy. Moppy can understand his dislike of her partners, but hadn't prepared herself for his jealousy extending to Sam and Thomas. 'For God's sake, aren't they too big for that?' when they hug and kiss Moppy.

It's slightly easier for her brothers, Graham, Peter and Dennis. They are not so intensely scrutinised. Graham has one daughter, Nicky, to his first wife Anne. Nicky is in England, working as a nanny and screwing her widower boss, but Graham doesn't know this. He lives with Gail who also has two grown-up children. Dennis is the bachelor and the receiver of everyone's confidences. There's always been a bachelor in Iris's family but Dennis is the first to be openly gay. He lives at Piha with Don. They have been together for ten years and these days both look a little grey in the face. Too many funerals, they joke. They are lucky to have escaped. Lucky that Jack and Iris have accepted them as a couple. Not that they didn't have their share of drama, but Jack will now shake Don's hand and Iris has come to enjoy their attentions. So much more than a daughter-in-law would bestow.

As far as Jack is concerned, Peter redeems the family single handedly. The same wife he married at twenty, Sally, and two children, Mathew and Louise. Good stable names. Good stable children. Mathew is at university studying engineering. Louise is in the seventh form and is planning to go nursing despite the low pay. Neither of them ever played truant, Sally informs Moppy, who even over the phone can hear the unspoken rider in her voice: but then they aren't from a broken home.

Lunch on Anzac Day is always at Dennis and Don's now. They make salads from their own garden and gather fresh mussels from the rocks. Graham and Gail bring quiches or pizza. Sally and Peter bring the bread. Iris brings the family favourites, apple pies and lamingtons. Moppy brings things the kids like, soy honey chicken wings or sausage rolls, home made with fresh herbs and pastry sprinkled with sesame seeds.

After lunch on the balcony overlooking bush and the water they usually have time for a quick cup of coffee, espresso, before the parade at Lion Rock. Jack marches with the other soldiers, while the rest of the family wait on the beach. Sam always wants to throw himself in the surf and Thomas always wants to run up Lion Rock. Moppy cries when they play the Last Post high on Lion Rock though she professes to have no time for sentimentality.

After the ceremony Dennis takes them to the RSA. The lady members bring round plates of sandwiches, the men drink beer and the women shandy, and Jack can be relied upon to say how proud he is of his family despite their idiosyncrasies. It's a safe familiarity for Moppy to rely on. A day when she can count on feeling less alone. When everyone tries to come to terms with the past.

'Are you coming on Sunday?' asks Iris.

'That depends,' says Moppy.

'On what?'

'On whether Vincent is welcome. The kids want him to come. They've already told him it's great out there. And Dennis doesn't have a problem.'

'We do,' says Iris. 'A big problem. It's not personal. But this is a day for New Zealanders. If you bring Vincent, we won't go.'

'But there's no point if you don't go.' Moppy slams down the phone. It's getting to be a habit.

Later she rings Dennis.

'Sweetie,' he says. 'Like I say. You've got to give them time. We had to. All the same, it's not nice for you.'

'No. Anyway I'm not coming. If they can't trust me and my judgement, they don't deserve my company.'

'Let me see what I can do to soothe the waters. After all, I've had practice.'

But Dennis cannot soothe the waters. He makes things worse by getting mad with Jack. Telling him talkback radio is rotting his brain, making him a racist.

Moppy and Vincent spend Anzac Day taking the kids to Motat. And everyone they walk past looks. Long evaluating looks. As if they are wearing sandwich boards. Moppy is on edge and sharp with Vincent.

'No, Vincent, Sam cannot have a coke. It makes him hyper.'

'One won't hurt.'

'Vincent, you're not his father. I said no.'

'You're so selfish. I hate you, Mum,' says Sam.

'You should have more respect for your mother,' says Vincent.

'I'll do the disciplining, Vincent.'

'I can't win,' Vincent says.

Tim was always calling her selfish. A selfish cow. Moppy could never understand why. Now the word selfish is a mantra for Sam and Thomas. Whenever she says no.

They drive up Mt Eden. Standing on the rim, Moppy points out the geography of her city. Where she was born, where she grew up. Vincent stands behind her, with his arms encircling her waist. Compensation, thinks Moppy.

~ oblique messages ~

At home Moppy discovers a ring of pebbles on her crushed shell path. One pebble carefully placed in the centre. She phones me to ask what it means. We went to Brownies together. But neither of us can remember the specified message. Was it go home or wait for me here?

There's a poem under the central pebble.

'Barb,' Moppy says. 'What do you make of this poem? There's no title. But there never is.'

She reads it out, a little awkwardly.

maps count
for nothing

in the distance
her mother in red coat

coming closer
she sees

the red coat
is a red tie

worn by a stranger
holding out

an ice cream
in his dark hands

'Well,' I say, stalling for time, 'the dark hands must be Vincent, but is he showing you the way or leading you astray? Things are not what they seem perhaps? I really don't know.'

'Do you think Ted might be watching me? Vincent does have a red tie. God, it's a bit creepy. I lost my mother once and then I saw her in the distance wearing a red coat. At least that's the vision I have now. But has the poem put the colour in my mind? I'm never quite sure of the sequence of events. Have I told you that story?'

'I don't think so, at least I can't remember it. Perhaps it's you writing the notes to yourself. Your subconscious.'

'I'm not that mad. At least I don't think so.'

I'm beginning to wonder myself. Did I at some stage write a poem in Ted's course about Moppy? Perhaps Sean has the necessary inside information? Still, I wouldn't have thought Sean to be the poetic romantic type. Nor the type to consider a lost mother significant in the scheme of things. Most of the time he's too drunk to be observant.

If I ask my prison pupils to describe getting lost, there is no shortage of words. Sometimes they describe hiding instead. All the details of the dark cupboard, a friendlier place than the foster mother's kitchen. In their poems, mothers or substitute mothers are more often seen waving straps than wearing soft red coats.

My own mother had a black coat. The most practical colour. She seemed to change when she put it on, becoming friendly and talkative with the knowledge she was about to leave the house. On the day of my older sister's funeral, however, she wrapped the coat tightly around her shoulders and never said a word. Janet died when I was five. Nothing dramatic – a bout of pneumonia. One moment she was there, hiding my dolls, the next she was installed in a sick bed in the living room and then gone altogether. I had a bedroom to myself. And dolls that remained still and mute on her bed.

That same year I became friendly with Moppy and Dennis. There was plenty of space in our house but I never invited them home. I preferred Iris's kitchen. Sitting at the table eating lamingtons. Dropping coconut on the floor and no one yelling.

~ the house as character ~

Jill was not part of our primary school days. She lived in the more exclusive and older neighbouring suburb. We met at high school, attracted to Jill's blonde coolness and sophisticated manners. Jill in turn liked Moppy's alternative style and my precocious way with words. Still liking to keep a handle on Moppy's life, if not mine, she suggests we all go out for dinner to the Indian restaurant up the road.

'Vincent will feel more relaxed there,' she says. 'But come for drinks first.'

A guided tour is obligatory for all first-time guests in their house. Robert's house really. A minimalist, architect-designed two-storey with huge floor-to-ceiling windows. Between the windows and the sea nothing impedes the view. There are no decks. The architect and Robert decided they would interfere with the purity. For this reason also there are no family photos on the walls. The art is considered, bought for the space it occupies. A Greer Twiss bronze sculpture that Moppy would kill for in the foyer, a large John Reynolds painting in the lounge.

If Laura Ashley was still fashionable Jill would wear flouncy dresses and have a house with friezes, but even their bedroom has not been corrupted with her taste. There's a king-sized bed, the stunning view and along one wall a curved plywood bench. It has cupboards and two places for the matching plywood chairs.

'Like a boardroom,' Moppy whispers to Vincent. 'Imagine making love in here. I'd have to dress up as a secretary.'

'What are you laughing at?' Jill asks.

'Nothing. Private joke.'

'God, save me from new lovers.'

'And where do the children sleep when they come?' an embarrassed Vincent asks.

In their room there is some sign of human habitation. Still, by all accounts they are very tidy humans. It's a carbon copy of the main bedroom except the beds are single and instead of a bench there are wall-to-wall shelves. The fabric used for bedcovers and the Roman blinds are the same as in Jill's room. A bold abstract design with sea colours, turquoise, green and blue. On the shelves sit books and neat collections, Barbie dolls and McDonald's giveaways.

'What a delightful room,' Vincent says. 'See, it is possible to have neat children.'

Moppy sighs. 'I'd like to remind you of one subtle but important difference. Emma and Georgia don't live there all the time, and Jill tidies their room.'

'And why don't you tidy Sam and Thomas's? Isn't that your job as mother?'

'Not in my book. I practise the stand at the door and throw technique.'

'But they're always losing things.'

'I know, but don't ask me to do it any other way. Besides, it's good training. In case I ever become a basketballer.'

~ multiplying clichés ~

Having had the guided tour already, I meet them at the restaurant which is dark and punctuated with red lamps. Moppy gets the distinct impression that the waitress is giving her the evil eye.

'Vincent,' she whispers, 'the waitress doesn't seem to approve of me.'

'Probably not. You have stolen something.'

'What?'

'Me.'

Taking charge, he orders for all four. A variety of dishes, Murgh Biriani, plain rice, Roghan Josh, dhal and chapatis.

Vincent eats with his hands, picking up meat with a chapati.

'Excuse me,' Vincent says, 'it really is the best way to eat curries.'

'So how are you finding New Zealand?' asks Robert. 'I suppose it's dull compared to London.'

'No. I like the quiet anyway, and now I've met Moppy.' He smiles.

Robert smirks. 'Yes, she's not bad is she, but she's a bit stroppy if you ask me. Needs a man who will keep her in control.'

'Behave, Robert, or I'll go home.' Jill turns to Vincent. 'Ignore him. Unfortunately I am married to him, but I can always rectify that.'

Moppy intervenes. 'Do you two mind not involving us in your domestic disputes?'

'Sorry,' says Jill.

'Tell me, Vincent, is that your real name?' Robert asks.

'No. It's Vikram. As in Seth.'

They look blank.

'*A Suitable Boy*. The novel.'

'Never read it. So why Vincent?'

'A good name, I think. I like Van Gogh's sunflowers.'

'Art as cliché,' Robert says.

We move on to safer subjects – work and the state of the economy – but Robert is restless.

'Are you a permanent resident already, or are you looking for a New Zealand woman to marry?'

'Are you planning on being obnoxious all evening, Robert?' asks Jill.

'I'm just asking a civil question. Someone's got to look after Moppy and her interests.'

'Excuse me, Robert. I am grown up now.'

Jill smiles. A fixed smile but a smile. Robert has lost interest anyway. He's eyeing up the waitress.

'Thank you gorgeous,' he says as he takes a plate from her hands. She frowns. 'Nice tits,' he says to her back.

~ the hangman waits ~

'Jill and Robert are your best friends?' Vincent asks on the drive home.

'Jill is. Not Robert. What did you think of them?'

'They seem very unhappy. I would not like such an atmosphere.'

'No. I think something is going on. They are not always that tense. Sometimes they can be quite funny and loving. Robert is a pig though. He sleeps around.'

'What do you mean?'

'I mean he has affairs. I think Jill knows underneath but she doesn't want to admit it. Even to herself.'

'Maybe she thinks it might be dangerous.'

'Why?'

'He strikes me as having the potential for violence if he doesn't get his own way.'

'I don't know. She's never said anything to me. I think she's mad to stay. But she wouldn't want to give up her beachfront house.'

'No. I must say I am not used to the idea of divorce. In my family no one is divorced.'

'Yeah, if you want to get rid of a wife you just set fire to her.'

'That's not fair or funny. Anyway it's only true of the lower classes. Rich men can afford mistresses. It's not a bad system. At least the wife retains her status and financial support.'

'That's true. Jill likes being a wife. I'm sure she gave up studying law because she didn't want to be in competition with Robert. But she wouldn't admit it. She's not the type to admit to mistakes.'

Getting out of the car, Vincent grabs Moppy's arm. 'I do not want to talk about them any more. I think they are not good friends for you. I want to make love.'

'We can't, unless you don't mind blood. I have my period.'

Vincent shudders. 'No. We'll just kiss in that case.'

Once, a delicious tongue in the mouth was satisfying. But now Moppy is disappointed. An addict. Once you've had a taste of the real hard stuff, you want more.

'I love you, Moppy. I could kiss you all night.'

Moppy does not reply. She is not so keen on his slow tongue.

~ laughing at the same frequency ~

Jill is sober the next day and angry enough with Robert to talk to Moppy.

'I thought I'd surprise him for lunch yesterday but I found him in his office, laughing with his secretary. She was sitting very close to him. Like I used to. He said he had already made arrangements for lunch. So I stormed out.'

'Doesn't necessarily mean anything.'

'No? He reckons it was all perfectly innocent but I'm not so sure. They were laughing at the same frequency. Almost as if they were laughing at me... You'd tell me if you heard anything, wouldn't you?'

'Yes,' lies Moppy. 'But really you ought to ask him outright. He is your husband.'

'I don't know if I want to know. I'd have to do something if I knew.'

Moppy puts her arm around Jill's shoulders.

'It'll be all right. He'd be mad to jeopardise your marriage. To much to lose. What do you think about Vincent then?'

'I think you'd never have to worry about him philandering. He kept his eyes on the door the whole time you were in the toilet. As if you might have escaped. I was annoyed. I'm not that unattractive. But I think you'll get bored with him.'

'What makes you say that?'

'I was watching your face while he talked...slowly. Your eyes were all glazed over.'

'Oh God. Sometimes I want to scream. He's so deliberate.'
'That's it.'

~ beware of red dresses ~

'A cocktail party? But I've got nothing to wear,' cries Moppy.
'Please, allow me to buy you something.'
'You can't. Can you?'
'Of course. Who else do I have to spend money on? And it pleases me so much to see you dressed up.'

Vincent insists they go to Parnell. These days Moppy shops in malls, though she wonders if she is getting too old to wear mass-produced clothes. The Parnell shop is full of muted colours and fabrics that swing even on the hanger. If further evidence is required of the exclusiveness of the clothes, observe the tones in the shopkeeper's voice.

'Are you looking for anything in particular, Madam?' There is a slight nuance of confusion beneath the confidence. She is not quite sure where to place this couple in her marbled interior. Not tourists, or Remuerites.

'What do you think of this, Vincent?' Moppy holds up a black crepe dress with all the attention paid to the low-scooped back. She secretly loves her unblemished back. 'Strong,' one long-ago lover called it.

'No, too long. I prefer this.' He holds up a skimpy bright red dress. The material has a slight sheen to it, the arms are cut away. It is short and straight.

'Don't you think it's a bit small?'
'No. Try it on.'

Moppy does what she is told. The dress does surprising things for her imperfections, skimming over her waist and stopping short to reveal her legs. Moppy pinches her upper arms. She regrets the slight invasion of flabbiness.

'Wow.'

It is not the dress Moppy would have chosen for herself. Not a dress you could wear to a film festival or to a café, but...

She averts her eyes as Vincent pays. In its expensive brown paper bag the dress is heavier than expected.

'How does it feel to be a kept woman?' asks Jill when Moppy brings it around for inspection.

'That's a bit cutting, isn't it? Why can't I have some small pleasures? Aren't you the one who lives in a seaside mansion?'

'You know perfectly well it wasn't my choice to build such an extravagant house. Anyway, Robert and I are married. I'm just worried that you're getting in too deep. You know what you're like: you get to the stage where you can't extract yourself. It was the same with Tim. And Vincent's not right for you. He's too dependent.'

It's true. Moppy is getting tired of Vincent's constant phone calls, morning and night, as if he can't breathe without her.

~ tadpoles and frogs ~

Some say her body's made for it. See the way she glides, mouth open for business and other diversions. Bones softening, small and pliable between liquid fingers. Her sense of gravity easily abandoned.

Some say she could live for ever in this sea, eating what comes her way, but already her legs are kicking against the current, against lakeweed entanglements.

On a whim, I send the above prose poem to Ted, mentioning my writing and my friendship with Moppy. A reply comes back.

> I say
>
> see her rise to the surface
> eye lids shutting out
> the blinding sun
>
> I say
> see her leap frog
> away

He always was terse in tutorials. However, on the bottom of the page a scrawled note: *I'm following your career with interest, if you wish me to critique any of your work, I'm more than happy to oblige.*

~ the arty cocktail party ~

The cocktail party is in the Art Gallery. Vincent's firm is entertaining clients. A private showing of photographs. No one is all that interested in looking at the walls. Guests are there to partake of the sauvignon blanc and the morsels of food and flattery.

Vincent clutches Moppy's arm.

'I'm so proud of you. You look so beautiful in my red dress.'

'Does this mean you want it back? I could take it off. Now if you like.' She starts to unzip the back.

'Don't be silly. This is business. Anyway it's yours.'

He steers Moppy in the direction of a man she would describe as a hunk. Tall, dark curly hair greying at the temples.

'Moppy, this is Rodney Spence.' Rodney's wearing a thinish grey silk suit which seems to flow from his shoulders.

'Delighted to meet you, Moppy,' says Rodney. 'Vincent's told me all about you.'

'But not me about you. What do you do?' asks Moppy.

Rodney holds a piece of polenta topped with red pepper delicately between his fingers. 'Architect.'

'Oh, you did Robert Fisher's house.'

'Indeed. Friend of yours?'

'Mm. Well Jill is.'

'And what do you think of their house?'

'Stunning. But not for me. I prefer to live in a bach. Which is just as well as I don't have any money.'

'What do you do?' His voice is polite and without curiosity.

'I'm a mother, a tutor, a sales assistant, an ex-wife.'

'And lover,' Vincent interjects. It's the first time Moppy has known him to be so assertive.

'And artist when I get the time.'

'Another one. The world's full of wannabes.'

'Of course, but it's true.'

'It comes down to priorities. Obviously being an artist is not so important to you. Anyway, stick with Vincent, he's crazy about you.'

'Talk about arrogant.' Moppy hisses to Vincent when Rodney sidles off. 'And I didn't notice you defending me. All you did was claim me as your lover.'

'Well it's true, isn't it? Although one day I'd like to be more.'

They concentrate on the photographs. The light falling on male flanks reminds Moppy of a McCahon. Her favourite.

'I've got some nude photos of myself, you know,' she says to Vincent.

'Really? Can I see them?'

'Of course. I was at my peak. Nineteen and without drooping breasts.'

~ the photographic past ~

The photographer, Jacob, was a German Jewish refugee. He wore rough jackets made out of sacking, and pants held up with an old tie. He lived in a shack in the Waitakeres, and slept on the floor in the corner.

The mystic of the artist pays off nevertheless – for men, at least. His pretty long-haired girlfriend was idealistic and thirty years younger.

Iris screamed when she saw Moppy hanging on the wall. That wasn't at all what she had in mind when she said the newly married Moppy could do with a few prints in their flat. I wonder how Iris recognised Moppy with her head cut off? Jacob was into breasts. The shape of them. The tip of the fingernail touching the nipple. I've still got one of Moppy and me sitting side by side. Deliberately out of focus. He wanted us to touch each other's breasts. All we could manage was a tentative brushing of arms.

Jill went there once and refused to revisit. Despite her attempts to blend in with us, she couldn't quite bring herself to appear naked before someone who lived on baked beans and threw the cans outside to rust. Moppy and I ignored the pollution. Coming from the boring suburbs we considered the photographs added artistic value to our reputations. And we would do anything for a permanent record of ourselves. Of course at that time I was not the size I am now. Still, Jacob went into rhapsodies over my soft rounded flesh, my ample handfuls compared with Moppy's angular bones and pert breasts pointing to the sky.

~ he hangs her up ~

Vincent is thrilled by the photos. Thrilled to be shocked.

'Can I have one?' he asks. 'I would like to get one framed. That way when you are not here I will have a beautiful reminder of you.'

How can Moppy say no? Vincent has bought her clothes and a portable phone so that she can ring him when she is naked in the bath.

He picks the full-length nude, the one without the head that so shocked Iris she ceased spontaneous visits to her only daughter. It's Moppy's least favourite, revealing her rounded stomach even before motherhood. It also reveals her full crop of pubic hair. After Sam's caesarean birth, the hair grew back sparse and unpromising. The hills of Greece, Moppy describes it as. Only a few gnarled olive trees left standing.

Vincent hangs it proudly in his bedroom. The sight of the photograph and Vincent eagerly pulling on his walk shorts to get the *Herald* puts Moppy off the toast he has brought her. She considers his skinny legs. Vincent is unaware of this deficiency. His hands are busy flipping the pages of the Houses For Sale as he looks for the perfect home for a reconstituted family. Three bedrooms, a separate lounge for the adults, and two bathrooms. No one wants to share toothbrush space with a person who is not blood or sex related. Must be within city limits. Mixed marriages are not popular over the Harbour Bridge.

Moppy wonders if she is panicking just at the thought of commitment.

There are times when she thinks she might indeed love him. That evening they take her kids to visit friends of Vincent's. A successful mixed marriage, Vincent says on the way. Sitting on the couch, all four adults watched Sam and Thomas and the two girls play Junior Scrabble, Moppy feels a rush of affection. She squeezes Vincent's hand. She runs her tongue silently over the words, I love you.

On the way home they start discussing the rerun of *Absolutely Fabulous*.

'I just love it,' says Moppy. 'It's the best programme for ages. So funny.'

'What is so funny about mothers getting drunk and smoking, and a daughter with no respect?'

'Oh Vincent, don't be so stuffy. It's supposed to be OTT.'

'O T T… What does that mean?'

'Over the top.'

He stops suddenly at the orange light. They all jerk forward.

'You are allowed to go through an orange, you know.'

'You are just like those women sometimes. So caustic.'

'Give me an example.'

He hesitates. Moppy imagines his head as a see-through glass clock. Slow gears grinding.

'Wait… What about when I was sick and you wouldn't come round and I asked you if I should ring the ambulance and you laughed and called me a hypochondriac.'

'Throwing up is hardly a national disaster.'

'My mother always looked after me when I was sick.'

'And then she sent you to boarding school overseas.'

Vincent carries the sleeping Thomas to bed. Sam walks without complaining. Moppy looks out the window for any sign of Tim. Though Vincent moves as gently and as slowly as before and whispers, 'I love you Moppy,' it takes her a long time to come.

Sleeping beside her, Vincent is so light she can hardly feel his weight. But he is there, snoring quietly, considerately. Moppy cannot sleep. Beside Vincent she feels huge and responsible. Just like when the kids were babies and sick, she thinks, and needed to sleep with us. And she remembers now that she would be awake most of the night, terrified of squashing them as Sam had once squashed his pet mouse. Smother love.

~ chicken soup and arsenic ~

The next week Vincent gets the flu. And visiting, Moppy tries to be kind.

'I've made you chicken soup,' she says. 'Not that I'm a Jewish mother, but it really is the best thing for colds.'

Vincent lies in bed wearing winceyette pyjamas. They are buttoned up to the neck. His sheets are flannelette. Beside the bed are a range of pills and drinks.

'I think I'll just sleep,' he says. 'It would be nice if you could make me a cup of tea later.'

'Okay, but I should warn you, I don't make a great nurse. Why do you think Sam and Thomas don't bother getting sick? It's ironic, really, because my mother was great when I was sick. She made me little cakes and she used to sew all our comics together into big books and bring them out as a special treat. My kids just watch TV or sometimes if I'm really feeling motherly I might go and get them a video.'

'I'd like to meet your mother,' says Vincent.

'I don't think she'd appreciate your germs. Anyway, we're currently not talking.'

'On account of me?'

'Sort of. I feel like a teenager just discovering my parents are flawed. I'm sure they weren't always like that. They were quite liberal when I was young. And Mum went on an anti-tour march once with Dennis.'

But Vincent has dropped off to sleep. Moppy sits for a while feeling sorry for herself. Who watches over her when she is sick?

The truth is she misses her daily conversations with Iris.

After an hour or so of watching him doze and feeling all the time as if he has one eye on her, she stands up.

'I'll ring you later,' she says. 'I've got to go.'

'Where?' he says.

'Anywhere, where I can breathe.'

~ dancing with the newly separated ~

She cannot recall the last time she danced, but he is standing in front of her holding out his hand. A few circuits of the waltz, a few clichés murmured in her ear and it's all coming back. The slide across the floor to the favoured ones.

Moppy, Jill and I went to an all-girls school. It was necessary for us to learn how to dance so we could graduate as young ladies, though of course in our school out west there were no such pretensions as debutantes. We got to dance with the boys down the road, the classes carefully matched in expectations. The boys lined up on the other side of the hall. The fastest on their feet got to pick the ones with the biggest breasts or the least acne. We were not allowed to decline any offers. Moppy was always one of the first to be picked. Sometimes she would avert her head as if she hadn't seen the boy on her left who actually got there first.

Unlike me, Moppy was never programmed to be a wallflower. I can see her hands remember the moves. He wants to fill her dance card with a lifetime promise. Slow foxtrots within the confines of his bedroom. Hasn't realised yet the traitorous possibilities of her feet limbering up for the tango.

~ a swift withdrawal ~

'Things are not working out for me,' Moppy says a week later when Vincent has recovered. They are having lunch at Tarantula in Ponsonby.

'What do you mean?'

'I don't think I'm ready to settle down yet. I've only just got out of one marriage. I want to have fun.'

'Isn't this fun?'

'Yes. It's a beautiful day, the sun is shining, but...' She can't look him in the eyes.

'Is it me?'

'No, it's the timing. I want time.'

'To do what?'

'To explore. Work out what I really want. You know, art and all that.'

'Other lovers?'

'I don't know. I just feel stifled.'

'But I have been so good for you, to you.'

'Precisely, Vincent. It's like it is with Tim. Everyone says he must still love me because he is so good in terms of money, but he still wants to control me, to own me, and it feels the same with you. Every gift is a demand that I should love you.'

There is a long pause. Vincent puts on his dark glasses. Moppy looks at the other customers, wincing at the young couple holding hands. She has no recollection of any man doing this to her. Most of her breakups have been insignificant fadings away, or far too messy to conduct in a restaurant.

'How much time do you want? I'll wait for you.'

'I don't think you're listening to me. I want a break. I don't want to speak to you on the phone every day. To have to give an account of myself.'

'But I love you.'

part two

~ how heavy the sleeping child ~

With significant lovers they say you always remember the first meeting. The important details embroidered in fine colours. It becomes a kind of code, a sampler on the wall of memory.

Certainly Moppy's father likes to tell the story of how he met Iris. She was walking down the street with a new beau. Jack, recently returned from the war in Italy, was hiding behind the hedge. Perceiving she was the right woman for him, he yelled out some cheek. Iris met Jack again later, on the ferry to Devonport, and admonished him. He laughed. Perhaps she laughed too, persuaded by the waves. They were married within six weeks. How I envy such certainty. And the story itself. In my house there were no tales of such meetings. 'Worst day of my life. I don't wish to be reminded,' my mother replied when I asked her as a child. I know now she was talking not of their first meeting but of the second, when my father told her the details of her fiancé's death.

I vividly remember one meeting. James was at one of Ross and Amanda's parties. They were always trying to fill up their big old villa with people. I was staying with Moppy and Tim, having just returned from overseas. James was sitting on a large couch. His wife had left him with two young children. 'She is selfish, absolutely selfish and mad,' he said. He had large sad eyes and a plump childish face.

Now I remember nothing of our lovemaking other than him turning to me in the middle of every night to check I still desired him. Crying when I turned my back. 'Don't you love me?' He did it so often I stopped listening. I fell in love with his children though, sewing clothes and giving them parties with chocolate crackles and cheerios. What I liked most was going out, taking them with us. Bringing them home late at night. The youngest asleep in my arms. Too tired to offer resistance to his substitute mother. Heavy and warm. Sometimes he wet my lap. It filled me with desire.

Ironically I left James when he refused to give me a child of my own, watching over me as I swallowed my pill every night. I was young enough then to believe in my fertility and the idea of replacement.

Romantic novelists will tell you there is only one. In his own way Mati has given me the same message. A large black and white sketch of a tui with a backdrop of flowering kowhai. On the back was written, *I have been waiting for you and now I have found you, I can send my wairua home*. He handed the sketch to me at the last moment as I was gathering my things. Pushing it into my hands, smiling shyly.

I'm not quite sure what I can offer in return, or what he sees in me. This rather large woman with too much to say for herself. Today he was sketching me in class but he refused to let me see. Surely it wasn't a nude?

I think back to my old photographs. How my legs once twisted around themselves. How Moppy's are still recognisable.

~ every day a desperate man speaks ~

Moppy has stopped picking up the phone. Vincent's long slow words occupy the whole of the tape.

'Moppy are you there?'
'Please ring me. I just want to know you are all right.'
'Do you need any money?'
'Moppy, can we go to the movies, as friends? I miss hearing you laugh.'
'I love you.'
'I'm going to Australia for a week. I'll ring you when I get back.'
'I'm back. I've bought you a present. Would you come to dinner?'

Moppy gives in. Wishes she was stronger with words. Wishes Iris had not sewn the insidious seed of submission. Anything for peace.

Vincent runs to the door. Hugs Moppy. 'How lovely to see you. I've bought you some wine from Australia.'

'You shouldn't have.'

They sit at opposite ends of the couch.

'You are very quiet, Moppy. Are you all right? Is the wine all right?'

'It's fine. I'm just tired. The kids are getting to me. Fighting all the time. I need a break.'

'We could go to Fiji. You could lie on the beach all day. My treat?'

'No, I can't.'

'Why not?'

'You know.'

In the swept-up restaurant Moppy has ordered whole snapper in a Thai sauce. She is presented with an elaborate plate. On top of the fish is a parcel with banana leaf wrapping. It's tied at the top. Inside is plain rice. Presentation is everything but Moppy did not order salmon. She pulls apart the fish.

'I ordered snapper not salmon,' she tells Vincent.

'Does it matter? It looks wonderful. I don't want to spoil the dinner.'

'Of course it matters.'

Moppy calls the waiter over. He is horrified.

'I am very sorry, madam,' he says. 'The buttons for salmon and snapper are so close.'

'It's okay.'

Vincent watches the fork entering Moppy's mouth.

After the bill is paid the waiter says, 'My name's Paul if you want me again.'

'I hope you didn't leave him a tip.'

'Of course I did. Ten percent.'

'But he was so obsequious. And he gave me the wrong meal.'

'Don't be so petty.'

He persuades Moppy to come back for coffee. She gives in. It seems churlish not to since she is wearing the black chiffon shirt Vincent bought for her.

'Have you been seeing anyone?' Vincent asks.

'No. I'm taking a break from men. Paying attention to my friends, getting time for myself, you know?'

'And is there room in this life for me?'

'As a friend.'

Moppy wants to ask for her photo back, she feels as if he owns a part of her, of her history anyway, but she can't.

'You're going so soon?'

'I'm tired.'

'I suppose you only came for the dinner, and the shirt. I'm... what do you call it? A sugar daddy. The truth is, you never loved me.'

On the way over the harbour bridge she gets stuck behind an old van bearing a window sticker: *Repent. The end is near.* Is it a personal message, she wonders? Passing the van Moppy sticks her tongue out. She's a schoolboy let out for the long holidays, a catapult in his pocket, a glasshouse down the road.

And yet another gift to greet her. Words

if I knew the secret
I would let you
in on it

so much depends
upon the light
and the birds

and two fresh quail eggs wrapped in tissue. William Carlos Williams again. Moppy cannot conceive of eating such fragility. She blows their insides out and places the thin blue eggs in a bowl of marbled Italian ones.

~ sex, lies and coffee ~

'How are his kids?' Moppy asks Jill. I'm eating a large piece of chocolate cake and whipped cream. I like to watch Jill's face as I open my mouth. Her thinly disguised horror.

'Ghastly. Georgia emptied all my perfume in our shower. I can't get the smell out, and every time I go in there I start sneezing. Worst of all, Robert just laughed. He can't see it. They're just perfect little angels to him. I'm getting really fed up. How are yours?'

'Okay. Sam's infamous now. In the local paper, did you read that article about truancy? Sam's headmaster said it wasn't a problem in his school except for one incident. Sam's of course.'

'And what has Tim got to say about it all?' I ask.

'Oh, he ranted and raved in his usual fashion but he's been quite nice to me since Vincent and I split up. Apart from saying, "He isn't the first man in Auckland to suffer at your hands and he won't be the last."'

'I keep telling you he's still in love with you,' Jill says.

'Maybe, but it's not reciprocal, I can assure you. I don't think I could bear to touch him ever again.'

'And speaking of sex, how do you two cope with a non-existent sex life?' Jill asks.

'How do you know?' Moppy and I reply in complete unison. We all laugh and look at one another.

'Barb, is there something you're not telling us?' Moppy asks.

'What makes you think I'd confide in you two? Biggest gossips out. If I have anything to say I'll write about it.'

And what is there to say? That Mati and I are exchanging glances. Coming to an understanding based on the merest shift in eye position. It's all very old fashioned, and not without soul searching on my part. This is not a plot for Mills and Boon, a happy ending guaranteed. Mati's the real thing, a gang member in for murder, though he swears he was taking the rap.

'And what about you, Moppy?'

'Promise you won't go mad.'

'Moppy, you promised.'

'I know, but this one's safe. He lives in Whangarei. American. Billy.'

'Billy. And what do you know about him?'

'Not much. I've just left a message. He says he doesn't like mind games or rugby.'

'Sounds your type.'

'We'll see.'

What Jill neglects to tell Moppy, but has confided in me, is that her own sex life is less than satisfactory. Up until now good sex has been the glue that has allowed Jill to ignore Robert's caustic tongue and obnoxious children. For the first time Robert is claiming to be too tired. Or coming to bed so late she has no option but to fall asleep nursing his pillow and a growing unease.

And why does she not tell Moppy this?

~ Billy the Kid ~

Billy likes dogs and horses. He's breaking in a couple from the Kaimanawa. He says he likes kids too, but they all say that. Especially the ones without any.

'Horses,' says Moppy. She still hasn't got over the time Sam and Tim were on the back of a horse. Their teenage babysitter had brought it down the driveway to show Sam. He was three. Lisa was holding the bridle when the horse protested, his back legs humping, throwing Sam and Tim on the ground. There was nowhere in the narrow driveway for the horse to bolt. As she watched the hooves hover perilously close to Sam's head, Moppy screamed. Lisa managed to pull the horse away but not before Moppy had realised it was only Sam she was screaming for. Moppy often talks of it as being a defining moment. She was already pregnant with Thomas and considered it too late to turn the clock back.

'Can you ride?' asks Billy over the phone.

'No, they terrify me.'

'Just a matter of training, like riding a bike. What about camping?'

Moppy sighs with relief. 'I love camping. I take the kids every year.' Something she couldn't do with Vincent. He would never have coped with the long-drop.

'Sounds good. But listen, honey, I'm ringing from a cell phone. I'll ring you on the weekend and talk more.'

'I want a together lady,' Billy says when he rings back, 'but you sound a little nervous. Are you?'

'No, I'm doing the dishes while I talk.'

'Why? Aren't you allowed to take a break? Sit down and relax. Believe me, I've studied psychology. I can already suss you out.'

'And?'

'I think you are uptight. Lacking in self-esteem, which makes you competitive with men. I wouldn't mind betting that you've suffered some relationship trauma, probably way back, that you've never gotten over. Ya need to acknowledge the real you.'

Moppy laughs. 'It's strange,' she says. 'I feel as if we've known each other for ages and yet I don't even know what you look like.'

'You won't be disappointed. I'm dark and muscular. I was a boxer in college.'

Traitor. Iris would kill her if she knew. An American lover no better than a Pakistani. During the war Iris declared she would have nothing to do with the smooth-tongued snakes bearing silk stockings and chocolates. When pressed to join her landgirl mates at the local dance, Iris would make some excuse. Later, when everyone had gone, she would run outside to lie on the ground, smelling the earth. Vowing to save her virginity for some unknown returning soldier.

~ within the confines of the telephone exchange and the letter box ~

Dear Billy,

After our phone call I felt so close to you, I had to write. Is this an illusion on my part? Am I totally silly? I think you have a well-tuned intuitive sense.

I have to be careful because I trust people too easily. However, I do have a survival mechanism. It's called retreat at the first sign of trouble. I'm like a snail, carrying my house on my back. In fact every man I've known has commented on my heavy bag.

In answer to your question, I am a together lady but I'm not averse to wearing my skin inside out, revealing the stitches, i.e. I cry often but I am not ashamed of this. An old Maori woman told me I should never wipe tears from my face. I should let them fall where they will.

Love Moppy

Billy rings. 'I loved your letter. But why can't you be a light traveller? Why do you need to carry a heavy bag?'

Moppy has been arguing with Sam. He wants to go to the movies in town with friends in the weekend. By themselves. It's times like this she wishes she was still able to hide behind Tim's decisiveness, his clear no. Hers lacks definition and is easily translated into yes.

'Billy, I'm really tired right now and not in the mood.'

'Poor baby. You need some TLC. What about a massage? Wouldn't ya like my intuitive hands on your back?'

Moppy laughs. 'Can your hands reach through the wires?'

'Of course, baby, they're magic. Working their way over your back right now. Your skin is so smooth. My fingers between your shoulder blades. Going down your back bone. So straight and beautiful.'

How does he know? thinks Moppy.

'Later, when I know you better, I'll lick you all over. From your toes to your neck, getting stuck in all your juicy places. Now, honey, I want you to turn off the light, snuggle under, put the phone down and drift off to Paradise.'

Moppy spends the night tossing and turning. She sits up in bed at 4 a.m., silently screaming, *Go away and leave me alone*. When she does slip into sleep at 6, she dreams Billy is a ballet dancer, she is the swan, and Billy is lifting her high above the stage, so high she wakes up with a start.

Thomas is prising open her eyelids. 'Is there anyone in there?'

'Go away.'

'I want breakfast, Mummy.'

~ what is love ~

What is love?, my prisoners often ask. It's their favourite subject, though for most an unfamiliar visitor. There is a moment of sadness as I shrug my shoulders and realise I have no easy answers. My heart is as hollow as theirs. An empty womb. My own body attacking itself. Perhaps if I had met the right man earlier, before too many stray tissues embedded in the wrong places.

Mati doesn't seem to doubt, though. I could tell he'd fallen for me when he read his short story in class. The description of the woman, not beautiful in the conventional sense but possessing a lust for life revealed in her ample figure, was clearly me. Mati described her as having a spirited approach to life and eyes that lit up at the merest hint of humour. Not that I like to think of myself as vain but there was something in the feeling. The woman had short dark hair rather than my long and wild grey, so no one else in the class got the association. The woman in the story was a dancer. The man, jaded and cynical, was deeply touched by the way she expressed herself. While he was reading Mati kept lifting his eyes to mine.

After Mati read I felt compelled to touch him in some way. I handed him a poem and let his hand cover mine, briefly. I could almost feel the others in the class about to say 'teacher's pet', but Mati's respected in there, by guards and inmates. If you asked, they probably wouldn't be able to tell you why. I think it has a lot to do with the way he holds his head. It takes a long time for most inmates to look you in the eye, but the first day we met Mati shook my hand and gave me a dazzling smile as if he expected me not to judge him. Like he considered we were equals. Then my eyes were diverted by the sight of two cockroaches scuttling past. Mati shuffled over to his chair and sat down, eyes on the floor. Like he had suddenly realised the truth of his situation.

~ like water for chocolate ~

In a weak moment Moppy had agreed to come with Vincent. As friends, she said, but *Like Water for Chocolate* was a dangerous choice of movie. Watching the unrequited one weeping tears into the wedding cake while sitting next to another unrequited one licking an ice cream. Such power the unrequited one possesses. Making all the guests at the wedding weep copiously as soon as they partake of the cake. And later cooking quail in rose petal sauce. So small and delicate, the quails. And the aphrodisiacal effect on the virgin sister, so overwhelming.

'Did you leave quail eggs at my place?' Moppy whispers.

'When?' Vincent whispers back, as if this is a common event.

'No, it can't have been you. I just remembered I was at your place. Unless you're Superman.' She giggles, thinking he is a bit Clark Kentish. Wrong colour of course but similar skinny body and shyness.

'*Ssh.*' This comes from a woman behind.

Moppy can feel Vincent shrinking in his seat. 'Sorry,' she whispers.

Moppy loves the extravagance of the ending where the lovers finally get to consummate their love in a room lit by hundreds of candles. So passionate in their loving that the house ignites. Consummation and consumption. Are they different?

Moppy is burning up herself. She's expecting Billy to phone her later to make arrangements for their first meeting on Friday. Vincent is in a bad mood after the movie. He didn't enjoy it.

'Magic realism is not for the rational,' says Moppy.

'Don't be so patronising. I just thought it was stupid. OTT as you would say.'

She is glad she insisted on meeting him at the movies rather than allowing him to pick her up. Making a proper date of it. She has one hand on her car door when Vincent says, 'Aren't you going to give me a hug then?'

'A quick one,' she says.

As she drives off she watches him watching her. A small forlorn man standing in the middle of the road as if he's waiting for a bus. To run over him.

Sellotaped to her door is a note.

up close
the exotic
often disappoints

while in your own
back yard an elegant
white throat throbs

But there are no tuis in my back yard, thinks Moppy. She looks in the telephone book to ring Ted, have it out with him, if it is him, but his name is not listed. Not for the first time she wonders if Ted watches her coming and going. She resolves to sleep with the curtains closed. Even so, she feels curiously aligned to him.

Moppy is in the bath with a face pack on when Billy rings.

'Can you ring back in ten minutes? When I'm in bed?'

Ten minutes pass. After half an hour, she rings him. The phone is engaged. She tries every ten minutes. Finally at twelve she rings Faults.

'Can you check this number, please? It's been engaged for two hours.'

'No, there's nothing wrong with the line. It's engaged.' The woman's voice sounds amused. Moppy is not.

~ we women obsessed ~

Telephones are mere instruments of convenience, the male writer says to me. Whether you answer them or not depends on the current state of loneliness.

In our teens, Jill's father, being a doctor, had a phone, whereas Moppy and I lived in houses where the only visitation from the outside world came via the radio. The telephone is an unnecessary expense, our fathers both said as if they were in cahoots. And who would ever ring here? Excuses for the real reasons. My father didn't want my mother ringing the pub or perhaps our neighbour, the widow Rose. According to Moppy, Jack was more concerned to prevent Moppy from being too accessible.

The determined always find a way out of silence. Moppy would run down the road on the pretext of getting Iris a loaf of bread clutching two cents stolen from Iris's purse in one hand and the number of a boy in the other. An explanation perhaps of why Moppy has never been afraid to make the first move despite discovering certain dangers in such boldness.

In particular, the day a truck parked beside the telephone booth drove off with the canopy attached to the roof. Moppy stood screaming, unable to get out, while the wooden frame and the glass cracked all around her. Luckily the driver heard the commotion and stopped before she became another statistic. A freak accident. On the other end of the line her boyfriend, Geoff, was quite ineffectual, but it gave him such a fright that he proposed going steady. She stepped over the glass carefully and ran to my place to tell me. Always something to be gained from disaster.

Though Moppy and I have both graduated to possessing a telephone directory listing in our own names, Moppy still claims that the telephone is patriarchal. 'Even when I'm not in love,' she says, 'it's always there needing to be answered or placated in some way.' Willing it, pleading it. Glaring at it sitting there stubbornly silent.

Moppy has read Adrienne Rich. She is not

*ignorant of the fact this way of grief
is shared, unnecessary
and political*

But feminism has made no difference here. Moppy is still a woman, *obsessed with Love, our subject*. And in her head a dialogue. His voice whispering sweet words to someone else.

Of course I can sleep at night secure but not happy in the knowledge that my potential lover is where I left him. Waiting for me to visit. This changes everything.

~ still on the phone ~

Billy finally rings at 2 a.m.

'Sorry, did I wake you, honey?' he asks.

'Of course not. I've been lying here wondering who you've been talking to for the last four hours.'

'It was this damn woman who's been harassing me. She finally got through to me. I couldn't get rid of her. I told her I didn't want to see her again. She was crying and carrying on so I couldn't just hang up. I had to talk her through it. Then my mother rang.'

'From America?'

'It's true. You can ring her yourself if you like. I'll give ya the number. She's drunk though, so she might abuse ya. Stupid bitch. Going on and on. So I don't want you giving me a hard time also.'

'Can you blame me? Perhaps this is how you get your kicks. Talking to strange women.'

'Don't be so insecure. Anyway, if it's such a big deal you could have spoken to me earlier.'

'I couldn't. I had a face mask on. I didn't want to split it.'

'Is your face that bad?'

'I don't think so. I just wanted to look my best for tomorrow. Are you still coming down?'

'Yeah, but I'm feeling pretty shitty, like I'm getting the flu. I know you'll burst, though, if we don't meet this weekend, so I've booked me a motel.'

'Okay. Where will we meet?'

'How about Kelly Tarlton's carpark at 7.30. Okay?'

'Yeah. What kind of car?'

'Red Alfa Romeo.'

Moppy rolls the words in her mouth. Red Alfa Romeo.

'Would ya like me to help you sleep?'

'It didn't work last time.'

'It will this time. I promise. A trip to Paradise. But just a massage, okay?'

His deep drawling voice travels at a leisurely pace down the line and over her legs. All the time he is telling her what he is doing, where he is placing his hands. When Moppy's breathing slows down he tells her to ring him again in the morning.

'Did you sleep well?'

'Yes. You have a mesmeric voice.'

'I was stroking you all night. You're a sensuous woman. I'm really looking forward to seeing you. But don't expect too much. I'm not at my best.'

~ bullying in the playground ~

'He's got an Alfa Romeo, red,' Moppy tells me. 'And he's good at it, he says.'

In the fifth form, cars were important to Moppy and Jill, and to me, if I'm honest. We had a list of questions for boys we met at dances. They had to be in the sixth form, and have a sense of humour and access to a car. Ownership was even better.

'Do you remember those boys we met from Remuera? Picking us up in a Rolls-Royce?' I ask.

revisiting the sixties

in our street
a Rolls-Royce

two boys
in Daddy's car

picking up chicks
from the west

give them
a good time

white boots
brown corduroy minis

a waist back then
but the same nervous

giggle as now
not quite certain

*she should be playing
with the big boys*

*how far down
does the tongue go*

*he's good at it
he says*

*my voice high pitched
in the leather interior*

*I want to know
how do you hold*

*onto the ball
without*

*getting
stomped on*

~ the light falls on his bald spot ~

Contemplation of this moment has occupied Moppy all day. She finds it doesn't matter in the shop. It's not busy. She's just about to leave when Sean comes in. He looks as if he's been drinking.
'How are ya?'
'Good, good, how are you?'
'Terrible, Zoe's left me. Reckons I drink too much. But it's where I get my ideas, ya know? We artists can't live sober.'
'I do. Most of the time anyway.'
'That's the problem with ya, Moppy. Too conventional. You wanna get rid of your kids and get on with your work.'
'You can talk. You'd get more work done if you didn't drink so much. Anyway, I've gotta go. I've got a hot date.'
'Lucky, lucky man. Don't forget, babe, I'm here any time you want.'
She drives home, forgetting to pick up something for dinner on the way. As it happens the kids are pleased enough with baked beans. Sam and Thomas are aware of her preoccupation, but distraction allows them a certain freedom. Once she lost Sam on a bus, having forgotten he was sitting at the back waiting for her to give the signal to get off. She was

standing in the street in Takapuna, faintly confused, as the bus drove away. Not without resources, Sam got off in the city and persuaded a shop keeper to let him phone his father. Tim was not amused at Moppy's carelessness. Yet another lecture deposited on the answer phone.

Tim picks the kids up right on time at seven, but Moppy still leaves late so Billy will arrive before her. She parks behind the red Alfa Romeo. Under the street light she notes the man in the car has a large head, dark hair and a bald spot. The man gets out. He has a weightlifter's body, short and squat. His trousers are too tight, the stomach hanging over his gold and leather belt. Moppy gets out of her car. Reluctantly.

'Moppy, I presume.' Billy puts his hand out. His gold bracelet jangles. He looks equally disappointed.

Surely he can't object to my looks, Moppy thinks. No one else ever has. She is wearing a long floral skirt with a cream lycra top, more feminine than usual, but she has dressed for the environment – waterfront, clear starry sky, nearly full moon.

'Billy.'

Moppy attempts a smile.

'What do we do now?'

'I thought it was arranged. We go out to dinner. But I've gotta warn ya, I'm feeling really bad. I think I've taken too many anti-histamines. But I didn't want to disappoint ya.'

The restaurant is on the waterfront. Middle range. Licensed Chinese. His choice, so why does he squint at the soup placed before him? His double chin wobbles when he sips.

'I shouldn't have come. I'm out of it.'

'At least we've met each other. Can put a picture to the voice.'

But why doesn't that beautiful voice have an equally beautiful body? And even the voice is dissipated across the table, the words slurred and coarse. His eyes, though, are deep brown. If this was Mills and Boon, the kind you can drown in.

'Do you like movies?' Moppy asks. In her teenage years she read *Seventeen* and all the advice on how to talk to a man.

'No, not much. I have trouble sitting still. Really I'm an outdoors man. A Marlboro type. You say you like camping?'

'Yeah. I love it. A group of us go to the beach every year. I've got all the works – tent, stove and even collapsible shelves for the pots.'

'When I say camping, I mean back to basics, a two-man tent and a fire on the edge of a river.'

'Sounds fun. It's just that I have the kids so you always need more stuff.

Not that I see them much, they're old enough to do their own thing now and they're good swimmers so I don't have to worry.' But she is worrying. She thinks she sounds like she's stepped out of *Little House on the Prairie*.

'And what do your kids think of having a mother who likes talking to strange men late at night?'

'They don't know of course.'

'Relax. What about men taking you out? How do they feel about that?'

'It depends. I've only really been out with one man so far. They really liked him.'

'So what happened?'

Moppy laughs. 'He was too nice. He didn't have the same sense of humour or appreciate my art. Then he got the flu.'

'You like to be in charge, don't ya?'

'You think I'm bossy?'

'Yeah. Look at the way you ordered the wine, for instance. Men usually do that.'

'I'm sorry. Would you have liked something different?'

'Yeah, it's too dry for my taste.'

'Oh, God, I forgot you were American.' Billy doesn't laugh. Moppy says quickly, 'I just can't stand sweet wine, it makes me sick. Ever since Cold Duck.'

'Cold Duck?'

'Teenage terror of the seventies. Sickly sweet. But I liked the bottle. A bulbous shape, very good for candles. The first time I got drunk I was camping in Coromandel. Your kind of camping, in a paddock. I was with my first serious boyfriend. We lit a fire on the beach and started drinking Cold Duck. I thought I was a bird, I was running up and down the beach, flapping my arms and singing, I'm a bird, I'm a bird, I can fly. Obviously it didn't put Geoff off me, 'cause we got married.'

Billy laughs. And Moppy recognises the rich tones of his voice again.

'So ya married your teenage sweetheart. How romantic.'

'It would have been, except he ran off with another man. Older and uglier than me.'

'Oh honey. That's terrible. No wonder your ego is a little fragile.'

He insists on paying for the meal and agrees to a walk on the beach. Moppy slips her shoes off and runs over the cold sand to the water's edge.

'Look, the tide's in, we could go for a swim. I haven't done that for ages. For years, in fact.'

'Yeah, sure, I'd love to, on another night. Right now I just want to go back to the motel and die.'

Sitting in the Alfa Romeo, Moppy feels sorry enough to rub his back for a minute. She is surprised by the substantial nature of his shoulders. Strong enough to pick her up and dance.

He drops her off at her car. 'Ring me in the morning then. I want to know you're all right,' Moppy says.

'Okay, I won't kiss ya and give ya my germs.'

Billy does not ring in the morning. Moppy looks in her art books for inspiration but she is too restless, too uncertain. She does not want to start work in case Billy rings, recovered and looking for entertainment.

Two days later, walking outside to her garden, carrying the cordless phone, she almost trips over a small cane basket. Inside is a bouquet of parsley, a plaited string of garlic and a recipe.

take every day
to ward off colds
and other undesirables

Moppy sits on her back steps, chewing a stem of parsley, watching her cat, Tyger, unsuccessfully stalk a thrush.

~ like seeing the film ~

All the world loves a lover and he had promised a trip to Paradise. In his Alfa Romeo.

Meeting the voice is like seeing the film after reading the book. According to Moppy's version the casting director got it all wrong. She wanted someone more like Al Pacino.

'It's true Billy has Italian heritage and gold bracelets,' she tells me over the phone, 'but he looks more like that short fat actor. The one who pushes his mama off the train.'

On the radio, a spokesperson for Friends of the Concert Programme is pleading for continued public funding for broadcasting. Explaining that television has changed our perception of reality. *Eyes are aggressive,* he says. *With radio we learn to trust our ears. Ears are gentle, wise and feminine.*

I hear this programme on the way to prison and resolve to take no account of the forehead with the word HATE tattooed on it. Not Mati but a new pupil, Ras. Mati has tattoos but his are more modest, some home-made dots on his face, a tui on his arm, and on the knuckles of his right hand the name of his gang. Aggressive enough, but his voice, soft as Iris's gingerbread, melts in my mouth. Already I am investigating laser removal of past loyalties.

Ras swaggers into the room, his arms swinging at the side. Though patches are forbidden, his long hair is tied back with a scrap of red material. The tattoo on his neck is obscured by a red scarf. He sits opposite, with his legs wide apart, and eyeballs me. I can see Mati is uncomfortable. On TV last night I watched a documentary about domestic violence. A woman in prison said she knew her boyfriend loved her when he beat her up for looking at another man. With practised sleight of hand the word violence can be substituted for the word love.

I ask if they have done their homework. To write about letting go. A weighted subject. Without waiting to be asked, Ras starts reading, staring me down the entire time.

> *when I get out of here*
> *I'll dangle her body*
> *over a cliff*
> *fuckin bitch, fuckin bitch*
> *fuckin bitch*
> *dobbing me in*
> *fuckin bitch, fuckin bitch*
> *fuckin bitch*
> *letting go feels good*
> *watching her body falling*
> *fuckin bitch*

I take a deep breath. This is a test. Designed to scare the hell out of me.

'Good sense of rhythm,' I say.

A collective sigh passes around the group.

~ taking what suits ~

Moppy, listening to the same programme, is the eternal optimist, taking the best parts like flattery from the astrology chart.

'You see,' she says later. 'I told you that you can tell from the voice.'

In the background a bracelet rattles, but Moppy frolics unconcerned in the pages of her next letter.

Dear Billy,

So we didn't ride off into the wild blue yonder forever and a day like I hoped, but perhaps it's just as well. The horse would have bucked me five miles down the track and you would be riding too fast to notice.

The trouble with having a rich inner fantasy life is that the reality often fails to match up. I was disappointed because you were not as I pictured you, in fact you're not really my type.

I can't help thinking you were also a bit disappointed in me. Perhaps you fancy small, plump blondes? If you found me flinty perhaps it's because I was unsure of the situation. Weighing everything up, I think we deserve to give each other one more chance. Why make a judgement based solely on personal appearances?

I don't want a bicycle built for two, I've got my own, but I'm not averse to the odd ride side by side in the country, singing amongst the blackberries.

Yours, Moppy

~ listening in ~

'Billy, are you all right?'
'Course I am. Why?'
'You haven't rung. I thought you might have rung on Saturday. I was worried about you.'
'I was in bed all day, sick. This week I've been away on business.'
'What exactly do you do?'
'I sell drugs.'
'Drugs?'
'Legitimate. Anyway what do ya want? I've just got home.'
'Oh. I wanted to know if you got my letter?'
'No. When did ya post it?'
'Tuesday.'
'No, never seen it. Someone might've stolen it. Ya never know around here. Pack of mongrels.'
'Are we going to meet this weekend?'
'Give me a break.' He sighs deeply. 'All of my life I've been surrounded by women on the take. I came to New Zealand to get away.'
'From whom?'
'This woman who wouldn't leave me alone. Endlessly on at me to marry her. She was into emotional blackmail – you know, if ya loved me ya would, it's important to me. On and on.'
'You lived together?'
'Yeah, for five years. Wasn't that proof enough? But all she wanted was a ring on her tiny little finger and one in my nose. I'm not getting into those games again, Barbara.'
'Barbara? Who's Barbara? My name's Moppy.'
'Of course it is, Moppy. I didn't call you Barbara. Why would I call you Barbara?'
'I don't know. My oldest friend's called Barbara. She's a poet. You don't know her, do you?'

'No, I never trust poets myself, they're all liars.'
'I'm not sure I can trust you.'
'Hang on, there's someone at the door.'

Billy comes back on the phone after a minute. Moppy is lying on the bed flicking through one of Jill's *Vanity Fairs*.

'I think you're ringing me 'cause you're frustrated,' Billy says.

'So I'll be all right with a good fuck?'

'For God's sake, woman, you admitted it the other day, why can't you admit it now? I don't mind playing with ya over the phone, if that's what ya want. It'll be a damn sight more satisfying than this conversation. Why don't I just lick ya all over right now?'

What the hell, thinks Moppy and lies back on the bed, letting his forked tongue slither across her naked breasts. Writhing over the bed trying to shed her skin which is itching with loneliness. 'Ah,' she sighs loudly when she has succeeded in reaching that state of oblivion. 'Thanks and goodnight,' she whispers, putting the phone down and spreading her new self diagonally under the duvet.

In the morning she discovers a note in her letter box,

it's not words
themselves
that need
to be trusted
but what is heard
under the rock

in the silence
between

Was he listening to my orgasmic cry, she thinks, or the man on the radio?

~ going all the way ~

'Thank God I'm not a Catholic,' Moppy says to Jill the day after Billy's phone call. 'It would be so embarrassing.'

'What I want to know is, why do these things happen to you? What is it about you?' Jill is genuinely mystified.

'I don't know,' says Moppy. 'Perhaps it all started with Mr Harrex. It's funny, though. I think the fact I was so innocent saved me. If my mother had found out what was going on with him it might have been much worse for me. You know? He was a really good teacher.'

Moppy was book monitor in form two. The job should have been mine by rights seeing I was top in reading, but Moppy was Mr Harrex's pet. We all knew that, even though none of us saw him sitting Moppy on his knee. *Skinny legs* the other kids called her, but Mr Harrex seemed to like them, stroking them with his large hairy hands all the way up to her white cotton panties. And under, ever so briefly. His face reddening. Standing up, saying, 'I'd better put you down before the headmaster comes in.' Years later Moppy said she had liked the soft slow feel of his fingers. Being picked. Had gone home and lain under the pink candlewick bedspread and tried to discover the soft warmth again.

Mr Harrex organised a class trip to Wellington on the overnight train. In the tunnels the boys ran up and down, shrieking and pulling plaits. Not mine because after Janet died my mother could not bare the sight of my long blonde hair. Too much of a reminder, she said, and cut it off roughly. The girls screamed. It was a competition to see whose vocal cords were the shrillest. Moppy won. Even then she was the boys' favourite. We shared a sleeping carriage. I lay in the dark, enjoying the rhythm and the feeling we were going somewhere significant. Moppy was on the top bunk on account of being the only girl in her family and never getting it. Mr Harrex came in and pulled Moppy's curtain aside. 'Goodnight, sausage,' he said. I pretended to be asleep but I could see his legs twitching as he stood there.

'What was he doing?' I asked Moppy when he left.

'Nothing,' she said. 'He just kissed me goodnight.'

~ a perverse persistence ~

'One thing's for sure, Billy has plenty of sexual imagination.'

'I don't want to know.'

'Really?'

'I'm not in the mood,' says Jill. She is twisting her wedding ring round and round. Moppy does not notice the tightness in her voice.

'Anyway it'll probably come to nothing. He accused me of being too wound up.'

'For God's sake, why on earth are you persisting? He sounds slimy to me.'

'It's his voice, the way he talks. It turns me on.'

'Perhaps he's a hypnotist.'

'Perhaps. I'm going to give it one more go. See what happens. You know how I can't resist opening the oven door to see if the cake is rising.'

'And sometimes the cake flops or you burn your fingers.'

'The alternative is not baking at all. Buying tasteless cakes from the supermarket.'

'Did you read about that rape case?' Jill asks.

'No. I try to avoid such topics.'

'You would. This prisoner put ads in the personal column. All these women wrote to him. They knew he was in prison but it made no difference. His letters showed such sensitivity, one said. She visited him in prison and was impressed with the way he talked, looking into her eyes the whole time. She even picked him up when he got out of prison. He repaid her kindness by raping her.'

'So what's your point? Billy's not in prison. I know that for a fact.'

But does she know what he does for a living? There are jobs not mentioned down at the employment bureau.

~ unsafe sex ~

'I needed the money,' said the woman in the magazine article, confessing her job in telesales was really talking dirty. Or listening dirty. Does it work in reverse? Can males sell their tongues for $100 an hour?

An ad pinned to a bulletin board in a coffee bar caught my attention. A serious coffee bar, you understand, so we are not talking sleaze here. *Are you a woman having trouble sleeping? Feeling wound up? I guarantee success. Requires client participation. Ph 0900 UNWIND*. That's me, I thought, and what did I have to lose but the price of a phone call and my dignity? It was September last year. I was finding it difficult to sleep. I kept seeing lambs in my dreams but they were not jumping over fences. They were lying on their backs with their legs in the air. Too fat to stand.

'Jerry here,' said the American voice after I had negotiated the sales pitch at the beginning. 'Thirty dollars for fifteen minutes,' he said, 'Fifty for half an hour.'

'Fifteen minutes should do,' I said.

'Lie down and make yourself comfortable,' he said. 'I'm just rubbing my hands with sweet almond oil. Getting them warm. You deserve the best.'

He didn't ask me what I wanted. Just assumed. Is that the difference between men and women? His voice was low, the type they use to sell ice cream over the radio on a hot summer's day. He traversed my back, slowly describing every inch. I wonder if he knew I was a substantial woman. It took a long time. I was nearly asleep when he told me to turn over. He started at the neck. When he got to the breasts he said, 'Put your hands over mine, feel the nipples getting hard.'

When he got to my pubic hairs, my snatch as he called it, he said, 'Twist those soft hairs around your fingers.' When he got to my sweet little bud, he said, 'Stroke it with me, tell me how fast or slow you want it. Am I doing it right? Now, I'm going to slip my fat hard cock into you while you keep stroking yourself. Oh, it feels so good, so tight, so fuckable, are you going to come with me, that's right we'll come together. My hot sperm is squirting into you now. Now.'

It was only when I hung up that I realised I hadn't asked him to wear a condom. Oh what the hell, I thought, you've got to live dangerously sometimes. After all, Moppy does.

The thing is, I told him my name. Stupid, I know. He rang me back. Said he'd never spoken to a woman like me before. Said he liked the sound of my voice so much he'd do it for free. He rang me a few times but I started to feel as if I was paying anyway. As the gay man says in the novel I'm currently reading, 'There is a constant cumulative cost.' He was talking about casual sex, picking up men in toilets or in bars. Not every heterosexual man has come to this realisation, but most women, lesbian or straight, have. In my middle age I've decided I want the real thing. Love and sex in the one body. Or nothing.

~ desert flower ~

Dear Moppy,

The sun is shining, my horses are prancing in the fields wanting me to ride them and I can't concentrate.

I'm sorry about the last few weeks, I've been tired and shitty, I guess the flu took more out of me than I realised. I really want to see your sweet face again, start again.

I am just as afraid of being hurt as you say you are. Men are no different. In fact I believe we are more sensitive than women. Me especially, even if I do come across as being strong. There is a difference but sometimes one will overpower the other and a bruise forms.

All I do know for sure is, I want to look into your beautiful blue eyes, and hopefully feel our souls exchange glances. I also hope we are able to undo the ropes that bind us to the past and express what we want and feel.

Sweet thoughts
Billy

For Moppy it's a matter of unravelling. The solving of various obscure facts. Who is Barbara, is his bracelet real gold, is he married, and what does he do for a living? Not for the first time Moppy thinks she has missed her vocation. If he didn't live so far away she would drive past his house. If she were not so busy she would go to the local library and look up the Whangarei electoral roll and telephone book.

'So, babe. How about we meet half way? Waiwera would be good. We can have a spa and see what sort of mood that puts us in. What do ya reckon, my desert flower?'

'Okay,' says Moppy on account of the desert flower. As a child Jack used to call her his 'lettuce leaf'. This weekend, Sam and Thomas are off to Hot Water Beach with Tim and Wendy. Moppy does not wish to spend the weekend alone. She will compensate for her loss by lying in a spa pool with a mysterious stranger.

She stops in Albany for ten minutes. It seems such a safe place. Small shops and hens running around as if no one has told them there is a prison down the road and a city over the back fence getting closer every day. What is she doing? she asks herself. In her bag she has packed a nightie, toothbrush, moisturiser and condoms. There can only be one intent from such a packing. She is not sure she wants to go on, but she tells herself, Too late now to turn back.

At Silverdale she finds herself stopping again. Buying a new lacy black bra and matching panties while playing over and over in her mind Billy's voice saying, *Hello my desert flower*.

By the time they meet in the carpark outside the hot pools the desert flower has ceased to bloom.

He says, 'You're late. I thought ya weren't coming.'

'I nearly didn't. I stopped in Albany and debated with myself. But here I am. Ready or not.'

'Well, no point being here otherwise.'

~ back to basics ~

The carpark is busy with buses bringing in groups of youths talking and laughing among themselves. Moppy's first date with Geoff was here at the hot pools. Sixteen, and just the two of them in his car.

Jill and I came in her boyfriend's car. I wasn't too pleased being paired off with big ears Ian. He kept trying to push my head under water like he didn't know what else to do with girls. It wasn't as if I was the size I am now.

Moppy marched right out of the changing sheds and jumped into the water beside Geoff. She put her hands on his shoulders while he towed her round the pool. I watched in envy. Later Moppy confessed it was she who first put her tongue into his mouth.

Despite the boldness of her tongue, they went around for two years before her virginity was broached. Pregnancy was never an option for girls from 5 Latin, even if we had to leave school early on account of money.

Moppy went to Family Planning, a borrowed ring on her finger, a lie in her mouth. It was all terribly serious, but there was a safety in the time frame that now seems absent. Sure Moppy has condoms and at home she has left a note under the telephone saying where she has gone and with whom, but is that enough? She's thinking of the young girl found dead in the city cemetery last night. Head bashed in to the point of non-recognition.

~ a sexual virgin ~

'Hey, don't look so worried,' Billy says. 'I'm not going to rape you.'

But why do his eyes graze over her body with sandpaper teeth?

There are no vacancies in Waiwera. Moppy follows Billy. His Alfa Romeo is much faster up the hill than her aging Starlet. By the time she gets to Orewa he has already turned into a driveway of a motel that offers a spa pool, Sky TV and a honeymoon suite which in the event turns out to be a circular bed.

'Well what do we do now?' Moppy asks.

'You need to ask?'

'Yes.'

'Well I'm gonna get my money's worth by having a spa. I could do with relaxing. You too by the look of ya. I could give you a massage first if ya want. I'm an expert.'

'Okay.'

Moppy buries her face in the red bedcover. It is unevenly soft, a brocade-like texture.

'You'll have to take your top off, woman. I've brought some oil.'

She pulls off her long-sleeved T-shirt.

'And your sexy bra.'

Thick fingers massage her shoulders.

'Boy, you're tense, babe. We'll have to do something about that.'

'Ow.'

'Just there, is it? Good. I need to go deep.'

'It hurts.'

'Oh don't be such a wimp. It's gotta hurt if it's gonna do any good. Now roll over.'

Moppy rolls over. She shuts her eyes. Billy tickles her nipples, then slaps her leg.

'Let's go for a spa before I get too turned on.'

The spa pool is in a small gazebo. Moppy runs along the concrete path, her white motel towel wrapped tightly. Billy saunters, swinging his towel as if he can't feel the cold at all. He is wearing skin-tight togs, black with square-cut legs. Moppy is wearing a purple one-piece cut low in the top and high in the legs.

'I'm gonna have to do something about this,' he says, rubbing his stomach and easing his body into the water. 'Mind you, you could lose a little too. Your legs are great but your stomach is losing it. I hate fat women. The States are full of wobbling bums.'

'Thank you very much.'

'There's no need to sound defensive. If we're gonna spend the night together, the least we can do is be honest. And Moppy, I like you. Right?'

'Right,' says Moppy.

They go for dinner. KFC. Moppy is as disappointed as the time she got a book on horses from her grandmother for Christmas. And he suggests going halves.

Later, back at the honeymoon suite, Moppy asks, 'What now?'

'First of all I'll give you a massage lesson. Get me in the mood.'

Moppy strokes Billy's back. It is hairy. She has never had a lover with a hairy back.

'Not like that. You have to move in deep. Visualise my muscles. Feel me.' He sighs deeply. 'That's the way. You're a quick learner, babe.'

'Thanks.'

She undresses in the bathroom and slips quickly beneath the cover. The bed's circular shape makes her disoriented.

Billy does not kiss the way Moppy likes. Vincent was too slow, but Billy sticks his tongue right down her throat. He sucks her nipples and twists her sparse pubic hairs round his fingers. He pulls. Then he quickly turns her over on her stomach.

'I like it from behind,' he says. 'Like horses. I'm a simple man.'

He plunges in deep. Over and over, his cock hitting the tip of her cervix. He is hard. Ramming it in. Moppy cannot see his eyes.

I could be anyone, she thinks, anyone at all. I am not Moppy lying here.

His withdrawal is sudden, abrupt. He makes a small strangled sound and pulls out. Rips off the condom and throws it in the wastepaper basket.

'How was it?' he asks.

Moppy does not reply. She is crying. Great sobs that wrack her body.

Billy is unfazed. 'Let it all out,' he says. 'Let it out. You're really a sexual virgin, aren't you – but not too bad, if only you knew what to do with it.'

He rolls over on his back and within five minutes is asleep and snoring. Moppy lies beside him, exhausted.

I've got to get out of here, she thinks.

Quietly she slips out of the bed, tiptoes over to the wallet left on the table and checks it for evidence.

A small card falls out. She reads the words, *Are you a woman having trouble sleeping?* Definitely, she thinks. There is also a piece of paper with a list of women's names and numbers. In his briefcase she discovers a large bag of marijuana, a packet of white powder and jars of unlabelled pills.

She picks up the telephone and puts it under the blankets next to Billy. On the back of his card she writes, 'I'd stick to phone sex if I was you. You're better at that and obviously experienced.' She leaves the card on top of his wallet. He can pay for the room, she thinks.

She opens the door and leaves. Billy does not move.

It's 2 a.m. when she gets home. Sitting on her doorstep she finds three brown eggs, one slightly cracked, the others perfect. No clues as to who left them. This is not a neighbourhood where the residents keep chickens. She's sure Ted hasn't got any. Moppy takes them as another sign. Fecundity perhaps? From what Sean has told her she knows he is sterile from a brush with cancer, so is it likely he'd remind her of that fact? She spends the rest of the night tossing questions of morality over her shoulder, and early in the morning phones me up and invites me for breakfast. A cheese omelette.

~ before they screwed ~

'You need proteins for confessions,' she says.

'What's to confess?'

'Perhaps I was wrong about trusting voices,' she says, but then she wants something in return for this admission of failure. 'That's not the issue now. I found your number on Billy's list of clients.'

I'm mortified, embarrassed, but Moppy and I go back a long way, she's seen my father drunk and I've seen her so desperate for a pee she used a cooking pot. Mind you, this was in a van in southern Italy.

And the I in the poem cannot always be trusted.

Before we screwed

Before we screwed
for the third time
in one night he said
'you are a sexual virgin.'

In this affair he is the one
with the stick, pointing out
the distinctive features
of my body. The erotic zones

*and the slight touch of erosion
but over all, 'not too bad
for your age, if only
you knew what to do with it.'*

*I suggest bathing in acid
carefully stripping back
to reveal my original form
but he has territory to conquer*

*no time for delicate
exploration and 'real women
like it rough,' he says
his cock ploughing a jagged track*

*through me, each thrust digging
up a deeply buried root
and when he comes he thinks
I am crying for joy.*

*After the plunder he snores
with the resonance of a satisfied
pioneer planning to name
pathways after himself*

*In the morning he wakes
to a virgin forest
dense and dark and no idea
where the tracks are*

~ a vow of celibacy ~

'Cappuccino?' Jill asks.

'No,' says Moppy. 'I think I need a wine. I've gone off cappuccinos ever since I thought about them in relation to Billy. All froth on top and underneath bitter and dark. With a flat white at least you see what you're getting.'

'So what happened with Billy? You've been very quiet about it.'

'I don't want to talk about it. Let's just say the sex was not good.'

'In what way?'

'Well it wasn't rape but it was violent. Like he hated me or all women. So you were right.'

'It doesn't make me happy. Believe me. You're not going to see him again, are you?'

'Definitely not. I've made a vow of celibacy.'

Jill laughs so much she knocks over her glass of red wine. It soaks into the white tablecloth. The waitress glares at them.

'Oh, highly Freudian,' says Moppy, who does not tell Jill about her escape in the dead of the night or about Billy's job. 'Anyway I'm serious.'

'Yeah, until you succumb to the next voice.'

'We'll see. Bet I can last three months.'

'How much?'

'A dinner on me.'

'You can't afford it. Anyway, what are you going to do with the free time?'

'I'm going to paint the house, be nice to my children and love myself.'

'You mean masturbate?'

'I don't know. Does that count?'

'Not according to Clinton.'

'Talking about sex, how's Robert?'

Jill pulls a face. 'Terrible. I can't do a thing right. He said it's about time I got a more stimulating job so I'd have something to talk about. According to him it's all my fault he's not interested in sex. If I was more spontaneous.'

'What does he want you to do? Dress up in suspenders and apron or disappear under the table and give him a blow job?'

'The latter probably. But who wants to when he's so grumpy?'

'Can't say I would.'

'Actually we were talking about you last night. He said he thinks you're addicted to excitement and that you deliberately take too many risks. That you like walking on the precipice. It doesn't make sense. If you were a poet like Barb, wanting material…'

Moppy laughs. 'Who knows? Maybe I'm stocking up. My life as a novel or film.' Her face takes on a glow. 'Hey, I've just had an idea. What about a series of collages made from scraps of material from lovers. Old letters, cards, flowers, photos and maybe some lines from Barb's poems. I could call it *barbed wire*.'

~ from the phone to the supermarket ~

Billy,

When I got home from our sordid little tryst I found three eggs on my doorstep. I don't know who sent them but I think someone was trying to tell me something. Like there's more goodness in your own neighbourhood. I suggest you crawl back to where you came from.

Moppy

PS. You're lucky I haven't dobbed you into the police for what I found in your briefcase. Believe me I thought about it, only my friend Barb talked me out of it. She didn't want to be involved and she certainly didn't fancy coming across you in Parry. If anything ever happens to me, I've left all your details with a good friend.

For the next few days Moppy pretends to be Garbo, wearing dark glasses and hiding behind supermarket shelves. At the same time she keeps a curious eye on the solo men. She's conducting future research. The idea is to look at what they gather in their trolleys. Disposable nappies are no good. Rat bait suggests they live in a hovel, fish bait that they're too keen on weekends with the boys, and *Rugby News* speaks for itself. Moppy is looking for the urbane man who has fresh mussels, fettuccine, brie, good wine and perhaps a small box of imported chocolates. A man who cooks for himself, is busy enough to have a life of his own, and a hint of hedonism.

She rehearses possible scenarios of meetings. Bumping into trolleys, making requests, but she's forgetting she shops in the married suburbs. A high proportion of the solo men do have nappies placed ostentatiously in their trolleys.

~ trying her hand with a Russian ~

In the restless lull between men, Moppy expresses an interest in teaching English as a second language.

'Why don't you come to my conversation class and see for yourself?' I ask her.

I want to focus on physical descriptions, so I start the session with a discussion on what men first look at in women.

'The body,' Sergov says.

The women claim to be drawn to the eyes.

'What colour? Sergov asks, as if he could change his bad women luck with coloured contacts.

'What is behind the eyes, Sergov,' I explain. 'The light and the feelings.'

He looks blank, but I can see the women understand.

'How did you meet your husbands or wives?' Moppy asks the class.

No one volunteers an answer until I point to Grace, the most outgoing pupil.

'In department store, going up.' She raises her hand.

'In a lift?' I ask.

'Yes, lift.'

'Quick work,' says Moppy before she realises this is too complicated to explain. 'What did he say?' she asks.

'Come for coffee. I said yes. He is handsome. Like Richard Gere but Korean. But now he is fat.'

They all laugh.

Heh Ju says, 'My husband chased me. I drive off but he jump on my car. I stop the car. He said I am beautiful. He come to home. My father like him. Said to marry. My husband is boring now. No job and he lazy. I was boring too but now in class I am happy.'

'Bored not boring,' I say and write it on the board.

'Are you happy because you make friends?' asks Moppy.

'Because of light in two teachers' eyes,' says Heh Ju.

'And how did you meet your wife?' Moppy points to Sergov.

'I have no wife now. In Russia I have two.'

Grace asks, 'Do you want wife?'

'Maybe New Zealand girl.' Sergov looks at Moppy and smiles. 'Then I can stay in New Zealand.'

'Don't look at me,' Moppy says and dives under the table.

The class laugh loudly.

She drives us home singing the song we sang in class, Eric Clapton's 'Wonderful Tonight'. On her doorstep she finds not eggs but two passionfruit. And another poem:

consider the passionfruit
the hard outer skin
the inner succulence

Our teeth sink into the yellow flesh.

'Who needs men?' she asks.

~ letting go again and again ~

But they do need us, I think as I am driving to Parry. In C block they are waiting for me at the iron gate.

'You're late,' Steve says.

'Sorry, I got held up at the top.'

There are guards and guards. Some more co-operative than others. And clearly those who think creative writing is a soft option. 'Most of them wouldn't know what a sentence was. Ha. Ha. Sentence, get it? So what do they write about? The thrill of raping?'

As I walk to our small room today, one guard says, 'You know the guys are much more co-operative after you've been. You make a difference.'

Ras smiles. An out-of-focus smile. His eyes are bloodshot, his pupils dilated. Obviously I'm not going to get any work out of him today. I ask him about the name tattooed large around his neck.

'Is Grace your girlfriend?'

'No she's the fuckin bitch that put me in here. And don't get too nosy. I made the personal growth lady cry 'cause she got too lippy.'

'Well crying's not a bad thing, is it?'

'Not if you're a woos girl, I s'pose. But us guys gotta be staunch, ya know.'

'Well I believe it's stronger to admit to weakness. It takes courage to show vulnerability.' I risk a glance at Mati.

Ras frowns. 'Did ya bring any muffins? I've got the munchies, bad.'

The others giggle.

'After we do some work. Mati, do you want to read?'

'This is from last week. Letting go.' His voice is soft.

freedom down the road

when I was a kid
we had lots of parties at our place, eh?
sometimes Mum would sleep in
we got to drink the dregs
have a drag of a fag
then sneak out
and run all the way
to the river

we weren't allowed there, eh?
never knew why
just another stupid rule
some kids hung a rope
in a tree
we flung ourselves
into the dirty water
falling down like a stone

letting go, screaming
to the muddy bottom
coming back up
creeping home to a whack
with a strap from Mum
for our wet clothes

it was worth it, but

A familiar tale. They all laugh. I talk about freedom and the sounds in the poem. About the natural voice. Mati smiles at me and gives me a small sketch to go with the poem: a river, a tree, a rope.

No matter how good the session, it's always a relief to reach my car. Three tuis waiting for me in the branches of a gum. My car covered in red blossom. I drive off, passing a small dog which looks like it is running away. His coat caramel and white, his head turned back as if to see if anyone is following.

~ a fatal flaw ~

If you fall off a horse and don't get back on you'll never ride again. So Moppy believes. And on a Saturday morning the newspaper is tempting to those lying alone in bed.

Positive professional, not dashing desperate or delusional but presentable, passionate and patient. Likes camping, cooking, classical music, commitment. Moppy circles this ad in red. She has always been attracted to alliteration.

Phil agrees to meet her in a steakhouse restaurant in town. Moppy is a little disappointed. Steakhouse was fine, fifteen years ago. Now she likes small cafés, Turkish or Italian. Somewhere dark. Phil didn't want to talk much on the phone. 'A waste of time,' he said. 'What was the point if you took an instant dislike to someone's ankles?' Moppy assured him that no one had ever disliked her ankles.

In the restaurant he tells Moppy that he's a school counsellor. 'I also do some private therapy at home,' he says.

'What kind?'

'Sex.'

Phil is presentable, he hasn't got warts on his nose or bunions on his toes. He's forty-five with a broad face, thick brown hair, a slow reluctant grin and a slightly wary look as if Moppy might be a serial killer. A trendy leftie living in a villa in Freeman's Bay, though he also likes red meat. Moppy slowly strokes the stem of her wine glass.

Phil has two children, girls about the same ages as Sam and Thomas. He pulls out photos to show Moppy, who wouldn't dream of showing him photos of Sam and Thomas. They are wearing tights with matching tops and floppy hats. 'Cute,' says Moppy, already slotting into the role of stepmother. Phil has his children every second week, shared custody, it's what you do when both parents work. He wants a relationship only on the weeks he doesn't have the children.

'An on again, off again kind of thing,' murmurs Moppy.

'I suppose so, but there's advantages in it. You don't get sick of one another and you get space to do your own thing.'

'You could be right.'

'I am, let's face it. How many reconstituted marriages work? I'm dealing with cases every day – doubly damaged kids. Far better to be less ambitious and keep the children separate. Anyway, take you and me.' (Moppy wishes he would take her.) 'I wouldn't be happy leaving my daughters alone with your oldest son.'

'What do you mean?'

'You must read the papers. It happens every day. Sexual abuse.'

'Not with my son. I can't see Sam being sexually deviant. We're very open in our house. I've always made a point of letting him know that sex is nothing to be ashamed of.'

'So you like sex?'

'Very much. And I miss it when I don't have it.'

'Do you own a vibrator?'

What do you say to a stranger? No I don't, but I do possess a good finger. Or it's none of your business?

Taking a deep breath, Moppy says, 'Actually I don't like vibrators. I find they tickle. And I don't have any moral objection to masturbation, but I prefer the whole experience of sleeping with someone. The intimacy of talking. The sound of your own voice gets to be so boring.'

Phil smiles. 'You're a gutsy lady, Moppy. I like your attitude.'

'It's working class, Phil. Calling a spade, a spade.'

'Really? You don't look working class.'

'No not now, but I'm a Westie. My father's a bricklayer.'

'You surprise me.'

They talk about counselling, about his play writing, about her art, about his sax playing, about approaches to parenting.

'A Renaissance man,' Moppy says. He insists on walking her to her car. 'And gallant.'

'I really would like to see you again,' he says. 'I've never met anyone like you before. So vibrant and alive.'

He puts his arm around her and bends to kiss. On the cheek. Moppy turns her face so their lips collide. She sticks her tongue in his mouth. He steps back, a strange look on his face.

'Goodnight, Moppy. It was nice to meet you,' he says.

Fatal words, thinks Moppy. If they say that to you at a job interview you know you've had it.

She meets Phil again in her dreams. He has a golden sax. He plays a soft haunting melody as they wander down a bank to a lake. It is a hot day, the sort of day for a chicken, strawberry and champagne picnic. Moppy is wearing a long voile dress in shades of pink and purple. At the edge of the lake she wriggles her toes. The water is clear. Clearer than air. Small black fish are darting around. 'You can see what you're getting into here,' she says to Phil. She puts one foot in, then withdraws it quickly. Phil has disappeared and under the water is an eel poking his head out of the sandy bottom. She looks around and sees another eel. They are morays, they have small sharp teeth and appear to be grinning.

'I just don't get it,' Moppy says, 'one minute we were flirting, the next he jumped back.'

'You probably scared him,' Jill says.

'Maybe it was my tongue. Too knowing. That's what the dental assistant said.'

'What?'

'That I was one of the few people who knew what to do with my tongue. She said most people didn't know where to put it when the dentist was in their mouths. Didn't help me learning Italian, though. I still can't roll my Rs.'

~ sex on the harbour bridge ~

In her dreams Moppy has more regard for her toes than to stick them into such dangerous territory. But in life? In life she's compelled to test the waters yet again. After three days she rings Phil.

'Hi, it's me, Moppy, remember? I just wondered if you'd like to go to the movies this week, if you're free?'

'No, I'm busy.'

'Oh.' She hopes she sounds nonchalant.

'Well look. I don't have the kids next week so you could come to dinner.' He sounds a little reluctant.

'Okay. Can I bring something?'

'Wine would be good.'

He said he was a connoisseur, she thinks, picking with a slight hesitation the very good red that Vincent brought back from Australia. She's swayed by the thought that he's a Renaissance man. And a sex therapist.

Phil seems surprised to see her, when he opens the door of his villa.
'Did you forget?'
'No, no.'
She's not so sure. Clearly he hasn't bothered tidying. There are papers all over the floor and on chairs. A typewriter on the table. No candles or flowers. Phil puts the wine in his wine rack and hands her a glass of cask white. There is food. Stirfried chicken, Thai style, with lemon grass and jasmine rice, perfectly cooked. Just enough for two. They eat silently.
'I haven't any dessert,' he says, 'it's bad for you.'
After dinner, they sit opposite each other on large burgundy cotton couches. He hands her a file.
'Would you like to read my play? Tell me if it's any good.' Phil sits watching and smoking. What can Moppy say?
The play is about a sex therapist and his affair with a patient who can only enjoy sex at a height. The higher the better. They get drunk one night and stop the car on the harbour bridge. 'Let's do it here,' the patient shouts as a truck rumbles up and squashes them.
Moppy laughs. 'It might be difficult getting a truck on stage.'
'But don't you get the point?'
'Yeah. Sex on the harbour bridge ends in premature ejaculation.'
'Very droll. The point is that romance always ends in disillusion.'
Outside, she shivers. Phil doesn't move closer except to open her car door.
She gets stopped by a road block on the way to the harbour bridge. She is expecting to be breathtested but a policeman shines a torch in her car.
'Good evening, madam. Anyone else in the car with you?'
'I wish there was.'
'Not the person we're looking for.'
'Who?'
'The rapist. He's just done it again. A twelve-year-old. Not far from here. Have you see anyone on the streets?'
'No.'
'Well, lock your doors and drive straight home.'
Moppy shivers again. For some reason she thinks of Phil. He seems a bit obsessed about sex. But unable to relate to a real woman. Still, it can't have been him. She's thankful Thomas and Sam are safe and asleep at Tim's. It's the same when she sees an ambulance. Always her first thought. Where are the kids.
Under Sam's gumboot on the porch is a note. She looks uneasily around. It's a still night. She can hear waves breaking and in the distance a morepork. She hurries inside before she perceives a foot breaking a twig in the bush.
Safe inside, Moppy checks the locks three times and reads the note.

what you long for
is in the longing

yesterday a tui
trying different tunes

no lover came

She turns out the lights and pulls the duvet up around her ears. Sometimes she's not sure about Ted's motives. If it is Ted. She wishes Ted was a normal neighbour, someone she could count on in an emergency or share a cup of tea with. Loneliness is not poetic. It's a dark mass in her stomach. She decides to confront Ted in the morning.

Moppy pushes the branches of a bramble rose aside. A reversal here, she thinks, wondering if she should kiss Ted on the cheek. Cure his stutter. Standing at the paint-peeled door she peers into the windows. There is nothing to be seen behind the orange net curtains. No movement. She knocks and knocks. No one comes. 'Are you in there Ted?' she yells. 'It's me, Moppy.' She waits five minutes then goes away. She's sure he's there. She can feel him listening.

~ the closed door ~

Circumstances have conspired to keep Ted out of the public eye. His stutter, lack of social conversation, choice of soda water rather than wine, distrust of postmodernism, dislike of most of the literary circuit, and his placing of himself in a backwater not known for an avant garde population. The overgrown path is not accidental or a simple matter of procrastination.

When it came to reading his work in public, Ted couldn't do it, despite his favoured short lines. His stuttering rendered him inarticulate. Lectures were also painful. The formality and the strictly one-way dialogue. But poetry does not pay, so he had no choice but to be a tutor.

The first time I went to one of his tutorials I felt deeply embarrassed for him. I longed to pluck whole words from the air and place them carefully in his mouth. Only his engaging eyes ensured we all came back the next week, relieved to find Ted more relaxed and the words flowing, a stream of literary anecdotes and digressions. He'd still trip up occasionally, as if he'd come to an outcrop of rocks, but we knew he'd get us safely to the mouth of the ocean.

The fact that he was okay with his students once he got to know them proved that his difficulty is not one of speech but of place. Low self-esteem perhaps. A difficulty in assuming the right or the place to speak. A matter of the tongue fitting. Or not.

~ fun and games ~

Jill is planning a party for Robert's birthday to which I'm not invited, not having a man to bring. According to Jill, couples are essential. She's been attending a drama class. Hence the theatre sports party.

Against her better judgement Moppy asks Sean.

'No way. I can't stand that prick. The high and mighty Robert. Really I'd punch him in the face.' Sean's never forgiven Robert for not getting him off a drunk driving charge. 'But anywhere else Mop, just say the word.'

'I'll have to try Phil. You never know, perhaps he's just one of those people who takes a while to thaw out,' Moppy says to Jill.

'Great. I've never met a sex therapist.'

To Moppy's surprise, Phil agrees. 'As long as I can take my own car and leave when I want.'

'Fine by me.'

Moppy gets there first. There are seven couples.

'So where's your new man?' Amanda asks. 'I always enjoy seeing who you're going to turn up with next.'

'He's coming.'

'Too scared to come alone with you, is he?' asks Robert.

'Probably, though he is a sex therapist and a counsellor.'

'Another nutcase then,' says Ross.

Phil walks in the door just as this last statement is uttered. He looks around at the minimal furniture as if he'd like a bean bag to sink into.

'You've probably got lots in common with Grant,' Moppy says as she introduces Phil, who grunts.

'Must have been working with teenagers too long,' whispers Grant.

'Right,' says Jill. 'This is not going to be a talky party. First we'll have a warm-up.'

'I see the drama lessons weren't wasted then,' says Ross.

'No.'

Robert winces as Jill's voice soars over the top.

'I want the men to lie on the floor on their backs. As close as possible. The idea is for the women to roll on top and get to know one another in a different dimension.'

Moppy is wearing a black crepe mini skirt, red tights and a red silky jumper. 'I don't think I'm wearing the right clothes for this sort of thing,' she says to Phil.

Phil grimaces and moves closer to Amanda, who is dressed discreetly in cream wool trousers and polo-necked jumper.

Robert lies down first.

'Closer, get closer,' Jill says.

'You've obviously never been in a urinal, Jill,' Ross says. 'Us real men prefer distance.'

'Not on the soccer field.'

'True.' The men shuffle together.

'Okay. Now women on top.'

Despite feeling this game is not politically correct, Moppy is in her element. The men all feel large, lumpy and reassuring. They smile, liking the idea of providing a protective barrier between the women and the floor. Except Phil. His lips are pulled tight. Ross pinches Moppy when she rolls over him. She ignores it. After, Moppy notices Phil and Amanda disappearing outside.

'I see my wife is trying to lead your man astray.'

'He's not my man and why did you pinch my bum, Ross?'

'Just wanted you to know I still find you irresistible. Even though you keep picking up dickheads.'

'I'm not sure how to take that.'

Ross has already drunk four glasses of champagne, the real stuff obtained from Robert's cellar by Jill. 'In the spirit of love, dear girl.'

A month after she separated from Tim, Moppy had bumped into Ross in town. She was on her way to a movie by herself. 'Let's go to dinner,' Ross said. 'You're far too attractive to go to the movies alone.' She was curious to see if Ross would make a move. If this was the beginning of the great play for the newly separated woman. Ross was charming but evasive, asking questions about her social life but avoiding any revelations about his own. They parted with a chaste kiss on the lips. Moppy was relieved.

'Remember when Amanda and I went to Australia to live and you were at the airport?' Ross asks.

'No,' she says, but she is lying. This was years ago, pre Tim and the children.

'Oh I thought you might have. I certainly remember you kissing me goodbye. Such a passionate kiss. The tears were rolling down your face. I nearly got off the plane.' He is serious.

~ but no kisses ~

Phil and Amanda come back in.

'About time we interrupted these two,' Amanda says. 'Ross would run off with Moppy tomorrow given half a chance.'

And I might take it, thinks Moppy. If I didn't have scruples.

'The next game is Musical Chairs, except the men are the chairs. When the music stops the women must jump on the backs of the men. We'll remove one at a time,' Jill says.

Phil buckles under Moppy. 'I'm not that heavy,' she says.

The holiday postcards are a little more demanding of creativity. Groups of two have to depict a postcard scene. Couples are separated. Moppy and Ross decide to be in India. Moppy rides on his back. Amanda and Phil lie on the floor, twitching and shivering. No one guesses they are tourists from the Mt Erebus flight.

'I think that's in bad taste, I really do,' says Grant.

Phil smirks. 'I thought this was a bad taste party.'

For supper Jill serves tapenade and crackers, sliced rare beef, tomato and pepper salad, cheeses and handmade chocolate truffles. Phil answers every question with a monosyllable and a strange kind of laugh. Ross says, 'Allow me' to Moppy and brings her little delicacies on a plate.

After supper Phil says, 'I want to go home now.'

Moppy walks him to his car. It's a fine starry night. Full moon. The kind of night for anyone to feel romantic.

Phil puts out his hand. 'Goodnight.'

'Aren't you going to give me a goodnight kiss then?' asks Moppy.

'No.' He looks at her as if she is absolutely mad.

Back inside Ross says, 'What a fuckwit. Thought you said he was a sex therapist.'

'That's what he told me.'

'Well he looked terrified of you, that's for sure.'

'Personally, I think he's gay.' This contribution comes from Amanda. 'Where did you meet him?'

'Oh you know, around.'

'It's pathetic, picking up these guys,' says Amanda.

'Yeah, you might land yourself in trouble,' says Robert. 'You don't know where they've been.'

'You can talk,' says Jill.

'Leave it,' says Robert, putting his hand over hers. 'You don't want to spoil a great party.'

'It's just that we don't want to see you get hurt, Moppy,' says Ross, quickly.

At home, words wait in the fruit bowl.

what use is a golden
apple anyway?

The kids are asleep, Nikki the babysitter gone by the time Moppy discovers the note. The only golden apples she knows are the ones from her childhood, her favourite Sunday morning story, *Diana and the golden apples.* She recalls how Diana allowed herself to stoop for the three apples thrown by a potential suitor. Worth it, the story implied. The price of a husband is losing the race.

~ frankly Moppy I don't give a damn ~

'What's wrong with me? I can't understand why he didn't want to kiss me again. It's not as if I'm ugly. Perhaps I've got bad breath. Do you ever check your own breath?' Moppy asks me.

'No, but I'm sure it's not halitosis. I just think you stepped over the line of his set of rules.'

'What do you mean?'

'I think he wasn't prepared for you to stick your tongue into his mouth. He probably can't cope with overtly sexual women. Ironic for a sex therapist, but what do you expect when you look in all the wrong places? Why don't you try for a job in prison, teaching art? You'd have all the men falling in love with you and you're guaranteed a captive audience.'

'Ha, ha. Is that why you like going there?'

'Well it's great to be appreciated. Mind you, I'm not sure if it's my muffins or my personality.'

'Men used to find me attractive,' Moppy says. 'I've never had a problem before. I hope it's not 'cause I'm getting old. It's not as if I'm fat with grey hair.' The words are out of her mouth before she thinks. 'Sorry Barb.' The apology makes it worse.

'Well, tact is not one of your strong points.'

'Sorry Barb. But I wasn't getting at you. I love your hair. You're wild like Germaine Greer, a fantastic crone.'

'Thank you again.'

'It's a compliment. But really, you'd tell me if I was losing it, wouldn't you?'

'Yes I would. But stop acting so spoilt. You remind me of Scarlet O'Hara. Stamping your foot. Phil sounded a dickhead anyway. Who cares?'

'All right. I get the message. I'll stop going on about it. But I don't think having an inmate for a boyfriend would be any more productive. No sex for a start.'

'Ah. Think of all the work you'd get done. Channelling all that sexual energy into your art. Works for me.'

'So have you got an admirer in there?'

'Many, but it's no big deal. They haven't got anything else to focus on so it's not surprising. Anyway, what's happening with your art?'

'Well you know – well you don't know not having kids – but I can never find the time. I'm still playing around with ideas. I just find it hard settling for one theme.'

'So combine.'

On the way home I wondered if I should have confessed about Mati. It was on the tip of my tongue, but something held me back. Such a fragile thing, love.

I think of our relationship as a premature child. We, the parents, cannot bring ourselves to put a notice in the paper. Instead I maintain a careful watch over the incubator and prepare myself for a possible death.

My mother was always warning me against tempting fate. In her case fate wasn't kind. An abusive father, an alcoholic husband, a dead daughter. Things are easier for me merely because I have chosen to be responsible for only myself. Even my work is self-directed. Now Mati has stepped in the one door I forgot to close. It's not an easy visit.

part three

~ Sunday lunch with Vincent ~

'I miss you,' he says. 'Do you miss me?'

'Sometimes,' she says, 'in the middle of the night.'

'When I go to bed I think of you. Always. I have your photo on my wall. I think of all the happy times. Going out with the children.'

'Are you ready to order?' interrupts the waiter. He is tall and speaks with a slight American twang. He glances at Vincent a little more intently than necessary.

'Where are you from?' Moppy asks.

'The North Shore.' He pauses before adding 'sweetie', and winks at Vincent.

'I think he fancies you,' Moppy says.

'I suppose that amuses you?'

'Well I don't see anything wrong with it.' Just because you're anal retentive, she thinks, but is not quite cruel enough to say.

'It's disgusting.'

'Lighten up.'

'I think these matters are serious. At least with me you know if I say something I mean it.'

'And I don't, I suppose?'

'No, I'm not sure you're capable of love.'

'I don't think that's fair, Vincent. You were smothering me.'

'Are you going out with anyone now?' he asks.

'No, not really. A few disastrous dates. What about you?'

'I've tried. Got as far as the bedroom with a woman but then I couldn't go through with it. Too many memories of you. And your dates? Were they from the paper?'

'Don't ask. I'm sorry, Vincent. I really am. Why is it that women want men who don't want them and not the ones who do. It's so stupid.'

'I agree. So does that mean you want me back?'

'You said you didn't want me back.'

'I lied. I still love you. Would you marry me?'

~ looking the wrong way ~

Moppy is driving home after lunch, decadence and guilt the currency of the moment. Decadent because of the glass of wine and the large piece of cheesecake. Guilty because of Vincent.

A 3-D billboard is positioned on a building in Fanshawe Street. A convertible car with the hood and the seats down. A couple embracing passionately. At that precise moment Moppy is not thinking about Vincent but about Tim. When they first met he had a convertible. There must have been passion involved too. She cannot remember. Taking the bend a little sharply, Moppy's car slews into the next lane. Just a slight movement, but enough for another car to crunch into hers.

Moppy pulls over onto the footpath.

'What the hell do you think you were doing?' asks a small rotund man as he gets out of his green BMW. The front passenger-side door of Moppy's car is pushed in.

'Oh God, I'm sorry,' says Moppy. The words are out of her mouth before she remembers the first rule of traffic accidents.

'Well at least you can see you were in the wrong. Look, it's okay, my car is only lightly scratched. As for yours, it just needs punching out a bit. Not worth informing the insurance company about. Probably won't cost as much as your no-claims.'

Moppy is crying. 'I'm sorry. I've never had an accident before.'

'Look, you seem a bit shocked. How about a coffee at Victoria Park? I'll follow you.'

'Okay.'

At least he sounds cultured, thinks Moppy. And I've plenty of time for once.

Over coffee, Gerald explains he is a lawyer. Specialising in divorce cases, so he's seen it all.

'Didn't stop me from getting into trouble myself though. I'm currently involved in a battle with my ex. She wants half of my business. She already has a good house, I pay for the kids to go to private schools and I didn't even want a divorce in the first place.'

'No, it's usually the women.'

'So what about you, Moppy? Are you happily ensconced in suburbia with two point five kids and a husband?'

'No. I lost the point five child on a bus, and I left my husband outside one day and he melted in the rain. So now I live in steady downward mobility.'

'Touché.' Gerald laughs. A lovely rich laugh that makes Moppy forget all about the dent in her car. 'So.' He leans forward. 'What have you been up to this morning?'

'I've just turned down a proposal of marriage from an lovely exotic man and had an accident, so I think that's enough for one day.'

'And why did you turn down the proposal?'

'Because I've already had two husbands and now I just want a string of lovers.'

Moppy is enjoying herself. This is the way to meet men.

'What do you do, Moppy?'

'This and that. I work in Just Art Books and teach art occasionally at night school. If I could afford it I'd be a full-time artist. But my work is not commercial. I'm into photography, collages and sculptures from debris I find on the beach. I like the idea of using cast offs. It's my thrifty working-class background.' Moppy wonders if she is making herself sound like the scullery maid meeting the master.

Gerald looks at his watch. 'Talking of cast offs, I've got to go. I was supposed to pick up my kids ten minutes ago. Next time we meet, perhaps it could be more gentle.' Moppy is aware of her upper body tilted in his direction and her traitorous eyes softening. 'How about we go to dinner next week,' he asks. 'My treat?'

Tim and the boys are waiting at her house. Tim wants to go to work, and Wendy is fed up with the Brady Bunch fighting.

'I see you're exercising your usual care on the roads,' Tim says, glancing at her door.

'Get stuffed,' she mutters, under her breath so the kids don't hear.

'By the way,' Tim says. 'I found this on your doorstep.' He hands her the familiar blue paper folded in two and a small grey stone. 'The kids say someone often leaves things for you. I'd be careful if I were you. Sounds like a nutter. But I guess that figures. Anyway, I don't want the kids involved in your strange games.'

'Thank you for your concern, Tim.'

She wonders if he read the note. He's not the most curious of men.

here no compass points
of familiarity

nothing to fix
your image

only this stone
encircled in white

'Sam, has Ted been away?'
'Dunno Mum.'

~ barbed wire ~

There are always those like Moppy who will opt for the unprogrammed, unpredictable advance. And others like myself who settle for something safer. Which is why I am here, watching the movie *The Boxer* with an old recently separated friend. Except his hand is clutching my knee during the violent scenes. Whispering *so sumptuous. Your flesh. An incitement to lust.* Making me forget to account for the solitary drive home. 'I love someone else,' I tell my friend, but how can I go into circumstances?

Even the motorway seems unreal, uncannily deserted, until I pass a body lying in a lane, alone on the other side. Face covered with a white sheet. A large pool of blood spreading from the heart. The police and the unmanned motorbike all stand some distance away.

I drive past slowly, not quite sure I am seeing what I am seeing. And at home I talk to myself. Lying in bed alone with my sumptuous skin. Identifying with the body on the road. Its terrible abandonment.

In the morning I discover the body was a woman's. A hit and run. I don't know why that makes it worse.

~ the formidable woman ~

'Talk about a cliché. Only you could cause an accident and then get invited out by the victim,' says Dennis, bashing out the inside of Moppy's car door.

'Well if it wasn't for that stupid billboard and being distracted by Vincent.'

'I'm glad you said no. He didn't sound right for you.'

'Nothing to do with his colour, I suppose?'

'What do you take me for? My best friends are minorities. I just think you need someone who has the same sort of rhythm and sense of humour as you. He sounded far too slow and reserved. And let's face it, his culture would have become an issue. Once he was your husband I bet he would have wanted to assume control.'

'Yeah, you're probably right. He loved me though. Still does, I suppose.'

Gerald turns up exactly on time. He seems shocked. 'How can you live so far out?'

'It's only Torbay. Not Siberia.'

He holds out a bottle.

'I wasn't sure of the restaurants round here so I bought this. It's a good vintage, very dry for champagne.'

Moppy groans inwardly. She tends to lose her caution drinking champagne.

The restaurant is in Takapuna. Small and dark.

'Since we're having champagne, I'm having seafood, scallops in champagne sauce. Okay?' Moppy asks.

'Certainly Moppy. Anything you like. I can afford it.'

Moppy regards Gerald's round endomorphic face and wishes he was her body type. Ectomorphic with a high forehead, glasses and an intensity suggesting Jewishness. Harking back to her unresolved holiday romance in England. But what difference does it make in the dark? And Gerald has plenty to say.

'I'm interested in painting myself,' he says. 'I'm self-taught of course, but I reckon I could do well if I just had more time. I particularly like nudes.'

'Don't we all,' says Moppy. 'You're a realist?'

'Yeah. I've no time for all the abstract stuff. People want something accessible. I'd love to paint you sometime. Your hair — so many lights in it would be a challenge. But I'm sure you get no end of these sorts of invitations.'

'Sure, there are a million men out there just waiting in line. And all of them want a talkative woman with two kids and wrinkles.'

'Only the most delightful wrinkles from smiling too much.'

'I think,' says Moppy, 'you are a flatterer. The type of man my mother told me to avoid.'

'Well the golden tongue goes with the territory, but I can assure you I mean it in your case. Look, why don't we walk along the beach? It's a cliché but the moon is full.'

Moppy doesn't have the right shoes on for beach walking, but clichés are clichés because they're so apt. She tries to push thoughts of Billy out of her head.

'It reminds me of Greece. Balmy nights and new lovers,' she says.

Gerald takes her hand. They walk in the shallows. Moppy tries to catch the phosphorescence on the edge of the waves.

'I think you are formidably attractive,' Gerald says, pulling her back and kissing her.

Not the type that asks permission first then. Still, asking does take away the surprise element, the idea of seduction, and Moppy is seduced. The champagne, the words, the kiss, the water and the moonlight all acting in conspiracy. Formidably attractive woman. What will Jill make of that?

'Do you think we should go to your place and get more comfortable,' breathes Gerald.

'But I've made a vow of celibacy.'

'Well you know what they say, vows are made to be broken.'

'Just a cuddle, okay?'

Moppy lies on the couch in his arms. His hands are sliding up the split in her skirt, stroking her thighs, pulling aside her panties. She should never have worn a skirt. Her period finished a week ago and she is secreting that dangerous egg-white mucus that carries sperm straight to the new egg. He slips onto the floor, bends to her thighs.

'Oh Moppy, that smell makes me feel like a man again. I want to kiss you there, kiss your sweet cherry.' His lips suck, his teeth nip, his tongue caresses. 'Oh God, Moppy, I've been wanting this since I saw you. Talk about love at first sight.'

'Don't you mean lust,' says Moppy. 'But forget semantics, you can't stop now. Have you got a condom?'

'I have, my temptress.'

Five minutes later Gerald pulls out of Moppy and comes with loud moans of delight on her stomach.

'I don't trust condoms,' he says.

Moppy is perched on the edge, too nervous to look up or down.

'That was great. Let's do it again,' he says.

Moppy agrees in the hope of being able to reach orgasm. Gerald doesn't have a problem getting an erection at will, but Moppy can't relax. She is thinking of Sam. Tomorrow she has an appointment with his teacher. Sam is not achieving his potential and neither is she.

She squeezes her vaginal muscles, pants and moans. Gerald is convinced. He comes as Moppy gets louder. Escape is possible.

'Gerald, I really need to get some sleep now. Perhaps you'd better go or we'll be awake all night.'

'Okay, my beautiful one. I'm going to Wellington tomorrow. I'll give you a ring when I get home on Saturday.'

Gerald doesn't ring on Saturday.

'Obviously you are too formidable,' Jill says. 'He's probably scared of you. Anyway, what happened to your vow of celibacy?'

'Well, you know, you've got to take it when it's offered.'

Moppy swallows her pride and rings a week later.

'Moppy. How wonderful to hear from you.' Smooth voice, thinks Moppy. 'I'm sorry I haven't rung. I've been so busy lately. Big court case and all. So how are you?'

'I'm fine. Are you doing anything tonight? I thought I could cook you dinner.'

'Moppy, I would love to, but I'm afraid I have to visit my great aunt. She's very old so I can't afford not to go. She lives in a huge house in Remuera all by herself.'

'Are you hoping to inherit?'

'Perhaps, but that's not the reason for the visit. Anyway Moppy I have to go. Another appointment, I'm afraid, but I'll get back to you, I promise.'

~ the rules ~

I wouldn't want you to think that I watch daytime TV as a rule, but occasionally I allow myself the luxury while I'm eating lunch. On Oprah

Winfrey today, two blondes who have written a book, *The Rules*. If you want a man who's not in prison, these women have the answers. According to *The Rules* one should never sleep with a man on the first date. Sure recipe for a one-night stand. On that basis, if Mati and I ever do get to sleep together it's bound to lead to everlasting marriage.

If the man of your dreams rings after Wednesday don't accept a date for the following Saturday. And never talk for too long on the phone. At all times, project an unattainable image. It works, the writers tell the audience, flashing their wedding rings. The single men they bring on the show laugh. They wouldn't fall for such manipulation, they say. They all want an honest relationship. Do we believe them? Since there are more single available women than men, the writers are onto a winner. Indeed their diamonds are large. I wonder if there is a similar set of rules for lesbian relationships?

I've never been in favour of one-night stands myself, though I'm still not sure how you tell beforehand. It's difficult for the gullible amongst us, like Moppy. Even more difficult when you recognise the familiar signs of a relieved departure. The way their hips sway as they bound down the steps in preference to walking backwards in order to see your face for as long as possible.

No such questions trouble my mind when I think of Mati. He is always where I expect him to be.

~ a potential lover evaluates IQs ~

'Guess who I'm seeing now?'
'Who?'
'A psychiatrist.'
Moppy has saved this titbit especially for me. I can tell by the excitement in her eyes. She's leaning forward almost into my coffee.
'You've gone too far this time. A psychiatrist. Are you mad?'
'Perhaps.'
'And where did you find him? Dare I ask?'
'Well, you know. I have my resources. You might know him. He works for the Justice Department. He's Polish.'
'Not Jozef Schernazy?'
'Yeah. You know him?'
'I've met him once. In Parry.'
'What can you tell me?'
'Only that he's perceived to be strange. Maybe it's because he's Polish. Maybe it's the fact that he specialises in sex offenders.'
'He is a bit different, but you know me, I don't go for the straightforward. Well I did twice, with Geoff and Tim, and look where it got

me. First of all competing with slim-bottomed men and then up an overgrown path in Nappy Valley.'

'Ha. Your problem is you don't seek men with the same interests, like Ted or Sean, both sitting under your nose.'

'I know, I know.'

'So tell me about Jozef.'

'We met for coffee last week. It was quite strange. He gave me his CV and told me he has a very high IQ, but he wouldn't tell me how high. According to him that would be unfair. Then he told me that I also had a high IQ, but not as high as his. How can you tell? I asked. From the light in your eyes, he said.'

'God, that's the second person to talk about the light in your eyes.'

'Must be true then.'

~ I insinuate some of my history ~

'I don't see why she can't go out with someone at least partially normal,' I say to Jill at our secret weekly meeting.

'What, get a married man, like you?'

'Now that's not fair. I told you he doesn't sleep with her.'

To get Jill off my back I told her I was having an affair. True in a way. An affair of the heart. There's no opportunity for sex, unless he goes to hospital. I can just see the headlines: Inmate discovered in hospital bed with overweight creative writing teacher.

I haven't told anyone about Mati. I have no taste for long conversations about my love life. I prefer writing to talking.

Moppy and I share some similarities though. A liking for art, literature and movies, and a propensity for disastrous relationships. One of mine was an Italian waiter I met on the ship to Italy. The trip was supposed to be a cure for Moppy after Geoff ran off. I was there to protect her from trouble. In the end we were about even. Giuseppe wanted to marry me. He loved my eyes. Like a painting by Michelangelo, he said. How could I resist?

When he came to pick me up from our cheap hotel in Naples to meet his mother, Moppy insisted on coming too. His mother lived in a less than salubrious area. Apartment blocks with washing hanging everywhere, peeling paint and loud voices. Giuseppe's mother was short and fat. Perhaps Giuseppe could see the potential in me. She pinched my arm and smiled, as if she was weighing up future grandchildren. Bound to be bonny. Just shows how you can be wrong.

We had already eaten huge plates of pasta at the hotel, but she brought out food – bread and some kind of sausage in a greasy sauce.

'Eat, eat,' said Giuseppe, 'you must eat.'

We sat down and ate under her watchful eye. She ate nothing, and neither did the two younger boys. They sat at our feet and stared. I was tempted to slip them something under the table.

By the time we could legitimately say we were tired, Giuseppe was drunk. Sober, he drove like a madman but drunk his driving was terrifying. Moppy and I were screaming for him to stop. He took no notice. I don't think I've ever been less in control. We made it back to the hotel, though he wiped out at least two rubbish bins on the way. He insisted on escorting us. Moppy stormed ahead. When we stepped into our room, he immediately fell down in a drunken stupor.

'Get him out of here now,' Moppy said. 'There's no way I'm sleeping in the same room as that maniac.'

I could see she had a point. Besides, he was snoring. We grabbed one leg each, hauled him out into the corridor, slammed the door shut and went to bed, giggling nervously.

By the time we got up at ten in the morning, there was no sign of him. We had no idea whether the manager had thrown him out or not. I tried ringing his mother but all I got was a torrent of rapid Italian.

'No Seppe, no Seppe,' she screamed. Did that mean he was dead or that she had decided I was too heartless?

'You're better off out of it,' Moppy said.

We went to Pompeii that day and met a couple of German men who took us out to dinner. It was my first taste of real pizza. The beginning of my love affair with Italy and the end of my love affair with Italian men. Unlike Moppy, once was enough.

~ the Polish psychiatrist drives like an Italian waiter ~

Jozef drives a small yellow baby Citroen. Instant attraction for Moppy. They are driving in the Waitakeres. It is their second date. She grits her teeth as Jozef weaves over the road.

'Would you like me to drive?'

'No, no I am fine.' Jozef's hands are waving around the car.

'Well this is a tricky road, so be careful.'

'Okay.'

Jozef's hands are large. He is wearing white jeans, white jacket and a black T-shirt. His dark brown hair is peppered with grey and he has a small bald patch at the back of his head. Unlike Billy's bald patch, Moppy finds this endearing, like the deliberate fault in a Persian carpet.

Over lunch in Titirangi she discovers a less endearing fault. Jozef eats with his mouth open. She can see his salad revolving, and his teeth. Luckily his teeth are good.

'Beautiful,' he says caressing her face, 'healthy skin. Unfortunately for me, I am diabetic.'

'Do you inject yourself?'

'No, pills only. I am lucky. I can't stand needles. But I don't mind injecting patients. Sometimes is necessary.'

Moppy avoids looking at Jozef's mouth. She wonders if this is a cultural thing. And if she should say something.

'Tell me, Jozef, why did you come to New Zealand?'

'Because I do not like idea of nuclear weapons or power. My mother was killed in Chernobyl.'

'She was living there?'

'No, in Warsaw. But three days after Chernobyl she die. She was asthmatic.'

'How awful.'

Moppy touches Jozef's hand. She suddenly thinks of herself as Princess Diana, offering comfort. Such self-consciousness annoys her.

'If there is a nuclear war or explosion New Zealand is safest place to be. And I think people of my intelligence are necessary for the world. So I am here. Lucky for you?'

'I'm not sure yet.'

'If you want an intelligent man, I am he.'

'But you have children in Poland?'

'Yes, a boy and a girl. The boy is ten, the girl eight. Very intelligent also, but their mother is not.'

'But what about your children. If there's a nuclear explosion?'

'I can only save myself. My children must stay with their mother. She is an artist and works at home. Anyway I have never lived with my children.'

'You never lived with your wife?'

'A different woman. The mother of my children is not my wife. She wanted an intelligent, handsome man like me for father of her children. It is best way I think.'

'Love has nothing to do with it?'

'Love is, how do you say it, non-existent, a trick.'

'An illusion?'

'Yes, illusion. You see, I need you for words. It is very important, I think, to select parents.'

'Like Hitler?'

'A sensitive subject. But he was wrong about race. I think intelligence is more important. Are your children intelligent?'

'Of course. Well, I think one has my artistic sensibilities, the other is more academic, like his father who's an economist. But what use is intelligence if it's not applied?'

'Applied?'

'Used. Anyway I think there is a large area of intelligence that is uncounted or uncountable.'

'Like what?'

'Creativity.'

'You are a woman, Moppy, but you are right. Measurement of creativity is a difficult science.'

Jozef lives in the city, in an old apartment block. Pigeons sit on the windowsills. The apartment is masculine and messy. Big black leather couch, a large desk covered in papers, a bookcase filled with mostly Polish books and small pieces of sculpture all in pewter grey. Moppy immediately looks for photos. There are none.

'Do you like my humidifier? Look how much water it has already. Auckland is too moist, I think. It is very bad for system.'

'But the hum would drive me crazy.'

'Well if I go crazy, I am best man to cure myself.'

'I don't think so. Haven't you heard of the cobbler's shoes?'

'No.'

'You know, a cobbler is a person who mends shoes. Usually his family have the worst shoes in the village.'

'So you think I could not cure myself?'

'No.'

'But, you think my apartment is good enough for a hug?'

'Of course.' Moppy puts her arms around Jozef. 'I am very good at hugging. New Zealanders are sometimes reserved, not like the Polish, I think.'

Jozef is not interested in a friendly hug. 'Can I kiss you?'

'Yes. You don't have to ask.'

'But yes. It is very important. We do not have any misunderstandings.'

'I think we will have many misunderstandings. You are a man, I am a woman.'

Still, Moppy has noted the art books in the bookcase. She has hopes, even if his kiss is brief.

~ it comes with a guarantee ~

'Can I see your breasts?'

Moppy unbuttons her black chiffon blouse. He puts his hands on the cups and looks closely. One finger slides under the material. Touches the nipple.

'All right?' she asks. He looks as if he is weighing them up.

'A mother's breasts. A little soft now. But real. Not like American women. So many fakes.'

'So good enough to make love to?'

'Yes. But first I must tell you something.' He looks uncomfortable.

'Should I sit down?' asks Moppy.

'Yes. But you promise not to laugh.' He takes her hand.

'I promise.'

'You know I have diabetes?' She nods. 'Unfortunately for males, one of the side-effects can be impotence.'

'I didn't know that.'

'Well,' he says as if she hasn't guessed already, 'I am one of the unlucky ones. Bad for me, but good for me. I have an implant. Another reason for coming here. You can't get this operation in Poland.'

'Oh?'

'Every time I want to have sex, I pump my penis up.'

'Oh, and when you have finished?'

'I deflate it.'

'So premature ejaculation is not a problem?'

'No. It does what I say.'

Moppy laughs.

'You promised not to laugh.'

'Sorry. It's a nervous giggle. I always do this when I'm nervous. I even laugh at funerals. If ever I was on trial for murder, I'd convict myself, laughing.'

'I see. An inappropriate response.'

'Women are prone to them. It goes with a lack of power.'

'Well you have power now. Do you want to try my expensive operation?'

'It works?'

'Of course. I've checked it out.'

Moppy does not ask who he checked it out with. 'Okay but I don't see what the difference is between breast implants and a penile implant.'

'Of course it is different. Mine is medical necessity.'

As if she is not surprised already, Jozef picks her up, carries her into the bedroom and lies her down on his bed. The cover is black. The sheets are pure white cotton. He unzips her jeans and slips off her blouse, then peels off his clothes. He is wearing old-fashioned white cotton Y-fronts. Moppy's face drops.

'Not sexy, I know, but they are most comfortable. My penis is longer than normal now because the implants do not shrink. I am gay man's dream but unfortunately for me I am not gay.'

Moppy tries to take an objective view. It is circumcised; long, thin and soft. Penises are so ugly, she thinks, but this is information best not revealed. Besides, she thinks the same about vulvas.

Jozef slips on to the bed beside her and starts playing with her fingers. Licking each one and then using his index finger to slide rapidly between her middle and index finger on her left hand. It's a strangely seductive move.

'Elegant fingers,' he says. 'You could play the violin. But what else are you made of?'

'Sugar and spice and all things nice,' murmurs Moppy as Jozef's tongue starts wetting her panties. She slips them off.

'Not much hair,' he says. 'I do not think I will get lost.'

'After the caesarean it never grew back, so I'm semi bald, like you.' Moppy wonders if she should have said that. Men are so sensitive about these things. But Jozef does not appear to be listening.

'Is this right?' He is caressing her clitoris.

'Yes,' says Moppy, trying to get into the mood. It has vanished now they are naked.

Jozef's fingers are speeding up. 'Would you like me inside?'

Moppy nods. She never speaks at these moments, afraid perhaps her voice will come out squeaky, doll-like.

He takes hold of his penis and pumps at the base. It stiffens. 'See, normal and hard. Is this enough to let me in?'

'I guess so. With a condom.'

'Ah.' He fumbles around for his jeans. 'See, a black one. Good for you. You can pretend I am a big black man.'

'Great. Just what I've always wanted.'

Moppy imagines this penis trying to find the right angle is one of the ones in Mapplethorpe's photographs. She visualises the erect black uncircumcised penis sticking out of a businessman's suit. The incongruity.

'I was in a gynaecologist's once,' Moppy says. 'He couldn't get the speculum in. I said to him, Two caesareans makes me a virgin, doesn't it? He didn't laugh so I said, It's been a while since I was invaded. By strangers or otherwise.'

Jozef's penis slips in. Timing is everything in jokes, but perhaps there is a language barrier also.

Lying beneath Jozef, Moppy tries to kiss him. His eyes and lips are shut. The face in orgasm often looks as if it is pain, thinks Moppy. Jozef groans. As quickly as he came, he slips out.

He caresses her navel. 'Good, for you?'

'Don't. I hate my belly button being touched.'

'And why is that?'

'I don't know. But you are not my psychiatrist.'

All Moppy wants is for him to leave the room so she can relieve herself of this terrible ache. Put her hand between her legs and allow the pulsing to subside.

~ the inevitable gossip ~

Moppy waits till nine o'clock to ring Jill.

'It's Dietrich Davis,' says Robert, handing the phone to Jill. It's an old joke. Neither Jill nor Moppy reacts.

'So how did it go? Did you seduce him?'

'Of course. Did you doubt it?' Moppy hears herself putting on an act. 'But I have something to tell you. Can you come for a walk?'

'Tell me now.'

'No. I can't over the phone.'

'Please, please.'

'Let's just say the word inflatable.'

'Inflatable?'

They are walking around the rocks, Takapuna to Milford. The weather is overcast and too cold for gays, thinks Moppy. The prospect of discovering Geoff hanging around Thorne's Bay with his latest lover still haunts her, though she hasn't seen him for years. The sea is beautiful in its malevolence. They can walk close to the houses here, and if lucky catch a glimpse of some well-organised family sitting down to breakfast. Sometimes Moppy walks the streets at dusk, before curtains get drawn, merely to catch a glimpse of what's going on. She hates the thought of being excluded. But in Takapuna the small baches with generous windows in the front have mostly been replaced by mansions with reflective glass, giving nothing away. Soon the only charm about this walk will be in the sea, the rocks and in the conversation.

The penis story is difficult to get out. Moppy keeps giggling, and then Jill starts, though she has no idea why. When the story is finally out the two of them are hysterical.

'Careful,' says Jill. 'We'll be locked up like witches.'

They are off again.

'Only you, it could only happen to you. Have you told Barb?'

'No and I'm not going to. You know what she's like. She'll write a poem and tell the whole world. You can't trust her at all. And you mustn't tell anybody.'

'Only Robert, please let me tell Robert. We need to laugh together again.'

Jill is impossible. So impossible she decides on a dinner party. This piece of news is too good for a cup of coffee.

111

Moppy comes late and alone. Jozef is working, or so he says. Robert is carving up Greek roast lamb. A recipe stolen from Moppy.

'How's your new man?' asks Robert. 'I hear he's got a thing about inflatables. Does he have a doll too?'

Moppy intercepts the quick warning glance in Jill's eye. 'Jill, you promised.'

'I'm sorry. It just slipped out.'

The men are looking admiringly at Moppy. Here's a woman who can hack it in the rugby changing room with a few good tales.

'The main thing is, does it work?' asks Ross.

'Better than yours, I suspect,' says Amanda.

Suddenly all the men are concentrating on the lamb.

Though Moppy wouldn't deny there is a certain thrill in being the subject of gossip, she is not sorry to arrive home.

'Is this yours?' she asks the babysitter. She's holding up a large sea egg, cleaned out and spikes removed.

'No,' Nikki says, 'I brought it inside. Perhaps a friend left it for your wall.'

The paper is stuffed in the opening.

Spikes on the outside
sweetness in

Moppy sighs. She's getting tired of metaphors. If he has so much to offer, why doesn't he?

~ poetry can't buy you love ~

Ted, if it is Ted, is not the first to think writing can buy him love. I've fallen down that hole more than once with poems. Hardly anyone sees poetry as being valuable any more. On a TV programme about sex most of the women questioned on the street chose a rugby player over a poet. And last month I was at the opening of a new library. My friend, a short story writer, was with me.

'Who are you?' the gatekeeper asked. He was wearing a Friends Of The Library badge. We were trying to sneak in early, thinking we had a right. After all, our books were in there, languishing on the shelves like nervous wallflowers. We thought we might visit them, stroking their spines with the same air of misbelief parents have when sighting their returning grown-up offspring.

The gatekeeper on receiving our names said to my friend, 'I've heard of you, I have the biggest collection of fiction in the country apart from the Turnbull.' He turned to me. 'But not you,' he said. Perhaps I was an imposter.

'I'm a poet,' I said.

'Ah. I have a theory, poetry died with Keats,' he said. 'Anyway, it doesn't matter now. Anyone's allowed in after 10 a.m.'

So there you go, a dead poet. Creatively speaking.

My first book, *Chewing the Fat,* was nowhere to be seen in the library or on the computer. Mati laughed when I told him. I guess if you're in prison, life takes on a different meaning. That's what I like about him. He gives me a new perspective, and for a writer that's valuable. Also he really appreciates my poems. Today as I was leaving, I slipped a book into his hands. *My heart goes swimming*. New Zealand love poems. Inside, a poem of my own and my home address.

the prisoner and the nightingale

on visiting days
I sing for him
old poems

my voice
stammering
over the rusty notes

and all the time
his shy smile
sneaking

past the guard
tying ribbons
around my heart

~ where's the kitchen knife? ~

'So has he had you committed yet?' asks Jill. She's taken a sickie and is visiting Moppy. A mental health day, she says.

Moppy looks at Jill's drawn face. 'Obviously not. In fact if I have any complaint it's that he shows no interest at all in tying me up.'

'I didn't know you were into bondage.'

'No.' Moppy laughs. 'It's just that he believes in the freedom and privacy of the individual. So I never know where he is. He never answers the phone. All I get is his answer phone suggesting I send a fax. Even if he's standing right next to it he won't answer it. He has a pager for work. But he can be very sweet. Last Sunday we went for a walk through Oakley Park. He knew all about the loony bin. Every 100 yards he'd stop and say, "Have we walked enough for a hug?" And just when I think he has forgotten me altogether, something arrives in the mail.'

'Like what?'

'Like this.'

Moppy shows Jill a page from a During Your Absence message pad. *During your absence* was circled. The date was written in. Alongside the time he had written 'now' and ticked *wishes to see you*. Signed Jozef, Hugs.

'Very cute and very strange.'

'Well he's not a New Zealander, is he?'

'What is it about the foreign with you? A Pakistani, an American, a Pole and who knows what else.'

'The Persian acrobat and the Egyptian.'

'I'd forgotten them, but of course I wasn't there. Still, I can understand it. New Zealand men leave a lot to be desired.'

'Tell me about it.'

'I can't. I just can't.'

Jill heaves her shoulders. She pulls a newspaper cartoon out from her bag. It suggests Camilla better watch out if she marries Charles because she would immediately create a job vacancy.

'So?'

'You know. It's repetitive. Robert had an affair with me while he was still married. I thought I was special, that it was real love. Now I'm thinking he's that kind. Non-monogamous.'

'What makes you think that?'

'I found a note in his briefcase. It was from "your B", thanking him for the ticket to Bali. Robert's going to a conference there next month and I wanted to go with him, but he said we couldn't afford it. The fucking bastard.'

'I'll say.'

'You knew?'

'No, I suspected.'

'And you didn't tell me? I suppose I'm a laughing stock around town.'

'It's not like that. Well, not with me anyway. It's his reputation, not yours. But what are you going to do about it?'

'Oh God knows. I suppose I should be grateful I don't have kids. I've given him ten years, and now I'm over forty and what have I got? A big fat nothing.'

Moppy puts her arm around Jill, but she can't help thinking that ten years ago Jill showed no sympathy to Robert's first wife. Karen got what she deserved for letting herself go, Jill had said at the time.

'You are entitled to half the house, Jill. You could afford a fantastic apartment in town. And anyway it's not too late to think about having children.'

'Anyone would think you wanted me to leave.'

'Whatever you do you'll have my support.'

'Just as well he wasn't there when I found the letter. I may have killed him. I was that fucking angry.' Jill never normally uses the word fuck.

'So what did you say?'

'Nothing. He doesn't know I know. I wanted to talk to you first. Figure out a strategy.'

'How can you maintain such restraint?'

'Acting. Remember our school plays? I was always the devious one. He thinks he's got the measure of me, but he's wrong.'

'I hope this isn't going to be another Warrior Queen scenario. Cutting up shirts or dropping manure in at the office.'

'No. But I want to pick my moment before I react. I'm not strong enough right now to do anything. Karen went all weepy and pathetic when she found out about me, and it turned Robert right off. Now I feel so bad. What a bitch I was.'

Jill is crying again. It doesn't suit her, notes Moppy. Her face is blotchy, her eyes puffy and red, at odds with her clear English complexion.

'You can always stay here, you know.'

This at least makes Jill smile. She looks around at all the paper littering the floor, at the boxes of Lego and the baskets of shells.

'I'd have to be desperate. Anyway, why should I go? I'm not the one playing around. As I said, strategy's the answer. So would you and Jozef come to dinner next weekend?'

'Why? What have you got planned? It sounds a bit uncomfortable.'

'Well you have to. Robert was supposed to go fishing, if I can believe that. I told him I'd already invited you.'

'And he agreed to change his plans?'

'Yes, that's the funny thing. In fact he looked almost relieved. She must have her claws in.'

Sam and Thomas have just come home from school. Thomas yells from the kitchen, 'Mummy, can I have a biscuit?'

'Yes, dear.' Moppy sighs. 'He always asks, even for a glass of water. It drives me mad. Sam never does. But sometimes Sam asks if he can go to a friend's place in a particular tone. It's like he wants to get out of it, but he doesn't want to take the responsibility. Maybe Robert's the same. They never grow up, you know. Makes me wonder why I bother really. Anyway, getting back to you, it seems to me that either you accept Robert for the polygamist he is or you leave him. Simple really.'

'For you maybe. You never loved Tim.'

'I loved Geoff. You know he wanted to stay married and have the odd affair with a guy, but no way. I could never touch him after I found out. I couldn't even hug him. He repulsed me. But I don't think it was the gay thing. It was the betrayal. And the lies.'

'I don't think you've ever really got over him. It's why you keep picking unsuitable men.'

'Yeah. I think my relationship with my father's got a lot to do with it too. Not that I blame him, but he was quite disturbed after the war. There but not there, if you know what I mean. I'm definitely attracted to men who aren't really available. Like the other night. At *Romeo and Juliet*.'

'*Romeo and Juliet*? The ballet?'

'Didn't I tell you? Dennis had free tickets 'cause the director's a friend of his and Don was sick. It was the last night so there was a party afterwards. I was lusting after this gorgeous man. Tall, dark and intense. Kind of Jewish, you know?'

'Aren't you occupied already?'

'Well who knows for how long? Just the kind of thing to have in reserve, I thought. Michael his name was. So perfect. A designer. I had instant visions of him fixing up the bach until I asked what he was doing there. "I'm Romeo's date," he said. Romeo's date! God. He knew too. He kind of smirked when he told me, as if to say, Got ya.'

'One thing about you, Moppy, is you always make me laugh.'

'No one ever takes my disasters seriously.'

Moppy is thinking of the night Geoff broke down in tears and told her he didn't know what to do. He was having an affair. With a married man. The guilt was killing him. Moppy had picked up the kitchen knife. She wanted to stab at something – him or herself. She picked up a cushion instead. The kapok flew all around the room. Geoff accused her of hysteria. Now whenever she or anyone of her friends is bordering on drama queen behaviour, the refrain is, 'Where's the kitchen knife?'

'I do,' says Jill, 'but right now, I'm the one with the problem.'

'That's right, you need the kitchen knife.' Moppy goes into the kitchen and comes back with her best German chef's knife. 'And a cushion.' She runs to the couch, grabs an old faded cushion.

'I couldn't,' Jill says.

'Yes you could. It's about time I threw it out anyway.'

Jill picks up the knife and stabs into the stained pink chintz. It's not kapok that spurts out but foam-rubber chips. They drop on to the floor rather than fly upwards into the air.

'You've got to do it like you mean it,' says Moppy, grabbing the knife and slashing the material. Sam and Thomas are standing at the door, watching.

'Are you all right, Mum?' asks Sam.

'Yeah, we're just getting rid of this cushion. It's ugly, don't you think?'

'Can we do it too?'

'When you've experienced betrayal,' Moppy says, wondering if divorced parents fall into that category.

~ the Mona Lisa reveals everything ~

It's funny how you find out the truth. I remember a conversation I had once with my father. In the days when I still considered it possible to talk. My father was slinging off at modern art. He was drunk. Da Vinci, he said. Now there's a painter. But Mona Lisa was not his idea of a sexy woman, he told me, though he admired the way she kept a secret.

There was such a nuance in the way my father said this that I realised he had a mistress, a longstanding one. The widow Rose to whom my father was and is such a good neighbour. Cleaning out her gutters on a regular basis, though my mother complains bitterly of the debris growing in hers.

My mother copes with her long-term grief and betrayal by shifting the focus sideways. She never has time for tears. Her fingernails are always sharp. When I was a child she delighted in scratching her nails over my blackboard and seeing me squirm. But in the street she adopts a gentle facade. She tells strangers that she has lived in the same house with the same man for over forty years and never even so much as looked at another man. She does not tell them that she has long since moved him out into my old room. 'So you can't come back even if you wanted to.'

Moppy, now, is definitely sexy, my father added. Always was, even as a young girl.

~ the chickens come home ~

'Jill, guess what I've found on my doorstep,' Moppy says to Jill even before she sits down at Navona's. I've already heard the story.

'I'm not in the mood. What?'

'Two adorable fluffy chickens.'

'Stranger and stranger. What have you done with them?'

'For the moment they're in a shoe box. Of course the kids want to keep them. But I haven't the foggiest idea about chickens. Jozef says we should fatten them up and eat them but I couldn't do it. We've still got the rabbit hutch, so I suppose I could keep them in there.'

'But why would anyone give you chickens?'

'Who can tell the workings of a mind? It's given me an idea though. I thought I'd pluck their feathers for a collage.'

'That's disgusting.'

Moppy does not want to ask Jill what she is doing about Robert. When Jill goes to order her coffee, Moppy tells me she is coming to the opinion that all relationships other than her own, of course, are tedious. The way people go on and on about the same old thing with nothing resolved and no forward motion observed.

'That's one thing I like about you, Barb,' she says. 'You keep most of your personal life to yourself. Animals have it sussed. I was watching the way the bigger chicken established its leadership once and for all with a quick sharp peck. So clean and final.'

I finger the piece of paper in my pocket. Wonderful the things I secrete close to my body.

Darling Barbara,

I prefer Barbara to Barb. I think it has more dignity which suits you. Thank you for the poems. I can't tell you how much they mean to me. I wish you were here every night to sing me a love song. Nights are the worst. But now I have you to think about. I lie in bed replacing the hard army blankets with those ribbons from the poem. Perhaps you feel them tugging when you turn over in bed. But I must not think of you in bed, it's too hard. Too long a time. Anyway my darling, it's dinner. Sausages and mash. Prickers and soap suds, I call them.

Till Tuesday,

Love Mati

~ a woman should look like a woman and serve porridge for dinner ~

Jozef is impressed with Jill and Robert's house. They are there for the ulterior-motive dinner, keeping Robert from his lover, and they get the same guided tour as Jill gave to Vincent.

'Sometimes I think this house has more personality than I do,' Jill says. 'A kind of severe but perfect top model.' In the children's room the Barbie dolls stare back vacuously. Each is dressed in a complete outfit. No missing shoes or hats.

'You allow the girls to have Barbie dolls?' asks Jozef at the dinner table.

'What's wrong with big tits and small waists. The feminists are only jealous,' says Robert.

'Actually,' Jill says, 'the girls don't play with them all that much. To tell you the truth, I like arranging them, dressing them up. We missed out when we were kids. Our dolls were babies. Preparation for the real thing – not that it's done me much good.'

'I wouldn't let my daughter have one,' says Jozef. 'She ask me to send her one from New Zealand but I said no. That shape is not natural for woman. A male fantasy. Real woman has big hips. Many of the top models are more male than female. They don't have periods. I like woman to look like she can produce children, like Moppy. A real woman.'

Moppy beams. Jill frowns. They all concentrate on the food. Jill has taken care to provide a meal with a New Zealand orientation. Oysters in the shell with coriander pesto, butterflied lamb and herbs, roast potato, kumara and peppers, fresh green salad and a dessert of ricotta strawberry pie.

'You've outdone yourself this time,' says Moppy.

'I knew there was a reason for marrying her,' says Robert. 'Apart from her beauty.'

'At the time,' says Jill, 'it was more to do with escaping from Karen than anything else. You just didn't want to be a full-time daddy.' She glares at both men.

'And what do you think of our New Zealand food, Jozef?' asks Robert, making good his escape.

Jozef is caught mid-mouthful. Not that that bothers him. His mouth already open, he resumes talking. 'You're asking wrong person. To me food is fuel. At home I eat mostly porridge.'

'Porridge?' asks Jill.

Moppy winces.

'Why not porridge? Oats are perfect food. Cheap, balanced and wonderful for bowels.'

'You could have told me not to waste my time, Moppy.' Jill is irritated. She's spent all day in the kitchen, fending off the visiting twins' sticky fingers and cursing Robert who'd maintained he had to work in the office.

'It's not wasted on me, Jill,' says Moppy, unrepentant.

'Or me,' I say, not quite sure why I have been invited, small talk never my forte.

'So what do you spend money on, Jozef? What's important to you?'

'Music. After listening to ravings of mad people and criminals, music is essential. Books too, especially poetry. Poles are big on poetry. A Polish poet won the Nobel Prize. A woman too.'

'And art,' Moppy chips in. 'You like art, don't you?'

'But of course. When I go back to Poland I will take a collection with me.'

'Back? But I thought you were staying here?'

'Not for ever. It is too conventional here. And uncultured. Even artists have no knowledge of history.'

'Are you talking about me?' asks Moppy.

'No.' He sighs. 'Women take everything personally.'

'You implied it.'

'No. I have no time for implying. To imply is disaster in my job. I must be accurate in my meaning.'

'Do you enjoy your job?' Jill asks quickly.

'Enjoy is not right word. The prison is a most uncomfortable environment. As for prisoners, I don't have, ah, sympathy for them. Most are lacking ability to realise the consequences of their actions.' Jozef pauses, waiting for someone to confirm or refute what he has said.

'Speaking from my perspective,' I say, 'nothing is as black and white as it seems, especially in prison. In my opinion half the guards should be locked up and half the prisoners freed.'

'Oh Barb,' says Robert, 'you're such a liberal. I wouldn't put it past you to fall for a rapist.'

'A murderer maybe, but never a rapist,' I say.

'Anyway, you can talk, Robert,' Jill says.

'What do you mean, I can talk?'

'I mean you're not exactly a mastermind yourself when it comes to the opposite sex.'

'You mean it was dumb of me to fall for you?'

'I mean you didn't realise and still don't realise I'm not the pushover I appear to be.' Jill's voice is steely.

'Okay, okay, I've got the picture. You've just read *Women Who Run With The Wolves* and you want everybody to know you've got a layer of fangs beyond those fine white teeth.'

'Not everyone, Robert, just you. I'm on a metaphorical journey to capture the white hairs from the bear's throat.'

'You're not going all new agey again, are you Jill?' asks Moppy.

'I don't know if it's new age or not. All I know is, it works.'

'Sounds like an ad for soap powder to me,' laughs Robert. 'What do you think of all this mumbo-jumbo, Jozef?'

'I'm scientist by nature and nurture and deeply sceptical of anything that cannot be explained rationally.'

~ to roost ~

Moppy and Jozef drive back to his apartment. It is the first time she has been invited to stay the night.

'So what did you think of Robert and Jill, Jozef?' For Moppy this is one of the great pleasures of going out with a man. The analysis on the way home, and again in the morning with girlfriends.

'The atmosphere was difficult. Is she having an affair?'

'No. He is'.

'Ah. That explains. Still, not so serious for a man. It is to be expected.'

'Not by me. My first husband had an affair and I dumped him without giving him a second chance. Mind you, it was with another man.'

'Poor you. Have you had test for AIDS?'

'Yes, but this was ages ago, well before AIDS.'

'Nobody really knows. But is that why you have had so many men? To make up for your bad husband?'

'No it is not. Anyway, you can talk. How many women have you had?'

'Ah, you cannot ask a man. Anyway, enough talking.'

Jozef's hands are sliding up Moppy's leg. Playing with the elastic on her black satin panties. I must concentrate on the here and now, thinks Moppy. And she tries, but when he is stroking her clitoris she feels uncomfortable, as if she is taking too long. Jozef is an impatient man. He has told her already how he likes to do two things at once.

'I don't think I'm going to come, Jozef,' she mutters. 'You can stop now. It's starting to hurt.'

'What is that you like, Moppy? You never say. Do you like kinky sex?'

'I'm just a simple girl from the western suburbs, I want your cock inside me, snug and tight. Slow-moving.'

He insists that she put her fingers on his, feeling him pump his penis, learning how to do it.

'There, it is going up. Am I good boy for you?'

In the white sheets Moppy does not sleep. She lies still and awake, keeping to her side of the bed. Jozef does not like to be touched in the night.

In the morning after Jozef has jumped on her again at 5 a.m. and after she has not come again, but then she never does in the morning, Jozef brings her breakfast in bed. Not porridge but croissants, soft and warm from the oven, fresh fruit and a candle lit.

'I could get used to this,' she murmurs.

'This is special and rare treat. And for next weekend when I will not see you because I am invited to Brisbane. See?' He shows Moppy a copy of the letter giving the conference details. 'Is this impressive enough to merit me a hug?' he asks.

At home Moppy finds a small bunch of violets.

from the garden
violets dawn wet
and open
for your taking

She pushes her nose into the fragrance as if it might obliterate the world. It is obvious Jozef has not even considered inviting her.

~ no tutu but a pirouette ~

Jill has changed her appearance. Her long blonde hair has been cut short, cropped at the back, and coloured a light strawberry-pink. She's also lost weight. She's wearing all black: tight suede-look trousers and a lacy top.

'You look fantastic, Jill. What have you done to yourself?'
'It's strange,' says Jill. 'I don't know where I've gone. I look in the mirror and see a stranger.'
'So what did Robert say about your hair?'
'He doesn't like it. Said I was too old to have my hair like this. I think he finds it threatening.'
'I'd be worried if I was him.'
'He is. I've enrolled in a jazz ballet class.'
'Perhaps I could come too. All I ever wanted was a pink tutu and ballet shoes,' says Moppy. 'But Dad said I had the wrong shaped legs to do ballet.'
'That's terrible. And anyway you've got great legs.'
'I think the truth was they couldn't afford it.'
'I hated it. Having my hair scraped back into a bun and the teacher was so bitchy. Mind you, I can still do a pirouette. See?'

Jill stands up and twirls around.

The man sitting at the next table claps. Moppy has been eyeing up his lean elegant face and his cropped grey hair. Just the sort of mature man I fancy, she thinks. The man stands up, bows at Jill and leaves.

'Whatever possessed you to do that?' asks Moppy.
'I wanted to see if I had the guts,' Jill replies. 'I've made up my mind to leave Robert.'
'When and how?'
'Next week, when he goes to Bali.'
'So what are you going to do?'
'I'm taking the next flight. And staying in the same hotel.'
'Are you going to kick the door down?'
'I'm not sure yet. I want you to come with me. Give me courage.'
'God Jill. Don't be ridiculous. I've got two kids and no money.'

'Fuck the cost. I'll book the tickets and hotel on Robert's credit card. Have you got a passport?'

'Yeah, and Sean owes me a week's holiday.'

'There you go.'

'So what would the Power of the Universe lady, Louise Hay, say about this?'

'Do you want to stay in the marriage or let it go? And I've just read *Feel The Fear And Do It Anyway*. It's time, Moppy.'

Iris is a bit suspicious when Moppy asks her to move in for a week to look after the kids.

'Why should Jill pay for you?'

Moppy's got a story planned. It's the teenage years all over again. 'She won a trip over the radio, and Robert's going to a conference.'

A generous woman at heart, Iris agrees to look after Sam and Thomas – 'as long as you two promise to look after yourselves.'

'We're not kids, Mum.'

'I wonder sometimes,' says Iris, 'I really do.'

Unlike Iris, Jozef does not exhibit much curiosity. Moppy gets the feeling he won't even notice her absence. Ring me when you get back, he says, as if distracted.

The night before she leaves, Moppy gathers the chickens, now twice the size, into a large cardboard box. They squawk and try to jump out, but she is determined. Hens are not her thing, and Sam and Thomas never go near them. In fact, Thomas is scared of them, as he is scared of cats. She closes the box and drives to Albany, hoping the children do not wake while she is gone. In Albany, round the back of the supermarket, she leaves them under a bush with all the chicken feed she has left.

'What else could I do?' she says to Jill on the plane. 'Anyway, at least they survived me, unlike Mum's budgie.'

~ taking what you can get ~

Bali is hot and dry. An antiquated taxi speeds Jill and Moppy past construction sites and hovels inhabited by chickens and mangy dogs. Scooters weave in and out of the traffic, blasting horns. There seems to be an absence of road rules, a lack of awareness even of keeping to one side of the road.

They have four days only. Jill has booked them into a hotel in Sanur. Robert is staying in the more expensive and fashionable Nusa Dua. No hawkers allowed. Still, the hotel Sanur is four star. Their room is large and airy, two double beds, a couch and writing desk, and a small balcony looking out onto a garden of palm trees.

Moppy imagines what it would be like living permanently in this space. She mentally moves in her furniture, realises only a quarter would fit and decides she really doesn't like cream-painted block walls or the absence of history. Standing on the balcony, she catches sight of a squirrel clambering up a tree.

'Jill, come and see the squirrel,' she says, 'it's so cute.'

But Jill is pacing the room.

'The bastard,' Jill says.

'Jill, you can't go on like this for four days. You'll drive me mad. Let's make the most of it. I might never get away again. And I don't want to listen to you moaning all the time.'

The beach is surprisingly clean. There's an area roped off for their hotel. Early in the morning the sand is raked. Outside the rope, hawkers offer watches, shells, material, massages. 'You want to feel good, miss?' 'You want to look good?'

Down on the water's edge a slim European man in his thirties is engrossed in a strange ritual. His arms and legs twitch in a kind of a dance. He's talking to himself in a loud voice, and laughing.

'Tai Chi,' suggests Jill.

'No, Tai Chi is silent. I think he's mad or on drugs.'

The man walks up the beach. The hotel workers standing by their ropes watch him carefully.

Jill and Moppy shun the coral-bottom sea bed for the seductive hotel pool. There's a bar in the middle on an island. They spend the afternoon floating around the pool, drinking cocktails, but neither is relaxed.

'Are you sure you want to go through with it? It could be really degrading. Why don't we just have a holiday on Robert and forget him for the moment?'

'No, I've made up my mind. Besides, I've done nothing wrong. I'm perfectly entitled to pay my husband a surprise visit. You don't have to come if you don't want to.'

'Of course I'll come. I'm being paid to.' Moppy is wondering if she can secrete her camera in her bag. To capture the look on Robert's face. It might work well in a collage.

They decide on an all-day tour through to Ubud the next day. There's just four of them on the mini-bus driven by a Balinese with the unlikely name of Elvis. 'Like Presley,' he says, plucking an imaginary guitar. Trevor and Pat are from Sydney. He's a butcher; she works in a bank. They're on a trial honeymoon. Neither Moppy nor Jill wants to talk. Especially on marriage. Moppy wants to feast her eyes on the country rolling by, the unreal-looking rice fields. The lushness.

'What are you two doing here?' Pat asks.

'We won a trip on a radio contest,' says Jill. 'We're hairdressers in Henderson.'

'Bet you can't get us a coconut,' yells Trevor.

'How much?' asks Elvis.

'Ten bucks. American.'

'No problem.'

Elvis stops the van at a grove of trees. He takes off his sandals and within minutes has shimmied his way to the top. A coconut tumbles down. Elvis follows. Though he appears to be slight, his hands have no trouble breaking the fruit open on a sharp stick. He hands it around. They all taste the watery milk.

'Good on ya, mate,' says Trevor.

'That will be ten bucks thanks, mate,' says Elvis.

'Got me there,' says Trevor, handing the money over.

Elvis takes them to a typical family compound. Walking through the gate, they come to a blank wall. They have to turn around to find the opening. 'This way evil spirits can't get in,' Elvis explains. Moppy thinks it's an excellent idea. But how do you differentiate between good and bad? And would that stop the poems she's beginning to treasure? An old woman with bare drooping breasts looks up from her chore of chopping vegetables. She smiles toothlessly. There are seven *bales* raised above the ground. Some have double beds, one is devoted to food storage, another to a black and white TV. There is a small temple with food and candles laid out. Like camping all year, thinks Moppy. It seems peaceful and orderly. As they leave Elvis slips some money to the woman.

The monkey forest has a much more malevolent atmosphere. The hawkers and the monkeys seem to be in concert, standing close, their hands outstretched, wanting.

'This reminds me of going to the zoo when Peter was having his tonsils out,' Moppy says. 'Mrs Taylor next door took me. She bought me a bag of peanuts for the monkeys. I handed the bag to one, expecting it to take a handful. It grabbed the whole bag. I was most upset.'

'And you're still naive.'

'Look, it was a traumatic experience. Then when I got home Mum was too busy with Peter to comfort me. He's her favourite.'

'Poor thing. You've never been the same since, have you?'

The trip is timed to end at sunset. A crowd of tourists wait at the cliff edge overlooking a temple on a rocky outcrop. A sacred place, Elvis explains. Peace descends even on Jill as they sit watching the sun go down behind the elaborate temple

'I'm doing the right thing,' she says. 'I'm sure of it. I'm not sure it's the right way, but it's too late now.'

~ too late now ~

They go by taxi to Robert's hotel in the late morning when Jill knows Robert will be at the conference. Jill has already rung and got his room number. The receptionist suggests a room on the same floor. 'No,' says Jill, 'I don't like number seven, can we have another floor please?' The room looks over the sea. There's shampoo and moisturiser in the bathroom, chocolates laid on their pillows, a bottle of champagne in the fridge.

'This is more like it,' says Jill.

'What do we do now?'

'I've got Robert's card and I'm in the mood for spending. Nothing cheap today.'

They walk into the centre of the town, discover a tourist's boutique, the prices ten times those of the markets. Jill buys a cream silk pants suit and insists on buying Moppy a long black knit dress.

'Where will I wear it?' asks Moppy as she twirls in the mirror admiring the flattering lines.

'To the next opening. You can say you're the mistress of a rich man.'

Swimsuits are next before their appointments with the hotel masseuse. Jill is determined they will look relaxed and stunning.

The masseuse is a slight woman, but her hands are strong. Better than sex, thinks Moppy, this permission to do nothing, say nothing, though she tenses when the woman goes a little too close to the tops of her thighs. Surely it's not an invitation? If so, Moppy doesn't take her up on it.

'To be on the safe side, we'll eat away from the hotel. The conference is having a special dinner at eight, so if we leave at seven or so we'll be right,' Jill decrees.

They eat nasi goreng in a small restaurant up the road.

'This is the life. No kids and no man, just good food and my best friend. Can't we go home tomorrow and forget about Robert?' asks Moppy.

'No,' says Jill. 'I'm determined.'

At nine they walk back to the hotel, knowing Robert will still be at the dinner.

'We'll have a drink at the bar, then go to our room and wait.'

Moppy has her standard dry white wine, Jill a brandy and ginger.

'I need this,' she says.

They are wearing their new dresses and their skins are taking on a luxuriant tone. A couple of men approach: 'How are ya?'

'Fine,' says Jill, a touch of ice in her voice.

'I think they want us to leave them alone,' the older man says.

Jill softens a little. 'We're not really in the mood.'

'Couple of lesies are you?' asks the younger man, who is wearing white jeans and a red T-shirt with the sleeves rolled back. Not that's he got any muscles to speak of, thinks Moppy.

'Course we are. What makes you think we'd have the likes of you when we can have each other?' Moppy's just warming up.

The older one grabs his friend's arm. 'Let's go where we're appreciated, mate.'

'Yeah, go on home back to your cave,' yells Moppy to their departing backs.

'Ssh, we don't want to draw attention to ourselves. I can't afford to blow this.'

'Sorry, Jill.'

They drink in silence.

~ in the meantime, the diminishing powers of mothers and poets ~

Iris rings me up. 'Barb, dear, do you know what's going on with Moppy? She doesn't tell me anything these days. In particular this trip to Bali?'

I toe the party line. 'No.'

Some mothers have the power of taking away all your grown-up-ness in one word or gesture. Moppy knows never to ring Iris when she is feeling vulnerable because she cannot dissemble in such matters. In one second Iris catches the hint of distress in her voice and her tears refuse to remain bound and controlled in their ducts. And when Iris speaks to me in her kind and concerned way, I want to curl up in her lap, like a cat. Feel her fingers stroking my hair.

'And what about you, dear? Have you found a nice man yet?'

'What can I say?'

I am on the brink of confessing all when I am saved by the sudden memory of Iris screaming at Moppy's naked photograph and the news of Vincent. I have too much respect for my eardrums to risk it. Instead, I tell her all about my latest book being rejected, how they want me to write a novel instead. And how I'm worried I have nothing to write about. I read her the letter.

Dear Barb,

We enjoyed reading *The Reluctant Crone Goes Visiting* very much. The writing is original, funny and full of insight. Especially the Parry sequence. However, we must reluctantly decline to publish it as we do not perceive a viable market for it.

We would like to say, however, that we would be very interested indeed in a novel from you as we consider that you have a strong narrative drive in your poems.

Once again we are sorry, but please consider the idea of a novel.

Yours sincerely
Rodney Crabtree

'What about Mills and Boon, dear? They pay well, I hear.'
'I think I'm too cynical. All the good romantic writers seem to have longstanding husbands.'
'Oh, well what about short stories? They might be easier.'
'No, ever since I wrote that story based on my mother and got into trouble, I don't seem able to write them. Besides, I don't like the structure.' Only one climax allowed. It would never suit Moppy, I am thinking. 'No, I'll just have to come up with a novel.'
'You'll think of something dear, you're very clever.'

My mother does not appreciate me being a writer. Dictating over the phone how I should not write about family conversations or, even worse, family quarrels. My grandfather once told me he and my grandmother never argued. True, I cannot recall any cross words but I cannot recall my grandmother either. On our infrequent visits she seemed to spend all day in the kitchen. All I can remember is a dress she wore often. Shapeless navy with large white spots.

With each word I put on the page I feel the power of the family diminishing. Myself stepping from their world into another of my own making.

~ a knocking on the door ~

'Hello, hello.' Robert hangs up.
'Who was that, Robert?' Robert's secretary, Bernadette, lies on the bed in her new silk nightie.
'No one there. Probably Jill wanting to know if I'm where I said.'
'But why wouldn't she speak?'
'Doesn't want to give me the power of knowing she's checking up. Don't ask me how the female mind works. I just know how devious you all are.'
'Yeah, and don't you forget it.'
There's a knock on the door.
'Would you get that, bunnykins?' calls Robert from the bathroom.
The bunny, who is not unlike a younger version of Jill, moves on small nimble feet.

'Is Robert here?' asks Jill in a whisper. She cannot quite force her face muscles into a reassuring smile.

'Robert?' calls Bernadette uncertainly.

'Fuck. What the hell are you doing here?' Robert is wearing his red heart silk boxers. The ones Jill gave him for his birthday.

'Hello darling,' Jill says. 'I thought I'd deliver this personally to you.' She holds out a letter. 'Aren't you going to introduce Bernadette to Moppy?'

Moppy stands behind Jill, uncertain as to protocol. Bernadette doesn't hang around for introductions. She grabs the phone, runs into the bathroom, locks the door and rings her best friend in New Zealand for advice.

'Brazen it out,' opines Tracy.

Tracy has never been wrong before. Nevertheless, Bernadette has too much regard for her newly straightened teeth, so stays put behind the door, holding a glass up to hear the muffled voices.

'Obviously, there's no point in denying her presence. But it's just a one-night stand. You know how it is – away from home, and where's the harm if your wife, whom you love dearly, never finds out? And you know I love you and don't want to lose you, don't you, Jill?'

Bernadette opens the door. Both women say, 'You fucking liar,' at the same time. Moppy would clap if only they didn't look so stricken.

'God, Robert, you're such a cliché. Not even original in your infidelity. I'm going now,' says Jill. 'You'll find my position quite clearly explained in the letter.'

She walks out of the room, leaving Moppy to cast an apologetic glance at Bernadette. It's not her fault after all.

Robert follows Jill down the corridor.

'Jill, be reasonable, we can talk about this. I'll make it up to you. A trip to Europe.'

'Ha,' says Jill. 'This time you won't buy me off, Robert. I mean it. It's over.'

~ 'you did it, girl' ~

Moppy and Jill flop on the plane. Only then does Jill allow herself to shake. She feels incredibly tired. Even doing the seatbelt up is an effort. Moppy had warned her of this, adrenaline let-down. She hadn't slept all night, expecting Robert to come after her. No one had knocked on their door. Jill was relieved in one sense, demoralised in another.

Despite the tiredness, the tips of Jill's toes are tingling. Over breakfast in their room, not feeling it safe to venture out, Moppy had given her a card. On the front a woman weeping, *Never cry over a man*, and the punchline inside, *Just yell NEXT.*

'Motto of my life,' Moppy said.

'Absolutely,' Jill said. 'In fact I think you should keep it. It's perfect for you. Anyway, I don't feel like crying, or yelling out for the next man. I'm just looking forward to getting on with my life. Not putting up with the twins or being embarrassed about Robert's sexist comments.'

'I didn't know you were.'

'Of course I was, but I believe in loyalty. Still, loyalty can only go so far. He's not going to be pleased when he picks up his car at the airport.'

'Why?'

'I didn't tell you 'cause I knew you wouldn't let me do it, but I left some mussels under the seat.'

'Oh God, they'll stink.'

'It was my way of making sure I'd go through with it. Knowing I would never be able to get back in his car. I left a note on top. *Just thought you'd like these for your dinner, darling.*'

'I can't believe you did that.'

There being no available seats together, Moppy and Jill sit separately. Moppy doesn't mind. It gives her the opportunity to tell the whole story to the man sitting next to her. He winces over the mussels part. Ben is tall and skinny, about her age, she guesses, with dark curly hair, not receding yet, and grey eyes. He's a company secretary back from a trip to head office in Melbourne with a side trip to Bali.

'You didn't take your wife, then?' asks Moppy, wondering if that's not too unsubtle.

'Be a bit difficult,' says Ben, 'since she's just had someone else's baby.'

'Oh sorry. Do you mind?'

'No, not really. We just drifted apart. You know how it is. You marry young and by the time you're thirty you're sitting in a restaurant trying to think of something to say to one another. You're all talked out. So, no drama like your friend, just a slow drifting away, quiet as the tide.'

'Yeah, it was a bit like that for me too.' They both look down at the magazines sitting on their laps.

As the plane flies over New Zealand, Moppy points out Mt Egmont, 'Or is it Taranaki now?'

'It's a symbol of the future, clear and beautiful,' Ben says.

'You're a bit new agey for a company secretary.'

'Ah, but it's a publishing company, specialising in new age books. I have to be up with the play, and the play is profitable.'

'I can imagine.'

Jill's been landed with a sleeping elderly couple. They wake up for breakfast and start complaining. They didn't like the dirt in Bali, and Agnes got sick. Agnes smiles weakly, then launches into a huge coughing fit. Fred pats her on the back.

'There, there, take it easy. Don't want you choking to death on the plane.'

'Oh shut up, you silly old fool. I've got no intention of dying.'

'Talk about bad luck. I got mine over and done with before we left home.'

'And then gave it to me, you old bugger. Only thing you ever give me is your germs. Men are no use, are they, dear?'

'Not a good time to ask me right now,' Jill says.

'Got man problems, dear?'

'Not any more,' says Jill as cheerfully as she can without appearing indecent.

She turns to the article in the magazine about older mothers. Looking over, Agnes says, 'Don't think it's right myself, having babies when you're forty. You just don't have the same sort of patience.'

'One doesn't always have the choice,' says Jill. 'I'd like to have a baby now if I could. I think it's a good thing. I know who I am and where I'm going. And I don't have money problems.'

'Oh well, fair enough. Is your husband happy about it?'

'I haven't got one any more,' says Jill. 'I left him behind in Bali. But I'm determined. I might pick up a potential father at university.'

'You're joking, aren't you?'

'No, deadly serious.'

'Oh dear. Let's hope you meet a nice man before it comes to that. A baby needs a father as much as a mother, isn't that right, Dad?'

'Can't say I've thought that much about it, dear.' Fred looks as if he wishes Agnes wouldn't get herself into these conversations.

Luckily for Jill the plane starts to descend and Agnes is fully occupied on her lollies. She takes two and grips the sides of the seat. Eyes closed. 'Good luck, dear,' she says to Jill as they stand up. 'I hope it works out for you.'

~ divine fate ~

In the line for Customs Moppy introduces Ben to Jill. Ben offers to take Jill home. Moppy walks out expecting to see Iris and Jack and the kids. Instead, Tim is waiting with Sam and Thomas. Iris was sick on the weekend so Tim's had the kids for two days now and if the fighting doesn't stop he's going to throw them out of the car window. The kids leap all over her, and not just because she's brought them back Balinese masks and kites, Moppy thinks.

'Iris reckoned they hadn't had a shower for a week when she arrived. And their hair needs cutting. They look absolutely disgusting. Honestly, you could do better for all the money I pay you.'

Moppy looks out of the car window at the succession of neglected houses. Not much different from Bali, she thinks, except we have painted lines dividing the road.

'Is there anything else?'

'No doubt I'll think of something in due course. Anyway, how come you can afford to go to Bali and eat roasts?'

'Roasts?'

'There's a leg of lamb and a chicken in the freezer.'

'You're checking out my freezer? What were you looking for, a body?'

'I was looking for something to feed the kids when I picked them up. I hadn't counted on having them. Wendy's kids are away with their father's parents. And you haven't answered the question.'

'Jill paid for my trip, not that it's any of your business, and if you knew anything about cooking, roasts are economical. I make them stretch to two or three meals and even make soup with the bones. Okay, master?'

'It's okay for you, you're a good cook and know how to do that. I'm disadvantaged.'

'And I haven't been, in a work sense?'

'Not when you earn twenty bucks an hour teaching at night school, using the skills I paid for.'

Moppy does not inform him of the fact she earns more. It doesn't pay to be too clever.

'You paid for?'

'Yeah when I was working and you went to art school.'

'That's marriage, Tim, and I'm surprised that an economist doesn't take it into account that I was the one with the house when we married.'

'I do, that's why I haven't made you sell up. Why I live at some inconvenience in Wendy's house.'

'You're too kind.' Moppy laughs. 'It is a bit like a Wendy house, isn't it?' She notices a slight smirk creep reluctantly across Tim's face and remembers how their relationship was founded on their very differences. How they enjoyed verbal sparring once, until they began taking the insults personally.

'What's a Wendy house, Mum?' Thomas asks.

'A doll's house.'

'Yeah, Abby and Hannah play with suck dolls all the time. And our bedroom's got pink walls.'

'Okay, okay,' says Tim, 'I'll ask Wendy if we can paint it another colour.'

'Black,' says Sam. 'I want black.'

'I want blue,' says Thomas, 'like Mum's house.'

Black, blue, black, blue, the argument goes on in the back seat and in the front.

132

'Anyway, Tim, I only work sporadically at night school and I get half that at the shop. I don't get paid for being at home after school or school holidays, nor do I get paid when the kids are sick.'

'But why should you get paid if you're not working? Everybody expects something for nothing these days.'

'And looking after children is not working, is it?'

'Of course not. We've had fun in the last two days, haven't we, kids?' Tim turns around. Moppy observes Sam's face flinch momentarily.

'Yes, Daddy,' pirates Thomas.

'I missed you, Mum,' says Sam.

'Only because you can't get away with things with me.'

Tim's lips are almost non-existent. If he had been clean shaven when they first met, Moppy would never have married him. So she thinks now, anyway. Forgetting all about the bottle of Southern Comfort she'd drunk at her thirtieth birthday, the clock slowly eliminating the possibility of sweet-smelling babies, and Tim the unlikely saviour arriving in the nick of time with roses and willingness.

The tartness in the car is relieved for Moppy by the view from the top of the hill as they drive down the street. The sun is shining on the sea, the pohutukawas are still green, and in her letterbox, a small note.

in your absence
the tui has been silenced
I'm looking forward
to its return

She checks her answer phone. The anonymous voice intones, 'You have no new messages.' She rings Jozef and gets his answer phone. 'I'm back,' she says in a small, uncertain voice.

At least the poet and the kids missed me, she says to herself.

~ that's the way the world crumbles ~

The newly single Jill rings me in the morning.

'So tell me every single detail,' I say.

'I will but first let me tell you about Ben. Moppy introduced us. He's gorgeous, and guess what?'

'What?'

'We've got a date tomorrow. We've got so much in common. We like lying in bed on Sunday mornings, walking on the beach, fires in winter, artichokes and the colour blue.'

'Doesn't everyone?'

'Not artichokes.'

'And what's happening with Robert?'

'I'm not answering the phone. He's too slippery with words. I've changed the locks and delivered all his clothes and personal stuff to his office. As far as I'm concerned, it's finished. My lawyer's written to him telling him I'll be willing to give up any equity in his business if he gives me the house.'

'It'll break his heart.'

'Yeah, more than losing me, that's for sure. Of course I'll have to sell it, the mortgage is too large. But I'll be able to buy a villa in Devonport with the proceeds. I'm going there this afternoon.'

So how come Jill gets a new man in five minutes? Within a year she'll probably be settled in new domestic bliss in Devonport while Robert will find himself tied up with a clucky, penniless student. Divine retribution. Isn't that the prerogative of the novelist?

And there's Moppy still occupying all of her bed most of the time, spending her days taking photographs of dead insects and blowing them up. Laying pools of poison. Arranging a still life, a cracked china saucer rimmed in dead ants.

And here's me, hanging out for a prisoner. What better way to prevent distraction. No doubt psychiatrists have names for such acts. Avoidance of intimacy perhaps?

I sent Mati this poem, explaining perhaps unnecessarily how I wanted to rescue him, take him away from that dangerous world. The possibility of large boots squashing him in the dead of night.

a slow shuffling in
eyes
studying the floor

two fat
cockroaches
scuttling by

and slowly
as I read
your eyes lifting

into mine
and I searching
in vain

for tissue
and matchbox
though I knew

my mother
would scream
at what

I'd brought home

I haven't read this poem to the guys. Not that it mentions any names but they already call Mati 'teacher's pet', and I am teaching something. How to suss out underground communication.

part four

stealing from the dead

Moppy has become interested in the process of decomposition. Her cat disappeared the week she went to Bali. She stood at the back door every night for a week calling Tyger, not realising that her body lay hidden under a table in the carport. Eventually Moppy's nose led her to the revolting sight. It had been raining for days, so the floor was awash. With dead maggots as well as water, Moppy discovers, peering closely. She calls Tim.

'There are some things you need a man for and this is one of them. I tried, honestly, but I just couldn't go near it.'

'I thought you had a man.'

'Yeah but he's not here on a regular basis. Besides, he's Polish.' As if that explained anything.

Tim grumbles but comes round, removes it and walks into the kitchen, smiling at Moppy and me sitting at the kitchen table.

'Once again I've proved that you can't live without me.'

'Told you,' I say, when he leaves.

'Don't be ridiculous. He's got Wendy.'

'That's not love. That's convenience.'

The next day Moppy finds a dead hedgehog stuck half way up the hedge. This time she determines to get rid of it herself, gingerly picking up the body on a spade. It seems too difficult to put it in a rubbish bag, so she walks to the back of the section, past the shed, past the disused glasshouse, and throws it into the ditch between her house and Ted's. Then, she takes a photo of the carcass. Every day, she decides, at exactly the same time, 4.20 p.m. she will take a photo. Black and white.

She has stolen the idea of course. Perhaps one day the series will be as famous as Damian Hurst's dead cow in formalin or, on a New Zealand scale, Peter Peryer's photo of the cow with rigor mortis. What with mad cow disease, cows are a sensitive subject right now. Just as well it's a hedgehog. Moppy has a vague idea of putting the photos in a collage with her lovers' memorabilia. She tells me she wants to call it *hedgehogs and romance, the decomposition of the species*. That there are no new ideas anyway. It's what you do with the concept that counts. Obviously she's forgotten the barbed wire title.

After a week the hedgehog has stopped noticeably smelling, though there are still flies buzzing around it. The body has flattened and the spikes look harmless and soft. The kids don't know there's a dead hedgehog down the back. Moppy remembers Iris telling her not to go near hedgehogs on account of them having TB and fleas.

Iris does not wish to talk about dead hedgehogs or Moppy's new project on the afternoon she drops in with Dennis and Don. They are in the middle of a garden tour, she explains.

'I seriously wonder about Moppy's sanity,' Iris says.

Shortly after, Moppy comes around.

'I just wanted to make sure you lot were not talking about me,' she says.

'You'd be devastated if we weren't,' Dennis says.

Moppy laughs in that delighted way when she's the focus of attention. 'Too true.'

'You have a tendency towards morbidness, Moppy. I've no idea where it comes from,' Iris says.

'I have. I remember the stories you used to tell.'

'Like what?'

'How I nearly got eaten alive by rats when I was a baby.'

'I'll never forget that,' says Iris. 'I was running down the road after you, Dennis, you terrible child, always running away. By the time I got back to the garden there were two large rats approaching Moppy's pram. They came from the rubbish dump down the road.'

'Oh God, we used to spray them with spray paint we found in the dump,' Dennis says.

Don looks horrified and admiring at the same time. He calls Dennis his macho man.

'Best move we ever made, away from there,' Iris says.

'Remember Sam's pet mouse?' Moppy asks.

'How could I forget?' Iris says. 'Not that I ever saw it, but Sam insisted on giving me all the graphic details.'

'I don't want to know,' Don says.

'You're such a woos,' Dennis says.

'There I was terrified of standing on Sam's missing mouse, wondering how we'd find it in all the mess, when Sam hopped out of his bed and I saw it, on the sheets, squashed perfectly flat,' Moppy says.

'Gross.'

'He must have taken it to bed with him,' Moppy says. 'Talk about smother love. It was the funniest thing I've ever seen. Just like it'd been pressed.'

'You are cruel, Moppy.'

'If I remember right, Mum, you laughed when I told you. I was just so relieved. I hate the smell of mice. It's probably something deep in my subconscious because of those rats.'

'Probably.'

'I laughed even more when I found the gravestone in the garden. "Misgiff the mose. Died in bed."'

~ stealing from the more gifted ~

Jozef is also not impressed with Moppy's interest in decomposition. 'If it was sex!' he says.

We are all at an art opening. After years of trying, Moppy's art school friend Glyn has managed to get his paintings into a gallery. Glyn has grown his hair long since Moppy last saw him. He wears it plaited under a black beret. Attached to his arm is Sean's ex-girlfriend, Zoe.

Glyn has all the opening jargon sussed. 'Moppy how are you?' He kisses her on the mouth. 'Haven't seen you for ages. What do you think, eh? I've finally made it. I've sold most of them too.'

Moppy considers the large pieces of hardboard on the wall. Glyn has adorned some with the circuitboards of transistor radios, and given them grey melancholic faces. On one of them the body of a girl is cut off at the waist. She has long model-like legs. The circuitboard occupies the space where her head would be. Gold threads emanate from the waist.

'Couldn't afford canvas, eh', Glyn says, 'so I used what I could scrounge.'

'Very original,' says Moppy.

Jozef especially likes the headless woman. He spends a long time talking to a leggy blonde in the corner.

Jill and Ben pop in briefly. 'It's our anniversary,' Jill says, 'four weeks today, and we've seen or talked to each other every day. We're going out to dinner now.'

'Just as well,' Moppy says to me. 'They're a bit sickening. They can't see past each other. Mind you, a bit more attention from Jozef wouldn't go amiss.'

'Come off it. You got that sort of attention from Vincent and it drove you crazy.'

Sean arrives and hugs Moppy for a little too long. 'So, where's your new man?' Moppy points to Jozef. 'I'd get him away from that bitch if I was you. She'd steal the pimples off your nose.' He lurches over to the paintings. He is drunk. His voice getting louder. 'You're a prick, Glyn. You stole this idea from me. It was my idea, you bastard.'

Glyn looks startled. The gallery owner walks over to Sean and leads him outside.

'What was all that about, Glyn?' Moppy asks.

'Oh God knows. He might have mentioned his idea about the radios to me. It was one of those things, you know. You can never remember where the idea comes from. But anyway the point is Sean would never have done anything about it. He spends most of his day feeling sorry for himself 'cause no one's recognised his talent yet. If he ever had any it's gone down the plughole now. He's pathetic, a loser.'

'I think that's a bit harsh. He's got the shop.'
'Ha, if it wasn't for you running it, he'd be broke.'

Moppy is three years older than Sean, eight years older than Glyn. It was only after her divorce from Geoff and our big OE that she got the courage to go to art school. She left before graduating on account of being pregnant with Sam. Tim wasn't overly keen on having an artist wife either. The old story. Marrying someone who is different, then trying to change them, making them like you. At art school Sean was the one who was acclaimed. And Moppy wasn't far behind. Glyn, on the other hand, was considered mediocre.

~ the elusive orgasm ~

'I get the feeling you're not all that happy with Jozef,' I say on our Sunday morning beach walk. Moppy has dragged me here because Jill's preoccupied with Ben. With long mornings in bed. Trying to get pregnant, Moppy reckons.

'No. The sex is not so good now. He does the right things but I can't turn on. I keep thinking of the way his finger applies a persistent beat, like he's counting.'

'Counting?'

'Seeing how long I take to come. It makes me anxious. He doesn't like kissing either. He says it's just another form of manipulation.'

'He sounds madder than his patients.'

'You know when he's driving around he listens to tapes of experts talking about sex.'

'Really? Are they sexy?'

'Not really. Very theoretical. Do you think I'm asking too much?'

'Course not.'

'After sex, I'm not allowed to talk and he doesn't like me touching him in the night, unless it's for sex. I told him I wanted him to treat me as a canvas. Stretch me out and paint me with his lips. I thought he'd like the artistic connotations.'

'And did he?'

'He jumped on me in the middle of the night after Glyn's opening. Must have been pumped up and ready. He tried to enter me from behind. I laughed and he hasn't rung me since.'

'Good job too.'

'Maybe, but I was so lonely last night. Don't tell anyone, but I couldn't sleep so I got up at five and drove all the way to his apartment. I left the kids asleep alone in the house.'

'Why?'

'To see if he was there. I just can't stand not knowing'

'And was he?'

'I don't know. Sometimes he leaves his car outside, but it wasn't there. It might have been in the garage.'

'Did you peep in his bedroom window?'

'No, I'm not a giant. He's two floors up.'

'You're mad, Moppy. You'll end up one of his patients.'

'Quite possibly. He thinks I'm quite unpredictable. Maybe I'll kill him.'

'What, with the kitchen knife? Don't be so pathetic. If you want to see the seriously mad, come to my poetry reading on Friday.'

'Okay, I'll leave a message on Jozef's phone. A good excuse. He likes the idea of mixing with artists and poets as much as I like saying, My lover, the psychiatrist.'

I write to Mati when I get home, enclosing a feather picked up from the beach.

the loneliness of the sea

On Monday I am teaching comparatives in my beginners' class.

'I am more intelligent than my husband,' Heh Ju says. Surely this is heresy.

'I love my son more than my daughter,' Grace says. This is not heresy. The class nod.

'It's the same in New Zealand,' I say, 'but mothers don't say so here. In New Zealand daughters often fight with their mothers. I fight with both my father and my mother.'

The class smile. They love these kinds of disclosures. I remind myself I'm not supposed to be talking so much.

Grace says, 'I love mountains more than the sea.'

'That's sad,' I say, 'now that you live in Auckland.'

'The sea is very lonely.'

'Do you mean you are lonely by the sea or the sea is lonely?'

Grace gives up and talks in rapid Korean. I wait.

'Tides,' says Heh Ju. 'Up and down.'

'Under,' says Angel.

Their hands are undulating. I am not sure I understand completely, but I have a glimmer. Something to do with the vastness of it. The way you are nobody beside it. This aspect of the sea appeals to me. I tell my class about the pleasures of early morning walks on the sand. If I can instil a love of the sea, perhaps they will not strip the shellfish off the rocks with piano wire. Perhaps they will be content to lie on the sand burying their feet into the hot interior.

~ ranters and ravers ~

The poetry evening is a disaster. There's a guy wearing a flashing cleric's collar. He introduces me as the Jenny Shipley of poetry, though he's never met me before. I'm not sure whether he is referring to size or stature.

Unnerved, I start to read, but the punk rockers, the ravers, the druggies and the prostitutes who have wandered in off K Road are too busy talking to listen.

'Shut up and listen,' I yell.

'Why?' they yell back.

I like to think I'm a liberal, but this lot have no manners. The *after we screwed for the third time in one night* poem goes down well but the skinny woman in the front laughs loudly. I stop mid-stream.

'This poem is not funny,' I say.

'I know,' she says, still laughing, 'but if I don't laugh I'll cry.'

That makes me feel better. These days at poetry readings I stick to the comic and the social. Extracted hearts don't make a pretty sight on stage. They are also slippery, inclined to be dropped. I've seen the odd one slither off the edge.

Jozef and Moppy sit in the front row. Jozef is chewing chocolate cake. I am mesmerised by his open mouth.

In the car on the way home Jozef says, 'New Zealanders are so uncivilised. Have you considered writing on more serious themes?'

'Like what?'

'Nuclear war, the environment, politics.'

'Love has always been a subject for poets. Besides, haven't you heard of the personal is political?' says Moppy.

'Of course. An invention of feminists, so they could write about trivia.'

'You've obviously got a closed mind.'

'And you, when it comes to oral sex,' Jozef whispers.

In the back I pretend I can't hear.

'I don't mind oral sex on me. I'm just not overly fond of a penis in my mouth. Blame it on my childhood, I never liked ice blocks either.'

I wonder if Moppy is being deliberately provocative. Hoping I'll get the giggles. Jozef seems to have forgotten my existence.

'Ice blocks?'

'You know, flavoured ice on a stick.'

'But my penis is not cold.'

'Nevertheless I don't want it in my mouth. At least not now. Maybe when I get to know you better.'

'You hold it out like present for a good boy?'

'That's not how I mean it. I mean it as being a natural outcome of intimacy.'

'Intimacy, a word with how you say it?'

'Connotations?'

'Yes, connotations. I'm afraid feelings are not my strong point. For me love is knowing what to do in nuclear explosion.'

'I don't know how you can be a psychiatrist then.'

'Ah, for a psychiatrist feelings get in way of making good clinical judgement. And now my clinical judgement is to go home. I need a good night's sleep.'

'Can't you sleep with me?'

'No, not unless you allow me to have sex in middle of the night with no foreplay and no laughing.'

'Okay I promise I won't move or giggle. Sex is a serious business, Your Honour.'

'Are you making fun of me?'

'Never.'

He drops us both off at Moppy's. I stay the night, sleeping in Sam's bedroom. I'm not sure if the Nirvana posters add to or subtract from my depression. It's always like this after a reading. The lure of revelation leading to a false intimacy. The warmth of the audience asking how you know them so well, then the cold truth of it. Going home to sleep alone.

~ bring me the sea in your bag ~

Luckily for me there's a letter to take the edge off the night before.

Darling Barbara,

I wish you could take me home in a matchbox. Perhaps if you write to the man who shrunk the kids and get his recipe. I'm sure your mother would scream. Some days I think about escaping. The first thing I'd do is lie on the grass and look up in the sky. Oh God, if you had told me grass would be one of the things I missed the most I would have laughed. Mind you there is plenty of grass in here but it's a little dry. I've given it up anyway. It fucks your brain. I miss the sea too. I wonder if you can slip a shell into your bag. So I can hear the waves.

Love Mati

'Come for a walk,' Moppy pleads. 'I'm going mad.'

Sunset on the beach is the time for lovers. We look into their faces and at the way they regard each other physically. We have names, categories. Handholders, arm wrappers or stoppers. The stoppers are like the couple seen recently in a TV documentary. The cameras followed the older woman and the younger man around the supermarket. At the end of each aisle and sometimes in the middle, they kissed. I wondered if this excessive mutual admiration was purely for the benefit of the audience. Moppy said she thought it had something to do with the way they had cut themselves off from friends and family. They kept saying they couldn't live without each other.

Moppy tells me she can hardly remember walking along the local beach with Tim and the children, though she knows there must have been such times. She can remember constantly jumping back from the incoming waves of arguments and dissatisfactions. Shoring up the sandcastle and eventually losing it.

I wonder what Mati and I would be like. Would we be able to withstand social disapproval? After all, I cannot even confide in Moppy, my oldest friend. And time alone is vitally important. I think a man lying permanently on my grass would kill it.

~ never ever give up ~

Jozef doesn't ring for three days. Moppy walks past the telephone warily as if it might dial Jozef's number all by itself. She is practising the rules.

They work. A drawing depicting a bird with a frog in its mouth arrives in the post. The frog's front legs are tightly gripping the bird's neck. NEVER EVER GIVE UP is written on the bottom. It's the type of thing office workers fax to one another. Accompanying the picture is a page from a clinical notes pad.

Dear Mopi,

First: Please see picture. I can see many explanations for the initial statement e.g.
1) The bird tried to eat the frog who tried to strangle the bird. Therefore never ever give up even if you are half eaten.
2) The lonely frog eager to be kissed jumped too eagerly. Understanding his mistake, he stops the bird from swallowing him. Therefore even if you make mistakes there are ways out.
3) When his dreams of becoming a prince were not met by kissing, the frog tried hugging the bird's neck. Therefore never give up trying to become a prince. If kisses don't work maybe hugs?

Moppy faxes a response from the shop.

> I quite agree one should never give up trying to become a prince. Here is a spell woven by a wise woman.
> Step 1) Using modern technology communicate regularly with the desired princess with honeyed words and not forked tongue.
> Step 2) Arrive often at princess's castle with small bribes of sweets for guardsmen.
> Step 3) When the princess presents herself, open your arms to show you hide no weapons and wish simply to hug.
> Step 4) Kiss said princess on the lips.
> Step 5) Be prepared to slip off frog skin.

In case of doubt Moppy includes a picture of herself on the bottom, scrawled with the words 'rumoured to be a princess'. Bound to work, she says to herself.

~ neither frog nor prince ~

Jozef has no desire to be a frog or a prince, no desire to be transformer or transformed. Nor has he any desire to be traced. After sending the fax, Moppy can't sleep. She is waiting for Jozef to arrive as per her instructions.

He rings two days later.

'How are you?' he asks.

'Okay, but I haven't slept well lately.'

'Why can't you sleep?'

'I don't know. Maybe the dead hedgehog is spiking my dreams.'

'Well the best thing to do is relax before you get in bed. Take a bath, have hot milk drink, play relaxing music.'

'I think you're missing the point. But I guess you're a typical psychiatrist. Throw a few pills at the problem and it will go away.'

Jozef sighs. 'So why can't you sleep?'

'You never return my calls.'

'I am busy.'

'Too busy to ring?'

'Yes.'

'Did you get my fax?'

'Yes, but it is not for me. I don't believe in fairytales or religion. Even my children do not have Father Christmas.'

'I thought you were with another woman. I was imagining you in bed with her.'

'Poor you.'

'Don't you have anything else to say?'
'No. I can't control what is in your head.'
'This works for you?'
'It is policy of mine to remain objective and calm. My job depends on it.'
'Well artists can't live like that. It is necessary for us to live on the edge. But it doesn't mean that you're any more sane than I am.'
'Perhaps not. But I couldn't do my job if I was not superior to my patients. Have I healed you?'
'Not really but at least I know you're still alive. Are you coming to the magazine launch next week?'
'Of course. Tuesday?'
'Mm. Will I see you before then?'
'No.'

Later Moppy thinks she should have talked about imagination and the power of magic, how the imaginative can empathise with the feelings of others, how magic can inspire and transform lives, but the time to defend herself is past.

She spends the weekend reading a book on the origins of romance, and pines for the romantic ideal of courtesy. Knights and ladies. If she could choose, she would be Morgan Le Fay possessing the power to dissemble, to be beautiful or old.

In the middle of a piece of hardboard she places the flattened hedgehog photo and edges it with the words of ex-lovers and husbands. Some of them appear in bubbles from the hedgehog's mouth. *Such a formidable woman, a pleasure to bump into, you always were selfish, you are a sexual virgin*. Even a torn-up photo of herself as Geoff's bride. She is wearing a medieval-type dress and veil and can't believe how innocent she looks.

On Sunday, Jozef rings. 'I must see you,' he says. 'Can I come over?'

'Yeah. I need a break from my collages. I'll cook dinner, mussels and pasta.'

When he comes, he spends an hour on the phone talking about a patient. Moppy carries on reading. They hardly speak.

By the time they get to bed they are both tired. In the middle of the night, Moppy feels Jozef urgently reaching out for her. She has her back turned to him. They slip together. Moppy likes the silence, the dark. He moves slowly, gently, as if he does not want to wake her. His hands clasp her breasts, his fingers caressing her nipples. This time she comes. An orgasm from somewhere deep within. Diving down a bottomless lake. Jozef sighs and goes back to sleep.

'Was that good enough to suck my cock?' he asks at 6 a.m.

'No.'

'Why?'

'Because I haven't had breakfast and I don't eat meat in the morning.' Moppy laughs her distinctive, throaty, laugh-at-yourself-and-at-me laugh.

'I'm going to work,' he says.

'Maybe later,' she says as he is going out the door.

He's not listening. He's already reading his patient files.

~ foreplay inhibits my interest ~

On the day of the magazine launch Jozef rings Moppy at work.

'About tonight. Do you want me to come?'

'Of course, in more than one sense of the word. Why? Are you busy?'

'No, it's just that I've sent you a letter. You may not want me there.'

Moppy feels a little chill inside. She remembers the hedgehog. Its flatness. Even more she feels like Sir Gawain knowing today's the day he's to encounter the Green Knight's axe. Still she says, 'Well of course I want to see you.'

To ask the contents of the letter feels presumptuous. She watches the clock tick slowly around and grabs her bag the moment Sean comes in. He hugs her.

'Hey Mop, are you okay? You look a bit pale. Not your usual cheerful self.'

'Yeah. I'm in a hurry, see you later tonight.'

She drives home as fast as possible, though as always on Beach Road there's a slow driver blocking her way. She runs to the letterbox and rips open the letter.

Mopi,

Thought and thought but I am not going to continue as your lover.
Reasons:
1. Not very sexually attractive to me.
2. Too complicated emotionally.
Reasons for 1:
Too sexually inhibited, i.e. Don't want to suck my penis or mounted from behind and too much demands for want foreplay (feel I have to pay rather than genuine interest from you. So boring I usually count, up to a thousand before you come) and no signs of perversion which would be genuine as it is nonconformism. And sorry, but I can't forget you laughing at me when I was horny.
Reasons for 2:
You are illogical and change the roles; this handicaps me. If there is

not enough structure I don't have control over situation and cannot manipulate or dominate intellectually in way I am used to. Male pigism?

I could repeat the above to satisfy female expression, i.e. feeling, but I won't as this is not an invitation to some kind of trying to change you or us. Sorry to disappoint you by giving up but I do.

Ever since I was twenty I have wanted a woman with genuine sexuality who is intelligent, warm and can follow a complicated discussion. I have been together with about 220 girls. After all, I am not an ugly or stupid man. Of course this before my current situation. I have never any sexual diseases because I have concentrated my seeking to girls in good social groups. For example of four girls that I was unfortunate to be the first man (really it's no pleasure to break a hymen) one has become a dentist, one a doctor, one a gynaecologist and one a psychologist.

I thought my wife was the person I was looking for, but after marriage she changed, i.e. never initiated sex. She no longer wanted to go to sex deviant clubs and demanded expressions of love, like flowers. I never tell a woman that I love her. Even my wife. Also I never tell women my sexual desires. Too easy to be fooled.

I think that if I filled your letter box with flowers or poems and was consistent in expressing desire for you it would enable me to make you do very much to please me sexually.

But it would not be genuine thus not satisfying for me.

Jozef

'What do you think, Barb,' asks Moppy, handing me the letter.

I have to read it twice. Not that it's not clear. Just that it's hard to get my head around.

'He's mad,' I say, 'and dangerous. Imagine him working with women.'

'I can't believe it,' Moppy says. 'Why didn't I see it? It's creepy. So foreplay is a form of payment. No wonder I was having trouble coming. What gets me is he's a doctor. It's as if the facts of a woman's body don't count. He probably agrees with female circumcision.'

'You're lucky to be out of it.'

'I told him he could come to the launch.'

'God, Moppy, why? Surely he won't.'

'I also found another note.' She hands it to me. 'A bit of a relief after the letter. To know some things stay the same, and weirdly appropriate.'

yesterday a possum
eyes disoriented

landed at my feet
for a moment or two

we both stood still
having no etiquette

for the situation

~ Persian acrobats and Egyptian traders ~

After Naples, Moppy and I stayed in a camp ground in Rome where Moppy met a Persian acrobat. So she likes to tell people anyway. It makes a good story, the way he took her up into the rafters and had her swinging through the sky. Straight out of *Tales from the Arabian Nights*. Keep your legs straight and your chin high, he said, as he pushed her off her perch.

She was wearing white. But there was nothing dove-like about his eyes. They were fierce as he took her. She lay on the floor in his caravan, allowing herself to be plundered. In the morning I followed the trail of abandoned clothes from the van I was sharing with Moppy. 'Where have you been?' I said, sounding just like the wicked stepmother. Angry because I liked the Persian acrobat myself and Moppy already had an admirer in the shape of an Egyptian we met in the Piazza Navona. Poor and hungry we were, reduced to stealing chicken pieces from a supermarket in order to survive. The Egyptian came loaded with chocolate bars, the money for pizzas and an appetite for violence, we discovered later.

If he had had the means to smuggle camels into Italy, Moppy might be living in Egypt now, scurrying along back streets, her head and legs covered. Her mouth permanently shut. The day after the Persian acrobat left for Venice, the Egyptian came calling. He had Moppy pinned behind the table, his arms gripping hers, and was about to rape her when I returned. He said she was to be his wife and therefore must obey his every desire. I told him to fuck off. The word was new to my mouth but I liked the way it sounded.

As Moppy said, there is a difference between fierceness and violence. The Persian acrobat taught her how to skim through the air, how to look down on the world without a cramping loss of confidence. He took her into his arms to sleep through the night as a loved one, and in the morning knowing they were from different lands with different time zones he let her go free. The Egyptian would have shut Moppy in a gilded cage, his singing bird. Look, my arms are blue and yellow.

Given more time, who knows what the Polish psychiatrist might have done with her mind? The clitoris is a small, unnecessary thing. Why don't I cure you of your dependency?

When I read Jozef's letter, I was grateful for Mati. Even though he's supposedly a murderer. He told me he took the rap for another. A gang member cousin, older and dangerous. This is a familiar story inside, where walls enable a loss of memory, but when Mati looks me in the eyes I believe him. Loyalty is etched in his face. And patience. I could never imagine him doling out a ration of affection or counting up to a thousand. And I wonder where he learnt this.

~ a lucky escape, we all say ~

'You want me to bash him up for you?' asks Sean at the art magazine launch.

'No,' says Moppy, 'I'm more worried about his female patients.'

'There must be someone you can report him to,' Jill says. Moppy has dragged her along for moral support yet again.

'I just want to forget him.' Difficult when he is standing on the other side of the room chatting up an artistic-looking woman.

Around the walls of the art gallery are photographs of the homeless.

'Looking at them helps get my life in perspective,' Moppy says.

'I think you're in shock,' says Jill.

'Who's that woman he's talking to?' Moppy asks me.

'Merle Baker, she's a film-maker. But don't worry, she's sharp. She won't get into bed with him.'

'And I'm not, I suppose?'

'No, I think you're a bit naive if anything, but that's not a bad quality.'

'I reckon he looks like the killer in *Silence of the Lambs*,' Jill says. 'His poppy eyes. Anyway, I think you should thank the universe for getting you out of a bad situation.'

'I wonder why I don't feel blessed,' Moppy says.

'You want to do something,' I say. 'Nothing illegal but a physical act. It will make you feel better.'

'Did you bring a cushion?' Jill asks. I think she's enjoying this. Maybe the sweetness of life with Ben is becoming too boring.

Moppy looks at us. Without a word she marches over to Jozef. We follow. Three little girls.

'You haven't met me before,' she says to Merle. 'I'm Moppy and I just wanted to save you some time. It's no use talking to this man unless you prefer kinky sex to kissing or foreplay.'

Merle rocks back on her knee-length black boots. 'I was just talking to him,' she says. 'As for arse fucking him, forget it, baby. He's not my type. Far too old. My boyfriend's over there.' She points to a younger long-haired man wearing tight leather pants and a black shirt.

'Excuse me,' says Jozef. 'Can I speak to you alone, Moppy?'

'No, I think you've said quite enough for one day. Now bugger off.'

Jozef gives her a wounded look. 'I think you misunderstand. I was trying to be honest.'

'Fine,' says Moppy, 'since we're being honest, I never really enjoyed sex with you. Except for the last time. Ironic, isn't it? You were too removed from me. Too lacking in emotion. But I guess that's an asset in your book. Anyway, as you're here at my invitation I'd prefer you to go.'

Jozef hands Moppy the invitation to the launch. On the back he has typed, *We can't be lovers but I would appreciate invitations to launchings. Of course I am still looking for a warm and intelligent girl and if I meet anyone looking for an artist (but not an odd fellow like me) I will inform you.*

Moppy stares at him open-mouthed. He lifts his hand to wave, and walks out of the room.

'God, the arrogance,' Jill says.

'You were great,' I say.

'Thanks, but can you get me a drink? I've got the shakes.'

Sean wanders over. 'Hey Mop, come back to my place for coffee after. You can see my new paintings.'

'Is this a come up and see my etchings?'

'I'm just trying to cheer you up.'

~ hopscotch and hugs ~

Of course Sean also wants a ride home, having written off the last uninsured car and lost his licence for drinking. He lives in an old villa converted into three flats in a street off the wrong side of Ponsonby Road. If there is a wrong side these days. The unkempt flats give the impression that this is a temporary stop. The tenants waiting for better things. Lotto tickets stuck on fridges with magnets. Moppy knows the bookshop is losing money. Sean earns less than the dole. He has wall shelves crammed with books, pottery, photos, the history of a previous, more expansive life. The dirty cream wallpaper is hidden behind paintings. There is nothing consistent about the arrangements. An abstract geometric design placed next to a nude portrait.

'Is that Zoe?'

'Yeah. Not only did that prick Glyn steal my idea, he also stole my girlfriend. I should kill the fucking bastard.'

'Well that will do a lot of good. From what Barb tells me, the cells at Parry are not exactly conducive to painting.'

'Well at least I'd get some time and three meals a day, which is more than I get at the moment.'

Moppy takes in Sean's skinny frame and his long lank hair. 'Aren't you eating?'

'Not much. My takings don't extend to fillet steak and I just can't be bothered cooking for myself. What I need is the love of a good woman, and you're the only one I know.'

'Sean, right now I need a friend, not a potential lover.'

'Sorry, Moppy, but any time, just say the word, you know?'

'Sean.'

'Yeah, sorry.'

'And fucking stop saying sorry.'

'Right, sorry.'

They laugh.

'Sean, it's not you sending me notes, is it?'

'What the fuck are you talking about?'

'Someone keeps sending me poetic notes. I suspect it's Ted McCarthy but I just wanted to check with you.'

'What, are they porno?'

'No, short poems. Kind of love poems.'

'Want me to bash him up?'

'No.'

'I'd like to give you a painting,' Sean says after he has drunk another glass of whisky.

'You can't, you're too poor. You could sell it. I'd buy one, but I don't have the money either.'

'No, no. I want to give you a painting. Any one you like, just pick one.'

Moppy picks a painting on hardboard based on the game of hopscotch. It's slightly skew-whiff as if the artist was drunk. Moppy likes the colours, gold and brown, and the reminder of a lost innocent world.

'I just love this. Can I really have it?'

'Sure you can.'

On the back he writes, To my good friend Mop, perhaps one day who knows? He adds three xxxs.

'Give us a hug before you go.'

He grinds his pelvis into hers. Moppy pushes him away and kicks his shins.

'Ow, what did ya do that for?'
'If you have to ask.'

Waiting at home for Moppy is a small parcel. Wrapped up in purple paper, a book, homemade, the pages bound together with purple ribbon. On the thick cover, a painting of grapes. Inside, poems handwritten, all the poems Moppy has received. On the last page a new one.

in another world

I would give you
the gift
of time
to do with
as you wish

forgive me

I am mortal
for your birthday
this is all
I have
to slake

your thirst

Moppy lies down on her bed to read it, aloud. She runs her artist's hands over the handmade taupe pages. Over the black ink words, as if they are Braille. She'd forgotten all about her birthday tomorrow.

~ not even Dear Moppy ~

It's tempting to use the information I have against Jozef. It's his private female patients I'm concerned about, not the prisoners, but even in the days when feminism was at its strongest I was never a card-carrying member. I don't mean I'm not a feminist, just that I've never been a belonger. Thus I have no access to those files, hot and cold for doctors, if they still exist. Anyway, Moppy assures me he wouldn't hit on a female patient. He likes the rational woman with a taste for kinky sex, if she exists.

The least I can do is write a series of poems. I take them to prison. Introduce them as being about a friend of mine. It's ironic, reading these poems to a group of men, some of whom are in for rape and one of whom is in love with me. I wait until they are settled with their muffins before I begin reading. Justifying the exposure by my belief that the best thing I can do for these men is to bring a bit of the outside world into their lives. To confront them with a woman's point of view. Uncomfortable though that might be.

The Psychiatrist and the Artist

i
'love is knowing
what to do in the event

of a nuclear explosion'
he says but she's not listening

so intent is she on diving
into his heart

(the quickest way
to learn a foreign language)

not realising, even
in the split second before impact

he has drained
all moisture from the air

deeming 'kissing
an unnecessary intimacy'

his mouth too rocky
for swimming

ii
sex was never
that good anyway

a quick pump, a jerk
he's out, deflated

and pointing to the rules
fifteen minutes sleep

*no twitching, giggling
or talking*

*from the undisciplined
mad in the back rows*

sex is a serious business

*iii
always this patient
was recalcitrant*

*refusing to swallow
his bitter semen*

*without a spoonful
of love*

*and later refuge, whispering
amongst friends*

*one sly tongue
to another*

*'he looks like the killer
in Silence of the Lambs'*

There is a silence afterwards. Broken only by Steve who's in on preventive detention and thus not too far from *Silence of the Lambs* territory himself.

'Gee he sounds weird. Anyone we know?'

Ras says, 'You want me to send the mob around to his place?'

They all laugh, except for Mati who says, 'Barb, you will be careful out there. I don't like the sound of that prick.'

I drive home thinking it's nice to have someone worrying about me. Not something I or the inmates take for granted.

~ getting things in perspective ~

Does Moppy take motherhood for granted? Sometimes, and sometimes she forgets. In another room she hears someone yelling, 'Mum', and looks around for this mythical creature. Like suddenly coming across yourself in a mirror. Is that really me? Waving your arm to make sure.

Two weeks after Jozef she is sitting on the sunlit floor reading the paper from cover to cover, paying no particular attention to the personals. Tim and Wendy are away for the weekend. Sam is outside playing with a friend. Thomas is up the road, buying milk. Moppy could have got it herself when she got the paper but Thomas needs something to do on weekends. He is not self-sufficient.

There is a knock on the door. A man asking, 'Do you have a son called Thomas?'

Moppy frowns as if she is trying to recall. 'Yes, but what does he look like? He's only this high.' She waves a hand in the air.

She thinks the man is going to report some bad doing. Stones being thrown at his car, for instance. She has had these kind of conversations before. But only about Sam. Never Thomas. She is preparing to protest innocence on behalf of her son.

'Thomas,' the man repeats.

'Yes,' says Moppy slowly. 'He's up the road.'

'Well he's had a little accident.' The man has a kind voice. He's tall, with thinning brown hair.

'Oh?'

'He's all right,' the man says quickly, 'but he wants you. I'll take you in the car.'

'Okay.'

She runs outside looking for Sam. He's bouncing on the trampoline with three other boys.

'Sam, I'm just going up the road. Thomas has had some sort of accident. Stay here.'

Waiting in the car are three children, older than Sam and Thomas. 'Hullo,' says Moppy. 'Hullo,' they reply. Quiet children, thinks Moppy. She remembers her father once helping a boy at Point Chev beach. The boy had fallen off his bike. He had cut his leg, quite badly. There was blood everywhere. Jack was calm, wrapping the leg in a towel and driving the boy home. But Thomas hasn't got a bike, and why didn't this man drive him home? Stranger danger, thinks Moppy.

'What's your name?' asks the man as they get to the top of the hill.

'Moppy.'

'I'm Bruce. Moppy, this isn't as bad as it looks.'

Moppy feels all the blood draining from her body. Blocking off part of the road is a fire engine. There is a line of people standing outside the shops on the side of the road. And lying in the middle of the road, a small figure. Moppy climbs out of the car. Though she doesn't in fact want to see what must be seen, she runs over to the body.

'Thomas.'

Thomas's dark grey eyes are brimming with tears. 'Mummy.'

A fireman steps over to Moppy. He puts his arm around her. 'Thomas needs you to be calm,' he says firmly. It is a very clear message.

Kneeling behind Thomas, a woman is holding a towel to his head. Then Moppy notices the blood, so much blood on the road, so much blood on the towel.

'I'm a nurse,' the woman says slowly, enunciating each word. 'He's okay. The ambulance should be here soon. He might have a fractured skull. You mustn't pick him up.'

'What happened?'

'He got knocked over by a car. Just ran right out in front of it, apparently.'

Moppy takes her eyes off Thomas for a second. A woman standing by the side of the road is mouthing, 'I'm sorry.' Her face punctuated by red lipstick is white.

Sam is running over. 'Thomas,' he screams.

Bruce walks over and takes his hand. 'It looks worse than it is,' he says, 'but don't scream, you'll frighten your brother.' He looks at Moppy. 'Can I do anything for you? You'll have to go in the ambulance.'

Moppy tries to think. 'Could you take Sam home and get my purse. And tell Sam to ring his Grandma, ask her to come here and look after him.'

'Fine.' He is the kind of man who can cope with a specific task.

'I'm sorry Mummy,' Thomas whimpers.

'It's okay, Thomas. It's not your fault. It's okay.' Moppy strokes his face. How long can an ambulance take?

The nurse says, 'Such a brave boy. He wanted to get up straight away. He said you needed the milk for your cup of tea.'

Moppy thinks she will never forgive herself. All for the sake of ten minutes' peace.

The ambulance arrives. Two men get out.

'What have you been doing to yourself?' the older one asks Thomas.

'A car hit me.'

While one is getting out the stretcher, the other is peering into his eyes and taking his blood pressure. 'What day is it?'

'Sunday,' replies Thomas.

Moppy allows herself to be proud for a second. She doubts Sam would know the day, injured or not. She forces herself to ask, 'Will he be all right?'

The ambulance man looks at her as if he is assessing her ability to cope. 'Are you his mother?'

'Yes.' Her voice has never sounded so small.

'Well he's alert, that's a good sign. But we can't be too careful.'

Bruce arrives back with her purse. 'I spoke to your parents. They are on their way over. I'll stay with Sam until they arrive. Good luck.'

Moppy just has time to say thank you before the doors close. The privacy is a relief. The driver heads off to North Shore, talks into his radio, then says, 'Just to be on the safe side we'll go to the Starship.'

'Well, you will have something to say next morning talk,' says Moppy brightly. No she will not go to pieces. After all, she even gets annoyed in the movies when the characters crack up. Screaming in an emergency is so self-indulgent, she always thinks. So frightening too. Her task is to keep calm, keep reassuring.

'Mum,' says Thomas, faintly irritated even in this state. 'I'm in the standards now. We don't have morning talk.'

In the hospital everything happens so quickly Moppy can't take it in. She does take in the Intensive sign at the door though, and the large team waiting.

'Hello Thomas,' says a doctor. 'We just want to have a look at you.'

They carefully move him onto the table. They are worried about his head. A nurse approaches with scissors. 'You don't like that T-shirt you're wearing, do you Thomas?' Thomas looks scared. 'I'll just get rid of it for you.'

So this is why you're supposed to wear clean underwear. Moppy would rather think of that than face the possibility of brain damage. Thomas is the one with so much promise, the one who will redeem her as a mother, the one who needs her.

The doctor turns to Moppy. 'We need to check he hasn't got any internal injuries first and then we need to take an X-ray. There's so much blood it's hard to see anything. But the good thing is, he's conscious and alert.'

Tim is not in his hotel. Moppy leaves a message, then rings Iris. Immediately she hears her mother's voice, she starts crying.

Iris is calm. 'Ring us the moment you know anything more, and don't worry about Sam. He's helping me make dinner. We'll stay as long as you need us to. Now, ring up one of the boys and get them to come and be with you. You need family at a time like this.'

Peter is not available. 'He's at the hospice visiting Nanna,' Louise tells her aunt. Moppy has forgotten Sally's mother is dying.

She decides on Dennis in preference to Graham. Dennis can be relied upon for a hug. And even though it's Sunday and Dennis has just put his wetsuit on and the waves are the best they've been for a month and the tide is right, he says, 'Of course I'll come, right now, Mop. I'll be there in an hour. Try not to worry.'

There is just Moppy and Thomas in the X-ray room. Already Moppy can sense a downgrading of interest from the doctors and nurses. Not another case to exercise lifesaving skills. Not another plot from *ER*. They are still waiting when Dennis arrives. Moppy is right about the hug. Dennis has been to men's groups. His arms enfold Moppy. He puts his hands gently on Thomas's chest.

'What a fright you gave your mother, Thomas.'

'It wasn't my fault,' Thomas says in a small, quiet voice. 'I was on the pedestrian crossing.' He is still a little scared of Dennis. His beard and his deep voice.

'It's all right, mate. Did your mother tell you about the time I got knocked off my bike by a car? Blood everywhere. I was unconscious, and look at me now. Nothing wrong with me, mate.'

'I don't know about that,' Moppy says. 'You are the most absent-minded person I know. Mind you, I always thought it was the –' She mouths the word, 'drugs'.

'Who knows.'

'It was your fault I got a burnt mouth too.'

'What are you talking about?'

'That day you got knocked off your bike.'

Moppy realises that Thomas's accident will remain. A scene in her mind just like Dennis's. Dennis was about the same age as Thomas is now. She could see his face covered in blood. But now it is a fine face, scarless and brown. Usually smiling.

'Okay, Thomas. Been in the wars, have you? I'm just going to take a picture of your head.' The radiographer is one of those no-nonsense types.

'X-ray,' murmurs Thomas.

'Nothing wrong with your brain then.'

'He likes to get things right.' And hates being patronised, thinks Moppy. Dennis takes her hand. The shifts of position are minute and careful.

'You are one lucky boy,' the radiographer says, bustling back with plates. 'I don't know what all the fuss was about.' She holds up the plate. 'See, a perfect, intact skull.'

Moppy lets out the long sigh she has been sitting on. Tears roll down her face.

An orderly wheels the stretcher back to the emergency ward. 'He's so skinny, there's nothing to him.'

'Probably why he didn't break,' laughs Dennis. 'Probably flew up into the air.'

'The nurse who saw the accident told me he just ran straight out from behind a parked car. You know how quickly he moves,' Moppy says.

Thomas is one of those kids who can't keep still. Or walk in a straight line. His legs twist and turn. On the footpath he often does an about-face. People look. Sam gets embarrassed. 'Walk properly,' he hisses when they are in public.

'I was not running. I was walking on the pedestrian crossing,' Thomas says. He will never admit to being in the wrong.

Like Tim, Moppy thinks.

~ one for each year of his life ~

The jeans-wearing doctor stitches the cut in Thomas's head. Nine stitches, one for each year of his life. She wants to keep Thomas in overnight. 'In case of concussion,' she says.

'I want to go home, Mum.'

Moppy negotiates, telling the doctor Dennis is a surf lifesaver and will stay the night. A white lie.

'She only let us go because we're white and middle class,' Moppy says in the car on the way home.

'Absolutely,' says Dennis. 'And because you seemed sensible. I can't imagine how she got that idea. We know, don't we, Thomas? Your mother is mad, isn't she? Not a sensible bone in her body.'

'From now on,' says Moppy, 'I'm going to be sensible. As payment for a safe son.'

'And who exactly are you going to make the payment to? You don't believe in God.'

'I suppose you're right. I'm just over-reacting. But I don't know how I'll sleep tonight. I can't get that scene out of my mind. The blood on the road. Thank God I didn't scream like the mother in that horrible road ad.'

'I always turn it off. The thing is, if you are screaming you get all the attention, not the real victim lying on the road.'

'But what if the victim is dead? Can the mother scream then?'

'I guess I will allow a concession in those circumstances.'

'Dennis, has anyone ever told you, you can be unbearably pompous. I'm surprised you don't wear a tie when you go surfing.'

'Dear girl. I'm having you on. In the face of death you've got to laugh.'

'Shut up,' Thomas yells from the back seat.

They are quiet for all of five minutes.

'You never did finish that story of how I caused you to burn your mouth,' Dennis says.

'Oh, after Mum and Dad took you off to hospital I got left with the Ballards. I was always scared of Barb's mother. She used to scream blue murder at Barb. She seemed to hate her. For surviving probably. Anyway, she gave me a pie for lunch. I sat there very quiet and ate it. That was what other children did.' Moppy turns around to the back seat. 'In our house, Thomas, everyone talked and laughed, but in other houses it was rude. I kept eating the pie, though it was very hot. Afterwards I felt the roof of my mouth blistering. It hurt for days but I told no one because everyone was running around after poor hurt Uncle Dennis.'

'Oh dear. What a sad story. Have you ever heard such a sad story, Thomas?'

Thomas shakes his head and smiles.

'Tell you what, Mop, I'll make it up to you. I'll stay the night. Keep you company. We could watch *My Fair Lady*. Have you seen it?'

'No I haven't. But won't Don mind?'

'Not at all.'

At home Iris has cooked the dinner. 'I found some corned beef in the freezer so I cooked that. Just in case you were going to have to stay in hospital for days. But all's well that ends well.'

The mashed potato made by her mother is comfortable and soft in Moppy's mouth. It slips down. She eats one small slice of corned beef.

Jack says, 'I must say we were really impressed with Sam. He helped your mother without being asked to.' It's the first time Moppy remembers Jack praising Sam.

Sam says, 'Show us your stitches, Thomas.'

'No,' says Thomas.

'I'm so glad you're okay,' Iris says. 'You gave us all a fright. You won't run across the road again, will you?'

Thomas frowns. His fine blond hair is still matted with blood. 'It wasn't my fault,' he yells in his high-pitched voice. He runs off down the hall to his bedroom and slams the door.

'See, perfectly normal,' Moppy says.

'Well,' says Jack, 'he has to be told you can't go darting out in the road like that. The police rang. The witnesses said that the driver wasn't speeding. They said Thomas ran from behind a car. He's so small and quick the driver probably never even saw him.'

~ coded conversations ~

Tim rings. He is relieved to hear Thomas is out of danger but he's angry with Moppy. 'It's all your fault. He's too young to be going up the road by himself. I suppose you were in bed with some bloke?'

'I was not.'

'Face it. You're not an adequate mother.' He slams the phone down.

Moppy bursts into tears. 'He says it's my fault.'

Jack says, 'He's a fucking idiot.'
'Language, Jack,' says Iris.
'I'm sorry, Iris, but it's the truth. It has to be said.'
'Dad's quite right,' says Dennis. 'Why is it your fault?'
'He said Thomas was not old enough to go up the road by himself.'
'Complete balderdash,' says Jack. 'He's nine years old, for Christ's sake. I was running my father's shop when I was his age. All by myself while the lazy bugger had his afternoon nap.'
'More likely his afternoon tipple.' Iris has never forgiven Jack's Dad for various misdemeanours.
'Yes, dear.'

Jack and Iris possess the language of the long-term married. Words have been compressed to a type of code which conveys a clearly comprehended history. Though Moppy would never admit it, she has this longing in herself. She imagines it is possible for someone to understand her perfectly. To forgive her, her sins.

After Thomas and Sam have been read to by Dennis and are tucked up in bed, Moppy makes coffee.

'So what's happening with the trick cyclist?' Jack asks.
'It's all over. Two weeks ago. He said I was too emotionally complicated and he couldn't manipulate me.'

Jack throws back his head and laughs. 'That's the funniest thing I've heard in ages. I'm proud of you, girl. If a psychiatrist thinks you're insane, you must be sane after all.'

'You had doubts?'
'Of course. Look at this thing.' He waves his hand at the wall. 'It's about time you took it down. All that time at art school for this. I'm sure it's not doing the wall any good.'

'I think it's wonderful,' Dennis says, 'but I also think it's about time you got your work out in the world.'

'I'm trying to. In fact I was about to do some serious work when all this happened today.'

'Well that's motherhood for you. You can never plan ahead and it doesn't stop even when your children grow up.' Iris looks at Dennis and Moppy with one of her significant glances. Being eyeballed, they call it.

'Yes, Mum,' they chant in unison.
'Well we'd better be going, dear. Your father doesn't like driving when it's late. Too many drunks on the road.'
'So what do you want for your birthday, Mum?'
'All I want is a bag of potting mix.'
'Mum.' Moppy is exasperated.
'You know me, I hate the thought of you spending money on me. I'd

d it on yourself. I don't need anything. Oh, I nearly forgot
hands Moppy a parcel, plainly wrapped in pink paper.
jamas to keep you warm, dear.'
is the one colour Moppy can't stand.
gs Iris and Jack goodbye. She doesn't always. 'At least they're not
winceyette,' she says to Dennis, picking them up and dancing around the table.

Despite the comfort of Dennis in the next room and the songs of *My Fair Lady*, Moppy sleeps in fits and turns. In the end she imagines a large remote control. She aims it squarely at the image in her mind. The fire engine skew-whiff across the road, the red-soaked towel, the small figure covered with a blanket. Click goes the control. The picture goes off and at 5 a.m. Moppy finally sleeps.

When she wakes she finds a perfect conch shell left on the window sill outside her kitchen. She picks it up, pulls out the paper and listens to the sea. 'How does he know?' she thinks.

*this whispering of the sea
so like the reassurance
of a heartbeat*

*so like the murmuring
of lovers in their sleep*

~ for a purpose ~

Moppy and Jill are driving to a new up-market op shop in Parnell.
'Of course there must be a reason for this happening. A deeper purpose. You have to see what you can make from this,' says Jill.
'Oh God, have you been reading Louise Hay again?'
'So what if I have? It's a way of seeing the universe in a positive light.'
'So what would you say to a mother whose child had been killed?'
Moppy has just attended the funeral of Sally's mother. The minister told the mourners of the death of his wife and son in an accident. 'If you open your heart to God,' he said, 'your grief will be lessened. And there is the comfort of knowing you will be reunited in heaven.'
'Pious bastard,' Jack said. 'Preaching to a captive audience.'
A young woman, a friend of Sally's mother, got up and started singing. Her pure voice filled the funeral parlour. Everybody started crying. Moppy had been in tears from the moment she saw Peter, his face wet, his arms around Sally. They looked so solid together. So exclusive.

Dabbing her face with a tissue, Moppy thought of the Maori grandmother she had met years ago at playcentre, the one who had told her, 'Tears must flow down your face, free. Never be ashamed of tears.' Moppy had been sitting on the edge of the sandpit at the time, watching Sam. She was pregnant with Thomas and dealing with the realisation that she was living with a man she didn't know. An unlikable stranger. She hadn't been aware she was silently crying.

'It could have easily been Thomas's funeral today,' she whispered to Dennis.

'But it's not, and Thomas is alive and well,' he said, squeezing her hand.

'Earth to Moppy,' says Jill.

'Sorry, you were saying?'

'I know you pooh-pooh my affirmations, but if it helps you get through the day what harm can it do?'

'Plenty, if you start telling people that they've got cancer because they need to be taught a lesson. Or that they are poor because they didn't get things right last time they were alive. Seems to me to be a perfect religion for the satisfied middle class.'

'I don't think I'm going to win this argument.'

'Not even with the support of Louise Hay and the power of the universe?'

'Well,' says Jill, grinning as she pulls into the only free carpark left in Parnell, 'the power of the universe is sure looking out for me.'

The shop is full of designer clothes. Even at op shop prices most of them are too elaborate or too expensive for Moppy. She settles on a pair of jeans while Jill buys a long chocolate-brown lacy skirt and top. 'Just the thing for dinner tomorrow with Ben. We're going to Antoine's. To celebrate our anniversary – three months. And it's big too.' She pulls the top out over her stomach. 'I'll be able to wear it if I get pregnant.'

'Already? Isn't it all a bit sudden?'

'I haven't got time to wait. And we're so sure. Both of us were from the moment we met.'

'Don't make me sick.'

'Come on, you've got the kids. Tell me, how is Thomas? Any after-effects?'

'No.' She pauses a little. 'But it does worry me he won't talk about it. Just goes berserk if I tell him to be careful on the road. He's so private I wouldn't know if he's having nightmares or not.'

'And you?'

'Having nightmares? No, but sometimes I wake up and see it all happening in slow motion. Hideous. And then I wish I had someone to say, "It's all right. I'm here."'

'What's happening on the man front?'

'Nothing at the moment. I've been concentrating on the kids, but they're getting sick of the attention. Get a life, Mum, Sam said this morning when I suggested taking them to the zoo. I tell you I'm getting tempted to visit Ted next door.'

'Really? Nothing would surprise me as far as you're concerned. Anyway, maybe it's not such a bad idea. He's a respected man, after all.'

When she gets home, Moppy goes looking for any sign of a note. There is no trace of visitors invited or otherwise.

~ an attraction to metaphor does not satisfy the parole board ~

Mati writes. His letter full of words crossed out with a thick black pen so I can't read what's beneath.

Darling Barb,

Yesterday I went before the parole board. Not for the first time. This time I had a new story. I told them I have a woman waiting for me. In cold storage. A good woman, whose roots are getting a little confined in her black polythene bag. I said that once I get out we are going to plant ourselves in the same patch of garden. The idea is our roots will become entwined. Supporting each other in cases of drought or flooding. They looked at me and asked if I wanted to see the psychiatrist. Definitely not I said. He's the mad one. It wouldn't have made a difference. They never let the likes of me go. You're supposed to crawl in front of them clutching the Bible. I said the writing class was the best thing that had ever happened to me. That you were so good at getting us to look at ourselves. I hope I didn't say too much.

Love Mati

I'm getting a little worried about being planted in the same garden as Mati. For so long now my roots have wandered where they will. Definitely not confined. Have I got the stamina for it?

~ lustful memories ~

Jill is shouting Moppy and me breakfast at Navona's. Jill orders eggs benedict. I order french toast and maple syrup. Moppy orders a whitebait fritter. It comes crispy and thick with whitebait, a fresh green salad on the side. A woman in the paper is writing about orgasmic food, but it is not enough to compensate Moppy for an absent sex life.

'You must know someone available, Jill. Barb only knows inmates.'

Jill laughs. 'I don't.'

'It's not funny. Nobody wants me.'

'Everybody hates me. I'm going in the garden to eat worms. I've heard this before,' Jill says.

'Yeah, when?' I ask.

'On Moppy's thirtieth birthday to be precise.'

'I must have been in Greece then. So what did she do?'

'Drank a whole bottle of Southern Comfort by herself, then lay on the floor bawling her eyes out. She was never going to get married again, nobody wanted her and worst of all she would never be a mother.' Jill rolls her eyes. 'Then she jumped on top of my boyfriend and stuck her tongue down his throat.'

'I didn't.'

'You did. Roland was never the same after that.'

'Well I did you a favour. He was a dork.'

'There's no accounting for taste.'

'Smell. It's all to do with smell. Apparently you are attracted to someone with different genes from you. So the gene pool is kept strong. Goes some way to explaining Tim,' says Moppy.

'So it was merely animal instinct,' I say.

'Yeah, I must have been dripping with fertile pheromones. Bouncing off the walls in his office. I blame Mum.'

'For what?'

'I took Tim home and she said he'd make a great father and that was that. It was like my cervix opened there and then and said, Put those sperm here, boy.' Moppy pauses. 'The irony is that he's not so good. Of course Mum was only thinking of practical things like money and stability.'

'That's not fair, Moppy. Tim may be boring and like to control you, but he's a good father,' Jill says.

'Depending on your definition of a good father,' I say. 'This guy in prison told me about his father kicking him off the roof of the house just because he spilt a bit of paint. He was twelve at the time. He told me he was a good father.'

'Tim's not as bad as that but he does have a quick temper,' Moppy says. 'I used to be scared of him sometimes. The change in his body language.'

'Well I hope it's not just lust with Ben and me,' Jill says.

'I always say there's nothing wrong with a bit of lust,' Moppy says.

'And look where it gets you,' Jill says.

~ imitating Moppy and falling for cream cakes ~

Without the physicality of a man close by, Moppy feels herself to be slowly disintegrating, like her dead hedgehog. Is this true for me also? Does it explain my lapse?

Last week, yet another literary party full of those looking for sex, gossip, a good review of their latest book, or a publisher who will like them so much they'll turn a blind eye to their lack of originality. Brian is on the outskirts of this group, not literary but a food critic. He's a big man, like Robbie Coltrane, attractive, though lacking the brilliant scriptwriter of *Cracker*.

'I can't understand poetry,' he said. 'All that hand wringing is a bit much. And the drunkenness. I guess it saves on therapy.'

'You've been to a poetry reading?'

'Yeah, I went once. There was a woman raving on about discovering her lover in bed with another man, and a young man howling at the moon.'

'Was it full?'

'The moon? I guess so. It seems to me there's the mad, the bad and the rare one with something to say.'

'And which category do you think I fit in?'

'Obviously the talented. I've read your stuff. It's not bad. Sexy, but it would be. I said to myself, There's a woman I wouldn't mind inviting back to my place for cream cakes.'

Sometimes all it takes is a word. Cream cakes seemed so improbable, so far from etchings, that I fell for it. Just because you're big doesn't mean your sexual parts have atrophied. Also I was ovulating at the time, mucus dripping, and I had had three glasses of sparkling wine. Bubbles always go straight to my solar sexus like they do with Moppy.

'I'll light a fire,' Brian said. The fire was gas, artificial. I was surprised to find that he lived on the golden mile in Takapuna in a respectable apartment block of six with balconies and pot plants. Designed for those who have given up on the idea of the coupled life. The place was messy. It endeared me to him. Obviously he hadn't planned a seduction. The door to his bedroom was open. His bed was unmade, the duvet lying on the floor. The kitchen was tidy, and possessed all the utensils that identify the serious cook: German knives, stainless-steel colander, wooden chopping block.

'Let's watch the flames and talk about poetry,' he said, but it was my legs he was feeling up. I wasn't sure how to extract myself. 'Such marbled perfection,' Brian purred. I'd forgotten to guard against temptation. How warm strokes and a seductive voice could soon lull you into a sentimental song.

We rolled onto the sheepskin rug. I tried not to visualise the sight. Two large white bodies pulling off layers. From there it was a short one-handed leap into the vagina.

Brian's fingers were articulate and knowing.

'I'm not going the whole way,' I said.

'Oh Barb, you're the stuff of legends,' he said.

It was easy to settle into something soft. Keeping the hands free but hanging at the sides, not allowing resistance. The floor parted for me. I hoped the occupants downstairs were out. Brian put his cock into my hand. Told me to imagine he was Michelangelo's David. My hands were shaking so much I let go.

The trouble was, I imagined Mati. Those eyes of his staring at me. He'll know, I thought. Poor Brian. 'So close,' he said.

Anyway, it would never have been more than a one-night stand. I couldn't do it to Mati. Nor can I tell him. This is between you and me.

~ so love and babies at first sight do exist ~

'It's turned blue,' Jill says as soon as Moppy picks up the phone.

She's turning into my mother, Moppy thinks.

'What're we talking about?'

'The test. I'm pregnant.'

'Really? Already?'

'Are you jealous?'

Moppy laughs. 'You've got to be joking. No way, not now I've finally got my kids to almost civilisation. I didn't like the baby stage at all. I think I'm more suited to older kids. So what does Ben think?'

'He thinks I'm wonderful, absolutely wonderful, and he proposed, last night. It was so romantic. He took me out to dinner to Antoine's, ordered champagne, wrote I love you on the cork and while I wasn't looking dropped a ring into my glass.'

'But you're still married to Robert.'

'I know. Everyone will say it's a rebound situation. By the time we can get married we'll probably have two kids.'

'Slow down. I'm the one who's supposed to move fast.'

'Yes, but we're aware of the clock ticking. We agreed it's now or never.'

'Are you sure?'

'Absolutely. The moment I saw Ben I knew. And it was the same for him.'

'It's not fair. Why doesn't that happen to me? What terrible wrong have I committed in a past life?'

Jill laughs. 'Nothing. Nothing's wrong with you. But Ben and I are soulmates.'

'I don't think I've ever had a soulmate. Really.'

'Art is your soulmate.'

'All very well, but art doesn't keep you warm on a cold winter's night or bring you tea in bed when you're sick.'

'Is that what you want, really?'

'My trouble is I want it when I want it and not necessarily when they want it. Perhaps I'm too self-centred.'

'Goes with the territory of being an artist.'

'But I just play around with art.'

'The point is you have the soul and the passion of an artist. But you need to recognise that yourself before you'll get anywhere.'

Moppy shakes herself out of envy. 'What's the ring like, anyway?' She's not really interested but knows Jill wants her to ask.

'Fairly small and plain. Certainly not a million dollars' worth. Just a gold band with a couple of set-in diamonds. A gesture, Ben said. A symbol of intent. I'm so lucky. But I put a lot of positive thought into it. You should do the same. Ask the universe.'

'What for?'

'A man like Ben.'

'Sure. He's lovely but I'd be bored within six weeks. Not quite the man for me.'

'He's out there, Moppy. You've just got to ask yourself for what you want.'

'Well I wrote a letter to this agency, you know, but they didn't reply.'

'What did you say?'

'Hang on, I'll read it to you.'

I am wondering if it is possible for you to help me meet my ideal man, i.e. the impossible dream all forty-something women possess, someone who is intelligent, compassionate, articulate and possessing a mature knowledge of himself.

I certainly have a lot to offer such a man but even if you knew of one I fear your fees may be beyond my means. This is because I have chosen to devote a large amount of time to my art. It's a matter of passion. I am told that the creative woman can be quite threatening to men but I am an incurable optimist looking for the braveheart who can accept my challenging nature.

I should say I am in my forties but I am young and silly sometimes. I try never to take myself seriously. My interests centre on the arts, theatre, walking, camping, talking and cooking, not to forget, though I sometimes do, my two sons, 12 and 9.

Please let me know what you think. I was interested in your ad re.

the medical specialist but not if he is a psychiatrist, as I recently dated a psychiatrist who said I was too emotionally complicated. Not true but neither am I a Barbie doll with an empty head.

Talking of heads, I have a reasonably attractive one and a body that fits me well. I can converse quite intelligently at dinner parties and I eat with my mouth closed. (Unlike the psychiatrist.)

Jill laughs. 'God Moppy you're mad. Have you ever considered being a scriptwriter for *Seinfeld*?'

'No.'

'Well that may be more productive. But like I say, if you put positive thought into it, it will happen.'

'You and your new-age Pollyanna. Piss off with your man to Paradise.'

~ designing the perfect replaceable mate ~

These days a writer friend of mine refuses to entertain interesting strangers, telling me such a leap into a big-screen romance is too dangerous. Safer, she says, to stick with long-term platonic friends, or animals. Neither will abandon you after the first brief encounter.

On the radio the Swedish scientist is explaining her life's work, creating virtual reality, namely Marilyn Monroe on screen. *Soon*, she says, *you'll be able to form your own synthetic actor,* key in the face, the tone of voice, the amount of knowledge desired from a best friend or lover.

The idea is not without appeal to me. An actor with Marilyn's body and the mind of a Jungian psychologist could be acquired with your gold card; a self-trained therapist with dubious skills and Hitchcock's face might be available, cut price, from the supermarket. Or there is always the option of designing your own lover. The thought of a virtual Mati breaking chains from his chest like Hercules and stepping out from the screen certainly inspires.

But why would anyone want to? asks the radio announcer. Either she has too many friends already or after sparkling wittily all morning she goes happily home to life as a recluse.

People are so unreliable, the scientist sighs. *And think of the convenience. Your best friend endlessly there for you twenty-four hours a day.* So enamoured, she's neglected the possibility of power cuts. And in a city like ours, power cuts are not to be discounted.

part five

~ 0900 Connections Anonymous ~

Moppy's taken a bite of the apple again. When I heard about Isaac, I knew she couldn't have met him any other place but in the personals. For a start she was cagey. 'We met at an opening – you know, that artist that everyone's raving about, what's his name…'

'Come on, Moppy, you're the most terrible liar. You found him in the paper, didn't you?'

She laughs, blushing and whispering in case the kids are listening. 'Okay, I confess, but don't tell Jill, now she's been converted.'

'Into what?'

'Into believing in love at first sight.'

'So what did he say?'

'No, this time I put an ad in.'

'But why, for God's sake? I thought you'd learnt your lesson after Jozef and after Thomas's accident.'

'Well that's just it, it's been ages now since the accident and I keep waking up at night, seeing it all over again. And then I start thinking about the boys becoming teenagers. The whole scenario, drink, drugs and driving. I don't know whether I've got the strength to go it alone. The only way I can get back to sleep is by visualising someone holding me. It would help to have a face to go with the arms. Besides, my horoscope said I was an emotional adventurer.'

'Methinks you protest too much. I think you feel incomplete without a man. They validate your existence.'

'Maybe. You know my mother said that I hated my father going out without me when I was a baby. I cried blue murder, she said, if he took the boys and not me. Unlike you, Barb, I'm not conditioned to being alone. Wherever I go, it's couples I notice, and there's Jill rubbing it in with Ben. Fuck me, even Sean's got a new woman or, should I say, girl.'

'Yeah?'

'Angie. She's all of about nineteen. An art student who thinks Sean is talented. God it makes me sick, the way women chase after male artists. It doesn't work in reverse.'

'I don't know, I've had the odd poet groupie hang around me at the bar.'

'For how long?'

'Well true, they do seem to slink away once I start reading and the audience starts laughing. As if you're taking the piss out of them, personally.'

'And aren't you?' She shows me her ad. 'Anyway, what do you think?'

Astonishing, attractive, artist, slippery and sensual awaiting the attention of intelligent, insightful, interesting man, 40–50.

'Good alliteration.'
'Isaac's a rich retired ad man. Into sex in a big way.'
'What do you mean?'
'He sees sex as being everything, a religion almost. He's very intense.'
'Be careful.'
'It's okay. He said he believed in a long slow seduction.'
'For God's sake, Moppy. I think you're addicted. You should form a support group.'
'What?'
'The Otherwise Highly Intelligent 0900 Connections Anonymous.'

~ paradise, the snake and all your dreams come true ~

Isaac lives in Paremoremo, on a narrow unkempt road. Moppy parks her car at the top and observes two white dragons on either side of a steep driveway. She remembers Jack telling her never to buy a house below the road. Bad resale value, he said, forgetting to take into account more important factors like suburb, sea views and schools. Moppy walks carefully down the wet cobblestones. Obviously Isaac is a gardener; she notes the flowers, red and white impatiens and purple native orchids.

A tall slim man she presumes is Isaac stands in the brick courtyard, holding a hose. Though it's not yet summer he is bare chested, adorned only with a sarong wrapped around his hips and a gold star of David around his neck. His hair is short, dark and curly, waving back from the forehead. Even the sun is shining.

'Moppy,' he says, kissing her hand, 'ma cherie, welcome to the House of Isaac.' He opens the heavy wood door. Inside is a marble statue of a naked woman. About three-quarters real size. Her hand extended as if to receive Moppy's coat. The walls of the hallway are lined with original paintings framed in heavy gold. Mostly oils and watercolours of naked women. Fawn shagpile-carpeted steps lead up to a long narrow room. Ranchsliders and a deck reveal a view of the upper harbour framed by dense native bush. Nikaus and rimus. 'What do you think, isn't it wonderful?' Isaac asks.

Moppy has already installed herself in the picture. Sunset on the deck sipping cocktails. Midnight in his bed making love. Within five minutes she is sitting at one end of the long cream couch. Isaac sits facing, with his legs nimbly in the lotus position. Moppy wonders how old he is and if she is meant to be looking up his sarong. At his lack of underwear. She almost giggles.

'You're an artist?'
'Yes,' says Moppy, 'well, part time anyway. It's difficult with kids. But I'm preparing something for the Visa Gold Art Awards. I'm not a painter, though. I'm more into mixed media.'

'I'm very attracted to artists, Moppy. They aren't usually constrained by conventions. But you, my dear, what kind of man do you like?'

'Funny you should ask. I've just read a book on the type of love story you choose and lately I seem to be attracted to the science-fiction scenario – aliens, in other words, men who I don't understand. Perhaps it's the challenge I like.'

'I can certainly offer that, but do you think you're really ready for a man like myself?'

'What do you mean? I don't know you.'

'I can't respond to a conventional relationship or to anyone who's judgemental. I like open women.'

'Well of course I'm open. I'm an artist. But that doesn't mean I like smutty jokes. I hate Benny Hill-type humour. One guy even called me a prude. But I'm not. In fact I think people who tell jokes about sex are often revealing some inner fear.'

'Absolutely right. Come, I want to see you relaxed, not sitting upright like this is a job interview.'

'Isn't it?'

Isaac laughs. 'I think you have a wicked sense of humour.'

She takes her shoes off and shifts along the couch.

'Let me feel your skin. You can tell so much about a woman.'

She holds out her arm. Isaac runs his fingers above it, close enough for Moppy to feel the air moving. His hand moves quickly to her ankles. 'Fabulous legs.'

'When minis were first in, I was sixteen and working in an office,' says Moppy. 'I had the shortest skirts of all the girls. When I was moved to another office all the men signed a petition to have me stay. Of course we didn't know about sexual harassment back then.'

'Thank God.'

'It was funny, though, because my mother told me years later that she used to take my hems down when I was at work. Half an inch at a time. I never knew.'

'So your mother didn't want you to be a sexual person and now you're rebelling. Am I right?'

'I hardly think so. Aren't I a bit old for rebellion?'

'Never too old, ma cherie. Look at me.'

'And how old are you?'

'What do you think?'

'Mid fifties?'

'Ah, ma cherie. You are right. And still so much to look forward to. So many new adventures.' His hand is snaking up the split in her skirt. Slowly, deliberately.

Moppy is sweating. Wondering if she is having hot flushes. Lately she has been dreaming of elaborate dwellings. Sometimes postmodern and minimalist in their furnishings, sometimes caves with low ceilings and cushions. Lately she has been thinking of painting her bedroom walls purple.

At the top of her thigh, Isaac stops. He sighs deeply. 'That's all for today. You are such a sexy woman but I want to prolong the pleasure. Okay, darling?'

~ delayed gratification ~

'You're not serious. Heaven knows what he's got planned if he manages to get his hands up your pants within five minutes,' Jill says on Sunday afternoon in her new house, a white lacy villa in Devonport, complete with Austrian blinds and scrubbed pine furniture. We're standing in the nursery, a sickly concoction of pink elephants and blue giraffes.

'He didn't put his hands up my pants. He stopped at the top.'

'Just like Mr Harrex,' I say.

'But I'm not twelve any more.'

'Aren't you?' Jill asks.

Moppy picks up the latest *House and Garden* magazine. She pretends to swat Jill with it.

'Watch it, I'm a pregnant woman.'

'How could we forget?'

Jill has been showing us all the new baby clothes. I allow myself a twinge of envy as I stroke the soft navy stretch and grow, appliqued with Winnie the Pooh.

'He said I was the most lively woman he'd met in ages and asked me if I wanted to come on Sunday for a spa pool party and, if I played my cards right, a finger fuck.'

We move into the yellow family room which opens out into a small backyard cottage garden. I notice there is already a swing planted.

'He didn't!' Jill says.

'He was joking – about the finger fuck, anyway.' Still, Moppy can't disguise her look of excitement.

It's perfectly clear to me how one can succumb to such advances. Where's the difference between a convicted murderer's handshake and cream cakes? But it's no joking matter. Mati's been moved to another prison down south. Maybe the authorities twigged. Saw a glance pass between us, smelt burning flesh. Love is not allowed to flourish within concrete walls. Sensory deprivation is all the rage. I arrived yesterday to find him gone.

He'd left a hastily copied sketch with Steve for me. A good but flattering likeness. On the back, he'd written, *Don't worry, I'll find a way back. Love, Mati.*

It was a bit of a shock. With an inmate for a lover you expect to find them where you left them, if not always in the same state. Even in prison they have parties. Potato peelings allowed to ferment in sugar can enable an absence of awareness. The clanging of doors just another monotonous sound like traffic. A flat chest suddenly acquiring a pleasing feminine roundness. Ironic that a common trait amongst inmates is their inability to delay gratification. And ironic that Jill doesn't have to endure celibacy. It annoys me the way she eats lunch, saving the slices of perfect avocado for the last mouthful.

'Isaac sounds like a bit of a free spirit,' I say, even though I have my own doubts.

'Mmm,' says Moppy. 'Whatever, I was so turned on after we kissed, I did something on the way home. Something naughty.'

'What?'

She laughs, and blushes slightly. 'Masturbated with one hand while I was driving. I nearly had an accident coming out onto the main highway.'

'Moppy. What are we going to do with you?'

~ a good navy wife ~

Dear Mati,

I have taken it into my head to become a navy wife. Developing a long-term patience. At night I lull myself into sleep by imagining you swaying on a bunk somewhere in the seven seas. Eventually, after many adventures, making your way to a port where I am waiting with my little white handbag and red scarf.

You'll see me there, waving my scarf on the dock, smiling and laughing.

Take care of yourself, Mati. Please hang in there and don't do anything stupid. You have so much to offer the world. Know that I am thinking of you.

Love Barb

Last night an inmate in Parry killed himself with a chisel. Now I find myself acting as censor, deciding what news Mati can do without.

~ sounds a bit fishy ~

Uncharacteristically Moppy changes her mind regarding the sauna and is about to phone Isaac with some excuse when he rings to tell her he is going to Los Angeles the next day to visit his daughter. 'So the party is off. It's bad timing, but I've decided I've just got to go. I'm psychic, you know.'

'No, I didn't.'

'Oh yes. I see auras.'

'Really. What colour was mine?'

'Purple. Very sexual. But the thing is, I saw red when Caroline rang out of the blue. I don't know her all that well. She was eight when my wife and I split up. I think she needs me. She said she was trying to sort herself out.'

'Oh. How long will you stay?'

'Darling, I might be psychic but I'm not that accurate. As long as I need to, but rest assured I will be thinking of you and I'll write. Astrid is going to look after my house and garden.'

'Astrid?'

'Don't sound so jealous, ma cherie. She's just a friend from Sweden. Of course she wants to marry me so she can stay in New Zealand, but she's dreaming.'

'I hope so.'

'I know so. Now I've got to go. Promise me you'll write. Look on this as a chance to get to know one another's innermost thoughts. Okay darling?'

We are sitting outside at the café on Long Bay watching Sam boogie board in on the unusually large waves while Thomas is at his hated swimming lessons.

'Sounds a bit fishy to me,' I yell into the wind. 'How do you know he's not just having you on?'

'Well I won't till I get a letter, I suppose. He promised to write. Just when it was getting interesting. Anyway, it gives me time to focus on my work.'

'Yeah and what's that?'

'My barbed wire series. I'm still trying to work out what it is I am saying and if that's my job anyway. You know, shouldn't I just do it and leave the analysis to someone else?'

'I reckon. I hate it when people ask me what a poem is about. I always feel I haven't done my job properly.'

'That reminds me, I got another note today. Quite different from the rest.' She takes it from her pocket. 'What do you think?'

*taking in
the white succulence
of flesh
translucent bones
easily ambush*

'I think it's cleverer than most of the others. A greater awareness perhaps.'
'Are you sure it's not you? It's your kind of style.'
'Don't you think I've got better things to do? Remember Ted was my tutor. His style's probably rubbed off on me. What do you think it means?'
'I immediately thought of fish and the fact Isaac is a Pisces.'
'Bones getting stuck in your throat.'
Moppy lifts her spoon into the froth and licks it.
'I notice you're drinking cappuccino again.'
'Well it's like sex, isn't it? Too good to deprive yourself.'

~ talk about a web of words ~

Isaac rings from Los Angeles to tell Moppy he has arrived safely. Send me a letter, he asks. She thinks about his impish smile, his tanned chest, the lushness of his garden.

Dear Isaac,

I guess it's a good thing having this distance between us. We can get to know each other without the physical distractions. I suppose phone sex is too expensive long distance. I'm not sure about letter sex. How would that work?

I feel as if you are playing me. As if I am your instrument. Your composition embedded in my veins.

Love Moppy

Darling Moppy,

New friend, whose strings I wait to pluck. You are a symphony I have not yet played but soon will. The distance between us is creating a concert. I shall reach deep into your hidden soul as I seek to discover the essence of you. To hear your song. I feel the softness of your hands, the taste of your lips. You are not far from me, nor I from you. You are close to me in ways new to me. Unfamiliar and exciting, like hearing a great composer for the first time. I have feelings to share and a deep desire to generate a response. Above all, I wish to provoke you into opening yourself, to go beyond the boundaries you imagine. This journey I am on is blessed with goodness. I shall return to seek out romance and passion and will dream every day of the possibilities of a love sharing all that each knows. I am seeking to discover a wholeness in myself as we travel one another's inner feelings, as we access the gift of another's soul and cherish it.

Visit me in your dreams. Write me your song.

A loving Isaac

~ of all things a baby shower ~

Jill invites us to a baby shower — not that Moppy added that particular detail when she passed on the invitation.

'I feel like the thirteenth fairy at the christening,' I say.

'Well I knew you wouldn't have come otherwise,' whispers Moppy, 'and I didn't feel like being stranded amongst these women.' These women being Amanda and Mary who are both clucking enthusiastically in the nursery.

'But I haven't brought a present.'

'You can write a poem, later,' Jill says. 'But I want a nice one.'

'Sentimental is not my style.'

'I'd go along with you there,' says Kay. She's Jill's drama teacher. Moppy remembers her from playcentre days. The two of them pretending to be supervising the kids while they moaned about their respective husbands.

'What do you think of this letter?' Moppy asks Kay after she has had four glasses of wine.

Kay frowns and raises her eyebrows. 'It looks to me like he's someone who's seriously addicted to romance. Frankly I don't think relationships are worth the effort any more. I never want to spend another night lying on the kitchen floor drinking gin.'

'Really?'

'Oh yeah, that's what I do when everything falls apart.'

'But you seem so sure of yourself. I would have thought you'd got it altogether, teaching drama and self defence. It's a lethal combination,' says Moppy.

'Ha, too lethal for most men.'

'So you live a celibate life?'

'Christ no. Sex is too good for the skin to give it up. No, I go for one-night stands. I tell you, rugby boys sure like older women, especially if you make it clear you just want a quick fuck.'

'Really?'

'Really. A good fuck keeps me going for a couple of weeks and in between I masturbate. Got it down to a fine art: every morning before the kids wake up. Sometimes I think I prefer it to the real thing.'

'What about women?' Moppy has always suspected Kay of being a lesbian in her Doc Marten boots.

'I've tried it. I really wanted to be a dyke. Most of my friends are. But I got so bored. They spend all day at it. And it's so intense. Men are much more uncomplicated when it comes to sex. Women get so emotional, including myself. Anyway, girl, take care, don't take him seriously is all I can say.'

Moppy being Moppy does take Isaac seriously. So seriously, she gets me to help write a reply. (I'm thinking of taking up work as a public scribe specialising in romance, revenge, goodbye and hello. I'll even do poems for extra. The literary whore. It's an ancient profession now sadly in decline, I suspect. Blame it on e-mail.)

~ getting the syntax right ~

Dear Isaac,

The daughter goes to the movies with her father. Her hands are wrapped in a white fur muff. She watches the great romance on screen. It does not require much imagination to see herself up there. The gazed upon.

Many pictures later she realises the cost. A concentration of lovers getting waylaid on her surface beauty. Reluctant to delve beneath. Confront her off screen without make-up.

Nevertheless I look in my letter box as if anything is possible. And anything is. A page of closely spaced promises. You want to reach deep into my hidden soul, to discover the essence of me. Being a woman unable to stand silence, I will tell you I am a mixture of lemon and vanilla, the quantities changing.

Love Moppy

Darling, darling Moppy,

Are you real? Pinch me with another letter. So poetic. I didn't know you were a poet. What other mysteries are waiting for me to uncover? I want you to enter my space naked. Lie down on a bed of roses. Open yourself to possibilities, unlimited by conventions.

A Loving Isaac

Dear Isaac,

In your letter you promise a bed of roses.
   You want me to be there for the opening. Prepared to be played upon. My skin moist and ready for plucking.
   The thought of the first performance sees anxiety etched on the forehead of the composer. Will I listen in ecstasy to your interpretation? Will we prove to be in harmony? If I weep for the rose bush, stripped and bare, will you collect my tears and sing to them?
   In the distraction of playing will you notice I am inarticulate, only able to make sense after, in the silence that follows? Too many questions. All we have at the moment is words insinuating themselves in between the sheets.

Love Moppy

PS. My drama and self-defence teacher friend reckons I shouldn't take you seriously. She thinks you may be addicted to romance.

Darling Moppy,

Tell me, are you difficult to love? Sometimes the ship I sail drifts with the current, at other times I take charge. I can see that with you I will have to be the captain navigating through the storm as you, the co-captain, are hiding under the bunk with your eyes shut. It distresses me greatly to think that you would allow a self-defence teacher to limit your courage. She probably wears black boots and is so busy kicking the balls of men that she cannot hear the music of the spheres.
   Moppy, you are a natural adventurer. You are brave in seeking another spirit. I believe it is asking too much of the self to be all things to the self. This is not what I seek, nor you, I think. Of course I am addicted to romance. I am not dead.
   Darling, my absent love, I want you to be all things to me, making all things possible, a Moses parting the Red Sea.

Love Isaac

Dear Isaac,

You ask, are you difficult to love? I tell you it is a matter of perception. Is it really my particular music you want or am I only the instrument?

I am not sure of being able to be all things to you. I swing from being an incurable romantic to a jaundiced cynic. I was jealous when my friend Jill told me about her proposal, it was the full story, flowers, champagne and a surprise ring. If you want to get to the sweet nut inside me you'd better come armed with a nutcracker and lots of patience. I only hope the nut has not got weevils in it by now.

I can't sleep so I'm up early writing this. The sun is just rising. The sky behind Rangitoto is pale apricot. I hope this means I might get a letter from you today. The postman is suddenly absent.

Love Moppy

Darling Moppy,

Sorry there has a been a silence. Nothing to do with you my darling but with myself.

Love Isaac

~ the lady doesn't sing to order ~

On the beach Moppy finds two seagull feathers. She holds them up to her head.

'Is that what I should do?' she asks me. 'Shatter eardrums? Shriek like a seagull or a Red Indian?'

'What are you talking about?'

'Isaac thinks I may have been sexually abused.'

'And what's he basing this theory on?'

'My silent orgasms.'

'How does he know?'

'I rang him last night. I was worried about the postcard he sent me. He said he was trying to work things out with his daughter. Apparently she blames him for her sexual problems. He asked me if I had any problems. I said I was normal, whatever normal was. And then he said he liked women to be totally uninhibited.'

'And?'

'I said I thought I was uninhibited but I didn't usually yell and scream, that I quite often had silent orgasms. He said he had this feeling about me. That I fitted the abuse profile.'

'Absolute rubbish and dangerous. He doesn't even know you, for Christ's sake.'

'Well we did have that one brief encounter. I did put my tongue in his mouth.'

'There's got to be a poem in this.'

'You dare. He already thinks I tell my friends too much.'

'Tell me, Moppy. When he's gone the way of all others, who'll still be here walking the beach with you?'

She smiles, and in a rare show of physical affection between us slings an arm around my shoulders.

From the corner of my eye I see Ted coming towards us from the rocks. Even from a distance I recognise his hunched shoulders. Like I carry in my head a file of the movements of people who are significant to me. Mati walks with a bounce. Ted bends towards the ground as if he prefers crabs and snails to blue sky and clouds. Moppy has not noticed him, but then in her perennial vanity she is not wearing her glasses.

'I've got to go,' I say. 'I've got a poem coming on.'

'Like you're in labour?'

'Absolutely.'

'I think I'll keep walking for a while. It's soothing, and I'm sure you don't need me at the birth.'

'Just don't take other people's hangups on board.'

'No Mum.'

~ a brief encounter ~

By the time Moppy does see Ted it is too late for either of them to turn away. Act normal, Moppy tells herself. Ted has picked up a piece of driftwood. Dark, about a foot long and twisted back on itself.

'Hello Ted. How are you? Haven't seen you for ages.'

Ted blushes. Contrasting sharply with his grey hair. 'F f fine. D d do you want this? F f for your wall?'

'Thank you, but I think it's an outside piece, for the back steps. Handy for leaving messages under, don't you think?' She raises her eyebrows.

'Mmm. G g g got to g g go.'

'I'll walk with you. The kids are at home.' She can see Ted making an effort to slow his breathing.

'How's Sam? I d d don't see him much n n now.'

'He's okay, apart from the occasional escapade and hanging around with a snotty boy I can't stand.'

'He's a neat k k kid. And T T Thomas? A A A After his accident.'

'As know-it-all as ever. Do you have kids, Ted?'

'N no. My wife c c couldn't.'

'Oh, I'm sorry. Don't you get lonely?'

'No. Not with my work and my b b b books. It takes p p p practice to live c c c...' He gives up.

'With yourself?'

He nods.

There's a long silence as they walk up the hill. Moppy resists the urge to colour it in. She's still ashamed for laughing at Dennis's stutter when she was a kid.

'You'll be interested to know, I had a brief encounter with Ted,' she tells me later.

'Was Rachmaninov playing?'

'No. Should he have been?'

'In the film, dummy. *Brief Encounter*. It's one of my favourites. God, I hate having to explain jokes. Anyway, did you ask him about the notes?'

'I hinted at it. But it seemed such a big deal to him just saying hello. I felt as if it was too delicate a subject to be exposed like that. Amazing really. It was like we had a whole subterranean conversation going on. An unspoken confession.'

'So did he invite you in for coffee?'

'No. We got to his gate and looked at each other. He lifted his hand, said bye and kind of scuttled off. I hate that about men. Most men anyway. So abrupt at endings. I always feel as if I'm standing with my mouth open. Still wanting one more bite. It doesn't happen with women.'

'No, we wait for the goodbye signals. The sunset or the fade away.'

'Well, if this was a movie you'd get up thinking, That was a bit weak. No grand gesture. But his stutter was getting better. We've broken the ice. And he's not so old-looking close up.'

~ fragile words ~

In prison I learnt that you cannot force people to speak, or stop them looking at the floor.

he thinking she would sing
an aria at this moment
is unprepared for muteness

tell me, tell me, he is pleading
but she who could never
roll her tongue

in Italian One
takes her pleasure silently
as if he might steal it

It's a matter of trust. Especially if you are trespassing. In prison the inmates listen for any nuance of judgement. The words should or shouldn't. They set tests. Wait to see if you complain to the authorities. Evaluate your staunchness. Whose side are you on, anyway?

You look them in the eye without flinching. You keep talking calmly, ignoring the way some walk, arms swinging in readiness. A small start, but you carry on from there, each week turning up smiling until they realise you aren't going to renege. That you can match their persistent sullenness with cheerfulness. One week they arrive grinning, almost puppy-like in their enthusiasm. The next you find them secreting poems into your hand or into your bag.

Most prefer not to talk aloud. The air in prison, thick with roll-your-owns, is altogether too dense and dangerous for fragile words like love.

For Christmas I send Mati a Christmas cake, homemade, and a book of photographs of the East Cape where he was born. He sends me a letter and some fine bone earrings, hand carved in the workroom.

Dear Barb,

Here I get to walk around on grass. I cannot tell you how wonderful it feels, as if all the sunshine and rain that grew the grass is entering my body. There are trees too, absolutely serene, and birds. But my dear one, these are poor substitutes for you. I feel I may have to take action to get back to Parry. But don't worry about me. I am getting on fine with everyone here. The atmosphere is lighter, though there is no one like Steve who I can really talk to. I feel tongue tied. I am doing my sketches but I can't write apart from this brief letter. For that I need you.

Love Mati

~ empty stockings ~

'Barb, you weren't asleep were you?'
'No.'

'I just wanted to run this letter past you. Okay?'

Darling Isaac,

It's Christmas Eve. I wish you were here. I know Christmas is not a big thing for you but it is important to me. Tomorrow my family and my best friend Barb are coming to lunch. I guess I will be too busy cooking the turkey to be lonely but right now I feel the absence of a partner. It feels sad somehow to fill the stockings by yourself. This wasn't how I imagined it would be. Mind you, I always felt lonely when I was with Tim anyway.

   I am still thinking over what you said. I think the reason that I am an artist is that I feel as if I am inarticulate. More visual than verbal. I would be interested in working on that with you. I wish you were coming down my chimney tonight as my Christmas present. Thank you for the nightie. I will wear it tonight and imagine you undoing the buttons, one by one, exploring each new revealed area.

Merry Christmas
Moppy

'What do you think?' Moppy asks.
'I want to know why you're asking me.'
'Because the letters you've helped me write have a certain tone about them, and maybe because it's half past eleven on Christmas Eve and I feel so alone.' Her voice is breaking.
'For God's sake, have you got the kids?'
'Yeah.'
'Well, then put yourself in my place and imagine that. I don't even have nieces and nephews.'
'Sorry, Barb. But maybe you don't miss what you've never had.'
'A fallacy, believe me.'
'So how do you survive?'
'Burying myself in words. Filling in the gaps. And if it's really bad, a special treat. Like tonight I've got the latest Carol Shields novel and a small box of Belgian chocolates all to myself.'
'Well, I've got to make the stuffing for the turkey yet, and truffles.'
'There you go, too busy for tears. Put on some happy music and get on with it.'
'Fuck, you'd make a terrible counsellor.'
'Tell me, are you laughing or crying now?'
'Oh, get stuffed.'

'No, that's the turkey's job.'
'I'll see you tomorrow.'
'Providing I survive lunch with Mum and Dad.'

~ Christmas in the burbs ~

At my parents' for lunch. An uneasy truce. My mother serves roast lamb, new potatoes with mint, and an old-fashioned layered salad complete with grated cheese, carrot and bottled mayonnaise. Looking at her sagging face, I feel an unaccustomed sorrow. She's hanging on to a husband who would rather be with the woman next door, and a daughter with whom she has nothing in common. In the silent kitchen are ghosts. Would-be sons-in-law and grandchildren.

I hardly recognise my father since he stopped drinking. Now or die, the doctor said. He sits silently eating, making an effort to ask, 'How's all this poetry business going?' and 'Can't you find a better place for your talents than prison?' My mother asks me to bring Moppy over one day with her kids, 'After all, I'm never going to have grandchildren of my own.'

'Not today, Betty,' says my father, 'it's not Barb's fault.' I actually want to hug him.

The atmosphere is cheerier at Moppy's. All her family are there except for Graham and Gail who have escaped to Christchurch. Tim's given Sam and Thomas a new larger trampoline and installed it in Moppy's back yard. Their cousins, Louise and Mathew, are teaching them backward flips.

'I'm going to have a go myself later,' says Moppy. 'When it's dark. I don't want Ted seeing me.'

'Wonder what he's doing for Christmas?' I ask.

'Don't take on that tone. I sent Sam over to invite him to dinner, but apparently he's going to his brother's. Who knows if he's lying or not. Anyway I did my best.'

'Fair enough.'

'Want to see what I got from Isaac?'

Moppy takes me into her bedroom and holds up a white cotton nightgown, buttoned down the front and hemmed in lace.

'Looks a bit virginal for you.'

'Yeah, but I like it. Better than what the kids gave me anyway.' She picks up a china ballerina doll wearing a pink tutu, and grimaces. 'Sam reckons they picked it out themselves. I bet Wendy helped them.'

I get an especially long hug from Dennis. 'You're looking ravishing today,

Barb,' he whispers. 'Have you lost weight? It must be all the pining away you're doing.'

Dennis is the only one who knows about Mati. I told him the week Mati got sent away. I had to tell someone and I figured Dennis knew how to keep a secret.

'Don't you think Barb looks great, everyone?' he says. 'That purple is stunning.'

'What about me?' Moppy asks.

'Sweetie, you always look wonderful,' says Dennis. 'But you know that, and Barb doesn't.'

Moppy's jealous, you know. Of the words I keep churning out. Of my lack of distractions. It's not that I don't have door-to-door salesmen willing to negotiate my slippery path for the sake of a possible conversion. It's just that I don't respond to them. Or to the phone either. It didn't come naturally. I used to jump to attention. My body tingling with possibilities. Lover, publisher, film-maker? Of course it might be different if Mati was able to ring me. It's hard to justify your ex-writing tutor on the approved list of numbers.

'I don't know. Barb's a sly one. She has her share of admirers.'

'My captive audience. It's true. Do you want to hear what one of my pupils recited at the Parry Christmas party? *Ode to my tutor, some would say shoot her, but I say salute her, and oh to be her suitor.*'

Everybody laughs.

'And what's he in for?' Jack asks.

'Rape,' I say. 'On preventive detention.'

Iris shudders. 'I don't know how you can go in there. Aren't you scared?'

'No. I always feel safe. Protected. It means too much for them to stuff it up.'

'If I had my way, I'd string them all up.'

'Listening to too much talkback again, Dad,' says Dennis in his low-key way of reproval.

'That looks perfect,' Iris says, as Moppy puts the turkey on the table.

We sit outside. It's a fine day. Peter has brought a door along and made a table with saw horses.

'How are your collages, Moppy?'

'Okay, but I've been distracted lately.'

'New man?' asks Sally.

Moppy blushes. 'Not really. Christmas shopping and the kids at home.'

'Why don't you forget about men and get on with your art?' Don says.

'Well, it's all very well for you to say that, darling,' says Moppy. She's never quite forgiven Don for taking Dennis away from her. 'I work better after sex, and at the moment I'm a little deprived. Not that there aren't future possibilities.'

'Moppy!' says Iris. 'Not in front of the children.'

Personally I don't think sex makes Moppy work better. She's too amenable to rolling around on the floor with her lovers. Shedding her skin to suit. It's always difficult to pin her down. To establish who she is and what she has to say. When accused of being evasive she laughs mockingly. 'I'm as open as a book. Read me.' But have you noticed how books change according to who's reading them? As if the words rearrange themselves on the page, taking all the necessary information from the thumbprint of the reader.

Poems are the worst. All that white space simply open to interpretation. For that reason I don't like to lend books. As for library books, beware if you're a library reader. Perhaps in my absence someone has completely altered everything and I've become the heroine rather than the narrator.

'And what about you, Barb?' asks Sally. 'What are you working on now?'

'A novel.'

'What's it about?'

'Can't tell you that. We novelists never reveal the plot half way through. It's bad luck, and anyway who knows what might happen? I'm as much in the dark as anyone.'

'Aren't you the one in control?' Don asks.

'No, that would take away all the fun. My characters can't be relied upon.'

We go for a walk to the beach after dinner. The first Christmas Day it hasn't rained for ages. The sun has gone down. The street lights make silhouettes of the pohutukawas.

'Should have come to Piha,' Dennis says. 'Got the flash.'

'The flash?' asks Sally.

'Haven't you seen it? The flash of green on the horizon as the sun disappears?'

'Obviously I'm missing something,' Sally says.

'Well you would choose to live in Meadowbank.'

'It makes sense for Sally and Peter, living close to work, but I don't know why you choose to live over here, Moppy,' says Jack. 'Now that Tim's well and truly gone. It's too tame for you.'

'For the kids, Dad. They like it here, and with Tim paying the mortgage I can't shift.'

'Still you always thought you were better than the rest of us.'

'It's very pretty,' says Iris. 'And safe.'

'Dad never changes, does he? I can never do anything right,' Moppy says when the others have left.

'Oh rubbish. You know he loves you. He's just got high standards for you.'
'I suppose. I hope I don't give my kids such a hard time.'

Even though I'm not sentimental I am in no hurry to go home to an empty cottage. To my own particular ghosts. 'So, did you get any other surprises?' I ask.

'Of course. He's as faithful as ever.' She hands me a card. On recycled paper a painted azure sea and a large golden sun.

from here

the horizon
so close

we could swim
to the edge

slip over

'It's a western view, I think.' Moppy says. 'So it's possible it is Sean, even though he denies it.'
'Hasn't he gone to New Plymouth with Angie?'
'Mmm.'
'Well then.'

~ no telling the score ~

Darling Moppy,

I cannot imagine that you are inarticulate. Each letter opens up another realm of possibilities. I am a person of the moment so there is no telling if we will prove to be in harmony or not. The jazzman plays, the dancers dance. The score is in the heart and in the head but nothing is written down, nothing is prescribed.

This man kisses you with love and in anticipation.

Isaac

PS. Tell me your fantasies.

~ putting yourself in the picture ~

December and January are slow months for me. No classes, and Moppy one of my few visitors.

'He wants me to tell him my fantasies.'
'Sounds sick to me,' I say.
'I don't know. It's the sort of thing lovers say to one another.'
'In my opinion fantasies should remain in your own head.'
'Well I thought I might cheat. Adapt one of Anais Nin's erotic stories.'
'Good thinking, Batman, but I tell you one thing, you're on your own with this one.'
'Don't you want to read it?'
'Maybe. If it adds to my knowledge of the human condition.'
'I think I'll have to get you a copy of her book. It's a great comfort on a cold and lonely night.'
'Moppy!'
'It doesn't make you blind, you know. Anyway, did you hear A.L. Kennedy on the radio? It was great. Ian Fraser said there was a lot of masturbation in her novels and she said there were two solitary arts and writing was one of them.'
'Well I'm sure Isaac would approve.'

Dear Isaac,

You ask me what I like. This is one of my fantasies. I am standing in Rome on a bus wearing a thin summer dress. I feel a man's hand touching me lightly through my dress. Touching my pubic bone, just above the clitoris. At first I think it is accidental but I stand still, afraid to move, and the pressure increases. I am becoming aroused. The bus lurches around a corner and I move closer to the hand. His fingers are caressing me now. Searching for the clitoris, stroking the lips. I feel the clitoris growing, demanding attention. He gives it. I look out the window. We're almost to my stop. As the bus pulls over, I come. I get off feeling faint. I daren't look around.

Love Moppy

Darling Moppy,

Your fantasy reveals some hang-ups. Mainly guilt. It seems you like the idea of not taking control. But this is something we could work on.

My fantasies are more heavily populated. I cannot bear to be restrained in any way. Sometimes I like to play the solo, sometimes

I am content to take a back role, to watch others. I especially like to play multiple harmonies. Sensuality and passion. Is it possible for us to be the leaders of a band?

Hopefully yours Isaac

This letter is the cause of great analysis between Moppy and me. Be straight, I say.

Dear Isaac,

I am interested in exploring sexuality with you, I feel you could teach me a lot. I sense you have an awareness of the skin that I am lacking. But being a woman I get feelings all mixed up with sex. I know I am presenting you with all my fears and insecurities. But it's important we don't misunderstand one another.

I want to know what do you mean by multiple harmonies? A ménage à trois, or quatre? I wonder what the purpose is? Are you addicted to sex? I am only interested in the intensity of one to one.

Love Moppy

~ words are all we have ~

Darling Beautiful Moppy,

But is domination, inhibition and repression lurking in the background? Darling, please do not try to influence or organise my love play. I only take what is freely given.

I am sensing a possible difference in moral opinion. Though I appreciate differences in a relationship, your letter questioning my preferences seemed an attempt at domination, setting limits before we have even made love. I am distressed at your stating your morality on paper without an opportunity for discussion, without even knowing my love thoughts.

When I am skiing down the mountain I do not want to come across a fence with a No Trespassing sign on it. For me life is a sensual and creative experience. My purpose is to create stimulus, to remain alive to all the senses. Knowing now that you have exclusive zones which your morality will not let you travel beyond is hard for me to accept.

It is even more difficult when we are out of eye contact. Whatever happens I have a loving feeling towards you.

Isaac

Darling Isaac,

If you have your fantasies fulfilled, does that mean a denial of mine? I am looking around for fences, trying to decide whether they are there for a reason, to stop you falling into a ravine, or merely to protect private property. In which case, can they be done away with?

I am using this time of uncertainty to start a new series of photographs. Years ago my friend Barb and I had some nude photographs taken by an eccentric German photographer. I thought it would be interesting to reproduce these. To see how our bodies have been ravaged by time.

Please Isaac be patient with me, and above all don't allow a few questions to ruin a challenging and interesting relationship.

Love Moppy

Darling woman,

I am hanging in there. I'm a bit confused but at the moment I'm looking forward to simply being with you, having fun and being challenged. I would like you to be aware that you need to be less threatening to me, at least from a distance. When the loved one is close enough to touch and smell, then words are not so important. At the moment words are all we have.

Moppy, I do not want a passive lover. It's a joint deal where both players explore the options. Reward your days with the awareness of the moment. Send your thoughts outwards like the rose that continues its perfume long after the picking and looks even more beautiful in its love setting than in the garden, just as you will look more beautiful in my love-bed.

A challenging Isaac

PS. I arrive home on Friday. Rest assured I will ring you on Saturday.

'But that's the night of my party.' I remind Moppy when she rings. 'You've got to come. It won't be a party without you. Actually I thought I might invite Ted.'

'You can't. Not if I bring Isaac. Anyway Ted wouldn't come.'

'He might. I am an ex-pupil after all.'

'Have you been telling Ted about me?'

'No.'

~ the scribe speaks ~

'Please, just one more photo,' Moppy says, 'and help with the last letter. It will be too late to send it but I can give it to him. I want the last word.'

She has me sitting in front of the window, one hand resting on the base of my throat, an area I find myself touching frequently these days. Ever since I discovered my thyroid gland was being attacked. A case of non-recognition apparently. Now I know how a soldier feels when he is gunned down by his own side. It happens more often than you think.

This ambush explains my sluggishness, my weight gain and my dry hair. The specialist said I would lose weight as long as my weight gain was unfair. He was too polite to ask if I ate too much. It's in the genes anyway. My mother is not a slim woman. She claims she didn't gain weight until after the menopause. It's not true. As a child I remember walking in on her once when she was dressing. I was attracted to the rolls of fat cascading over her pubic hairs. I wanted to touch her, to bury my head into all that unfamiliar softness. She screamed at me to go away. From then on her bedroom door was always locked.

In the morning I swallow my pills and stand in front of the mirror, but I have yet to perceive great chunks of fat falling off and melting like an iceberg. In Moppy's photograph I am wearing nothing but a watch. I wonder if I should send one to Mati. Would he pin me on the wall? A counterbalance to the Penthouse Pet.

'This is the last time. Now tell me what you want to say to Isaac.'

'I want to write about my Dad and the way he says meeting Mum was the best thing that happened to him and how she grumps and says, "It's actions that count." Usually when he hasn't mowed the lawns or helped her in the garden.'

Dear Isaac,

You say, sometimes words are all you have to build a house with. My father likes to play the romantic, whipping flowery words from behind his back on the slightest occasion. My mother never speaks the word love. For her, love is filling my car with the fragrance of vegetables and flowers. When it really matters, she says, words don't count.

We each want what we have not found. A mother who will say she loves you and a father who will fill your car with vegetables and flowers he has grown himself.

You will tell me you love me. I will tell you growing vegetables is an act of love requiring constant attention. A willingness to plunge hands into soil, to feel a lover's dirt beneath the fingernails.

Yours Moppy

~ the return ~

Darling Barb,

I am back in Parry. Not a promotion. I'm afraid you might be disappointed in me. I trashed my cell, broke everything including my TV and stereo. It was the one sure way of getting back to Parry. It felt good though, ranting and raving. I have been contained for so long. I hardly spoke to anyone down there. I spoke to you though, every day in my head. I didn't want their voices interfering. I'm in D block temporarily so it's not good. They may not let me come to class next month, but they will probably let you visit me. Can you send me another address to write to? I wouldn't want the authorities to find out. They'd stop you coming in a flash. Any excuse. Hope you're not too mad with me.

Love always Mati

PS. I bribed a guard to get this out. Write under another name.

What can a man do when all his power is removed but destroy his home? It happens all the time in prison. Walking down the corridors of Parry you can hear the unreleased screams, the mouths opening and shutting. Waves continuously rolling in.

And what a phoney I feel in there, knowing for all my empathy I get to go home at the end of the session, swinging my empty bag with relief. Sometimes heading for Piha to throw myself into the surf on a week day when there are no crowds to laugh at the fat woman. By the time I've battled with the rip and the waves and screamed at the top of my voice, I've forgotten their mouths.

Dear Mati,

Though you are swimming towards me, sometimes I feel I am also out there in the water, one arm over the other.

like Hinemoa
once you've slipped
into the night lake
there's no going back

only the hope
of a beloved one's arms
pulling you up
from the shore
keeping you

from drowning

~ laying the scene ~

On Friday afternoon Isaac rings. 'I'm here and I can't wait to see you.'

Moppy wants to invite him to her place, but she doesn't consider a floor covered with Lego to be a seductive element.

'I've got to go to a party tomorrow. Do you want to come?'

'No, I want to be with you, alone.'

'On Sunday we can be. But Barb will never forgive me if I don't come. Besides, there'll be all sorts of interesting people there.'

'Okay, okay, but what about tonight?'

'Tonight?'

'Can't you come to dinner?'

'I've got the kids, so only if I can get a babysitter. I'll ring you back.'

'Do, darling.'

'Barb can you do me a massive favour? Babysit tonight?'

'If I can use your name and address.'

'What for?'

'I can't tell you, but nothing illegal.'

Moppy waltzes back home at twelve o'clock.

'I take it by the flush on your face that you had a good time?'

'Oh,' she sighs. 'It was so romantic. We ate dinner outside on the balcony. Candles, wine and champagne.'

'And what did he cook?'

'Stuffed chicken breasts and for dessert a chocolate mousse, heart shaped.'

'Pretty good for someone who only arrived home today.'

'Well actually, he told me he came home yesterday but he wanted to get things clear before he rang me.'

'Oh yes?'

'I know what you're thinking, but there was no sign of another woman. I told him over dinner that I was only interested in a monogamous relationship and he said, "Of course my darling, how could I look at another woman with you around?"'

'But you've only known him five minutes.'

'Does that matter? My parents got married within six weeks of meeting and they're still relatively happy. When I went into the bathroom there was a little bunch of flowers with a note saying, "It's lovely to have you here."'

'Not nearly as original as Ted's.'

'Not everyone's a poet. Anyway Isaac's got a poet's soul.'

'Please! And after dinner?'

'He made coffee, the most wonderful special recipe, thick and sweet, and...'

'And?'

'And I'm not telling you any more.'

'Come on, I know you're dying to.'

'Okay. We didn't make love but he did feel me up. It was amazing. I had the most intense orgasm. I can't wait till tomorrow.'

'Neither can I, to meet this paragon.'

'If you weren't so cynical, Barb, you might have more luck.'

'And if you weren't so gullible you might have fewer disasters.'

'Oh, go home to your cosy little aloneness. To your safe poems.'

~ getting to grips with the facts ~

Moppy dresses carefully on Saturday night. A sleeveless yellow top and black satin trousers. When Tim picks the kids up he looks at her and asks, 'Where are you off to then? You look like you've got a hot date.'

'Barb's, if you must know.'

'So how come she didn't invite me?'

'Why would she? You've nothing in common. You think writers are bludgers.'

Isaac is waiting outside when she arrives. He grasps her hands and gives her a long kiss.

'At last, ma cherie. You look magnificent. Come and meet Tina.'

'Tina?' Moppy fights off a rising panic.

'My other daughter. She's just arrived from Hamilton.'

Isaac holds her hand as they walk into the living room.

Tina's dark hair is tied back in a ponytail. She has the small delicate face of a ballet dancer, and dark brown charismatic eyes.

'Hi,' she says, walking over and kissing Moppy on the cheek. Confident, thinks Moppy. 'Daddy's been telling me all about you.'

Isaac pours wine. 'White?'

'Please.'

'I'll have one too,' Tina says.

'Aren't you too young?'

'Dad, I'm twenty-one, for God's sake. I've been living on my own since I was seventeen so that makes me at least twenty-five.'

'Okay, but no more than one.'

Tina sighs. 'It wouldn't be so bad if he acted his age. Honestly, looking at him in his lavalava and bare chest you'd never think he was sixty-four.'

'Sixty-four? You told me you were fifty-four,' says Moppy. She thought that a big enough gap.

Isaac doesn't miss a beat. 'Tina. I'm trying to seduce this beautiful woman, not scare her off.'

'Oh Daddy, you never change.'

'Well do I look like I'm sixty-four?' He stands up and flexes his arm muscles.

'No. You don't,' she says.

'Good, let's eat then. Tina has cooked all this food herself and it's the height of rudeness not to pay due attention to the food.'

On the table is a spinach and cottage cheese pie with fillo pastry and a Greek salad.

'Yum,' Moppy says on her first mouthful. 'Reminds me of Greece.'

'My mother is Greek,' Tina says, 'and a wonderful cook.'

'Beautiful too,' says Isaac, 'like every woman I have had the pleasure to know.'

'And has your mother married again?'

'No, Daddy put her off for ever.' She laughs wryly. 'Besides, Greek women usually marry for life. But she's happy now. She has her own business. High fashion.'

Moppy notes that Tina asks no questions of her. Is it her age or is Moppy just another of Isaac's insignificant conquests? She concentrates on the strawberries. The first of the season, large and perfect but flavourless.

'Can you come back and stay the night?' he asks on the way to the party.

'Do you think I should?'

'Darling, promise me you're not going to get all suburban and moralistic. I thought we'd been through all that in our letters.'

'Well I did bring my toothbrush, but isn't Tina staying?'

'No, she's staying with friends. I told her we wanted to be alone.'

Suddenly he pulls over in a bus stop, grabs her arms and kisses her.

'What are you doing?'

'You looked so sexy, I just had to kiss you and say sorry but I think you should take off your bra. You can see the straps.'

Moppy wishes her arms were like they used to be, brown and firm. 'What the hell,' she says and wriggles around until she gets her bra-strap undone. Isaac glances down the V neck.

'Darling, you are magnificent. Now all we need to do is get your panties off so I can see you walking around and imagine your naked body.'

'Do you mind. I'm not having my crotch rubbing into the seam all night. It might give me an orgasm. Like the time I was wearing tight jeans and sitting on a merry-go-round with Sam at the Easter Show. I had to pay to go round three times. I pretended it was Sam who wouldn't get off.'

Isaac laughs a laugh so full of approval that Moppy pushes away the memories she has of Geoff who always wanted her to show herself off. Who, in opposition to her mother, once demanded that she recut her bikini bra to make it more it revealing. Not so much for him but for all the other envious men on the beach.

~ tell me about myself ~

'Wonderful to meet you.' Isaac shakes my hand. 'Don't you think Moppy's magnificent? She just whipped off her bra when I asked her. What sexiness. And you, you look wonderfully powerful, though there is an aura of red around you.'

'Red, what does that mean?' I ask.

'Danger. Is there someone around who would like to do you harm?'

'Perhaps it's the other way around,' I say. There is something equally repellent and attractive about Isaac. His unbuttoned shirt and gold chains remind me of the art salesman at the bar.

'I see you're troubled, my dear,' he says to Nan, whose husband Gary is in the kitchen playing the part of the drunken artist. Nan is plump and soft. Like me, except I don't wear low-cut tops.

'How can you tell?' asks Nan.

'I read auras. Of course anyone can if they're in touch with their inner selves.'

'So what else can you tell me about myself?' Nan asks, leaning towards him.

I think about my prisoners, how they often ask me to describe themselves to themselves. How even if they possess mirrors most of them lack the skills to interpret.

Isaac turns to Moppy. 'Can you get me another drink, darling?'

Moppy gets up. When she comes back Nan has moved into her seat and is sitting very close to Isaac.

'Thank you, darling. You don't mind if I talk to Nan in private, do you?'

Watching Moppy, I can see she does mind.

'No,' she says.

We move over to Jill and Ben. Jill keeps her hand on her stomach. Protecting her child from the talk, the smoke, the drink. Raspberry-leaf tea and water are her current favourites. Vigilance is important. She is not young. 'They call me an elderly primigravida at National Women's. But I'm not alone. I'm really looking forward to coffee mornings.'

'So you're not going back to work?'

'No, Ben and I have talked about it, haven't we, darling? It's not as if we need the money. Robert's left me well set up and Ben doesn't do too badly.' Ben winces slightly. 'We think it's important for a child to have stability for the first year at least. After all, this baby's the most precious person in the world.'

'More precious than me?' Ben asks.

'Equal, dearest one.'

Moppy looks over at Nan and Isaac laughing. Their heads are very close together.

'Nan and Isaac are getting on well considering they've just met,' she says.

'For God's sake don't look like you're jealous,' Jill says.

The room is crowded. Standing room only. This morning I shifted all the furniture into my bedroom. Glyn and Zoe are speaking with forced gaiety to other people. Gary is making a nuisance of himself with the dreadlocked Angie who came with Sean. He splashes port over Angie's skimpy white top. Jimmy, my ex-con friend, goes over to him and says, 'I think you've had enough, mate.'

'Leave me alone, you bastard,' Gary says. 'Who the hell do you think you are?'

'Younger and stronger than you for a start,' Jimmy says. 'And I've spent a lot of time in Parry so I wouldn't bother.'

Despite her great interest in Isaac, Nan keeps one eye focused on Gary. She possesses blind faith. Why else would she have spent thirty years putting up with affairs, drunken abuse and constant poverty? One day they'll write about me as the loyal artist's wife, she told me years ago. The sad thing is, his work is garish and naive, filled with primary colours and no subtlety. On the way to take Gary home before he makes an even bigger fool of himself, Nan says to Moppy, 'Fascinating man, Moppy. A catch. Such chutzpah.'

'Has the cat got your tongue?' I ask Moppy when Isaac is in the kitchen. 'You've hardly said a thing all evening. Most unusual for you.'
    'Yes, I'm fine,' she says.
    I notice the way Isaac walks. Like a cat, delicately as if he is stalking. I look at Moppy. She is sitting very still, as if she is concentrating on invisibility.
    'You've got to live your life as an artist,' Isaac says to Nan's replacement, Angie. I'm standing behind them, adopting a distracted air. 'Everything you do must be the best you can do,' he says. 'Food, conversation, loving and sex. No half measures.'
    'Talking of which, I want to go home,' Moppy interrupts. 'I've been waiting for months.'
    'But it's not twelve o'clock yet,' Angie says.
    'You've heard the woman,' Isaac says, getting up. 'She commands and I obey.'
    'Here's my number,' says Angie, handing Isaac a card, 'in case you want to see my paintings.'
    I walk with them to the car. Isaac says, 'Darling you were wonderful. All the men were listening when you said you wanted to be alone with me. Sensational.'
    'Remember how you used to believe you could fly?' I whisper in Moppy's ear as we hug. 'Think of yourself as a bird,' I say. 'Remember licking is not a sign of love.'
    'Why do you say that?'
    'I've no idea. It just popped into my head. Someone said it to me once and it seems appropriate.'

'What's happened to Moppy?' Sean asks when I go back inside.
    'She's become an upmarket ventriloquist's puppet,' I say.

~ fermenting juice ~

'Darling, do you mind if we just go to sleep? I'm suddenly exhausted,' Isaac asks.
    Moppy can't sleep in the wide bed. She lies awake looking up at the mirrored ceiling. The ghostly shadows. Isaac snoring. A morepork calling

from the bush. At five o'clock she wakes in the middle of a dream where Ted, taller and younger than in real life, had been popping words sweet as strawberries into her mouth. Crunching on *your succulent bones*, she wakes to find Isaac's head buried in her crotch.

With two hands he caresses her outer ears then pokes his fingers in her eardrums. Her world becomes self-enclosed. The roar of the sea inside her head.

Isaac releases the pressure. 'Do you know what this means?' he whispers.

'It means you're poking your fingers in my ears.'

'No, sweet. It means I want to put my cock in your vagina. It's a code. The nose is for the anus. The mouth for oral sex. For now, though, I want to touch you deep inside. To feel you clutching me, needing me. I want to heal you, to show you a new way.'

His penis is flaccid. 'It's always like this the first time. Despite my boldness, I'm vulnerable too. I'm sorry, darling.'

'It's all right. We could just cuddle. In fact it makes me feel better. Less pressured.'

'You're wonderful. But darling, you could think of it as a reluctant virgin. Try your powers of persuasion.'

Moppy cradles his balls with one hand while the other plays with the head of his penis.

Harder now, he negotiates his way in. 'Oh Moppy,' he sighs. 'I can't tell you how wonderful that feels. As if you've parted the Red Sea for me. One day,' he pants, 'we'll have tantric sex, the entire day. It's wonderful. The redemptive power.' He moves slowly. 'Do you know where your G spot is?'

'I'm not sure,' Moppy says. 'No one's ever planted a flag there.'

'Please Moppy, this is serious. Can't you feel it there?' And she does, high up in the clouds, an eruption followed by a red lava flow, leaving a permanent trail.

'Oh God, oh God.'

'Is that all you can say?'

She sighs. 'It was wonderful, really wonderful,' but Isaac is already asleep, his hand flung across her belly.

'We shouldn't have done that,' she says in the morning when he brings her a cup of tea on a tray with a pink rose in a vase.

'You're right, it was too soon. Did you know Hindus make love to their brides by hugging and caressing only, for ten days, before penetration?'

'No, I mean you should have used a condom.'

'Darling, I've had a vasectomy, it's okay.'

'What about AIDS?'

'For heaven's sake, AIDS is a conspiracy promoted by fundamentalist Christians.'

'What do you mean? People are dying of it.'

'People die on the roads too but it doesn't stop you from driving. For me condoms impose a deadening of feeling, completely opposite to sex which is all about being open, about moisture, the giving and taking of. And risk is a necessary part of it.'

Later they lie naked on sun loungers in his courtyard. No one can see in but they can hear the neighbours talking.

'I don't like the winter,' Isaac says. 'Usually I withdraw into myself. Summer is my time for loving.'

'Does that mean we have only the summer?' Moppy asks.

'Ma cherie, you're wonderful. Who can predict?'

He hands her a plum. The juice drips down between her breasts. Isaac gets up, comes over and starts licking. When he pulls her on top, she can feel her back burning. Didn't Katherine Mansfield say, *Risk anything*? She comes in time to the ball being whacked obsessively against the house next door.

~ if the tongue fits ~

Moppy's favourite play is *The Taming of the Shrew*. We studied it at school. Though some say this play is anti-woman, Moppy maintains Kate and Petruchio are equal partners entwining tongues in a hard fought-for alliance. The moon is the sun. Yes, yes, if you say so, says Kate smiling all the while.

Shakespeare has a lot to answer for. Reverse bulimia in Moppy's case. Swallowing back all the words and actions judged to be conventional. An obsolete lexicon lining the roof of her mouth. Living on nothing but lumps of sugared words slipped between her teeth.

Cleaning up, the morning after, I feel the lack of love so acutely, I phone the prison, explain I am Mati's sister with important family news. They fall for it. But then Mati and I are awkward speaking to one another. I'd forgotten the soft hesitancy of his voice, and mine so fast and blunt in comparison. But also some new anxiety in his tone.

'What's wrong?' I ask.

'The atmosphere is shit here,' he says. 'It's going to blow soon if they don't stop screwing us.'

I've read it in the papers, the bowing to the string-'em-up brigade, the stamping out of drugs. I haven't told Mati it's doubtful I'll be able to go back. Rumour has it that the new regime doesn't consider poetry rehabilitative. The ability to distinguish between a sonnet and free verse, not a positive outcome.

But why act surprised? The authorities have always suspected poetry. A subversive element.

~ the aftermath ~

Half way up the driveway Moppy's car stalls. She's glad Isaac has gone in after waving her goodbye. 'Like making love, my darling, you need to take time, rev the engine first, or you'll never get up.'

By the time she gets home Tim is waiting for her.

'Nice to see nothing changes,' he says.

'What do you mean?' Moppy wonders if sex is written on her face.

'You're late.'

'Ten minutes.'

'It's the principle. One minute is late. The only things you're ever on time for are planes and doctors.'

'Give it a rest, Tim. You upset the kids.'

'Don't drag them into it.'

'No sir, would that be all sir?'

'No. Since you've broken your agreement you can forget about me having the kids one night this week.'

'You two are always fighting,' says Sam. 'I don't like it.'

'Blame your irresponsible mother.'

Tim marches off, his shoes cracking over the shell pathway. Through the hedge Moppy thinks she sees a shadow move.

'Are you there, Ted?' she calls.

There is no reply. Must have been a bird, she thinks, and goes inside.

'Who wants to play a game?' she asks the kids. As if this will atone for her sins.

Outside, she stands by the trampoline doing her best not to wince as Sam executes a backwards flip. Her eye catches sight of a small black rock on the edge of the path, a piece of blue paper beneath it.

fingers crossed
like any skipper
picking his way
through black
rocks

A little more oblique than some of the others. Who is the skipper and what are the black rocks? Moppy vaguely remembers that sailors were said to cross their fingers to avoid being lured onto rocks by sirens. Is she siren or sailor?

Jill rings Moppy. 'Do you know Isaac's been married four times? Ben's sister knows one of his ex-wives and says you should be careful, he's a dangerous man.'

'Maybe once but I think he's changed. He told me that he falls in love too easily, but now he's older he no longer has the same attraction.'

'Ha,' says Jill, 'there were plenty flocking to his side last night.'

'You've got to admit he's definitely got sex appeal.' Moppy hesitates. 'Perhaps I should have kept it as an epistolary romance. After all, in our letters we were arguing and everything, running the full emotional gamut. And I didn't have to worry about other women.'

'But sex?'

'Well there's always phone sex. Oh God, we did have great sex this morning though.'

'You are using condoms?'

'Well no, it just happened.'

'For God's sake, Moppy, that's so dangerous. You may as well be sleeping with a gun under your pillow. You've got kids to think about.'

'Yeah, I know. I'll talk to him about it.'

'You don't need to talk about it, you just need to do it.'

'Well I will when I get back from camping.'

'He's not coming, is he?'

'Not in a million years, he said. No matter how much he might love me.'

'Love, ha.'

~ an inarticulate love ~

Dear Mati,

I'm sorry if I gave you a shock the other day when I rang. I am going camping with Moppy for a week. She needs me to bang in the tent poles and to protect her from the married Mafia. I will ring you next week. If trouble breaks out, keep your head down and remember to be your charming self.

I have been reading love poems. A whole book on them, but I prefer the women's work. A lot of the men's poems seem to be confused about sex and love. Two quite separate words. No such worries for us, but I am worried about Moppy. She is hanging out with the wrong man, I think. When I tried to say something, she said, 'But you don't see the way he is when it's just us.' How many times has this been uttered by the battered woman? Not that he's hit her. It's early days yet. There's no doubting he's seductive and unusual in his ability to talk openly about intimacy, so different from most Kiwi men. But this is what I don't trust. Perhaps I'm feeling hostile. I have just seen the film *Nil By Mouth*, a bleak picture of an English housing estate. Their equivalent to *Once Were Warriors*. Familiar territory to you.

Moppy says driving down Isaac's drive is like entering another world, like Paradise. And as dangerous. I'm not sure what reference this has to us, Mati, your world could not be further from Paradise. Perhaps I'm asking are things what they seem? Do I really know you? I remember your eyes, how they shone for me, and your gentleness.

After our conversation I wrote this poem.

the inarticulate telephone

Alexander Bell

made no allowance for
the difficult questions

do you, do you not
caught under my tongue

this dependent
on the angle of your gaze

information
like water

not easily given
to flowing up stream

Love as always
Barb

~ talking into a pillow ~

'So tomorrow I'll be cuddled up to myself on the airbed,' Moppy says to Isaac over the phone. It's late and she's in bed.

'Barb's going isn't she?'

'Thank God. The couples get a bit much, though it'll be different this year, no Robert and Jill.'

'I can't stand married couples,' Isaac says, 'especially the faithful ones. It's like a living death. No more possible adventures.'

'Well Ben and Jill aren't married.'

'Course they are. In spirit anyway. But it's not for the likes of you and me.'

'I don't know. I'd quite like a third husband. Just to add to the notoriety.'

'Don't look at me, darling. I've far more exciting plans for us.'

'Like what?'

'Let's just say this is the summer of your seduction. A fantasy journey. The discovery of your true desires. Your inner self.'

'Really? I don't remember booking my ticket.'

'Darling, you can't be an artist without this knowledge. How can you portray a woman if you yourself have never smelt and caressed one? Seen her open like a flower for you? How can you know about openness if you restrict yourself to the conventional?'

Moppy ignores the words weaving an opaque fabric around her head. They seem to have nothing to do with her.

~ the worm turning slowly ~

'It's probably just as well Isaac didn't come,' Moppy says while we are putting up the tent, this time with the help of Ben and Ross. 'He wouldn't have coped with the cold water.'

'Not to mention Sam and Thomas,' Ben says. 'Has he met them yet?'

'No, but he's promised to.'

'I'm looking forward to meeting this guy myself,' says Ross. 'He seems a character.'

'Character is right,' I say.

I'm worried about Mati but there is nothing I can do. Camping will take my mind off him.

Jill has passed the critical stage, so she tells us. She's in her last trimester. She wants to lie in the sun, read baby books and reflect. 'Everything has happened so quickly,' she says. 'Sometimes I think it's not real. I think I've stepped over into another world, into another person's life. It's really strange. The other day I found myself driving to the house in Takapuna. Thinking about what I was going to cook Georgia and Emma for dinner.'

'Well they do say pregnant women are a little unbalanced.'

'You're just jealous,' she says, and then quickly, 'I'm sorry, Barb, I keep forgetting. I've noticed pregnancy makes you very inwardly focused.'

'It's all right, really. I've decided to make every poem, every piece of writing, a baby. Anyway, I don't think I could be a writer and a mother.'

'You could,' says Moppy, 'but it's a hell of a lot more difficult.'

Without Robert, the camping scene has changed. Ross and Amanda solve their loyalty dilemma by agreeing to a week with Robert and his kids in a Bay of Islands motel and a week with Jill. Grant and Mary can't decide, so stay home. 'Typical teachers and counsellors,' says Moppy. 'So practised in being non-judgemental they can't make decisions.' She's much happier with the atmosphere, now that the couples clique has been corrupted by Jill, but she's initially concerned about Sam who is a social animal. In fact, without the other kids Sam gets on well with Jessica, Ross and Amanda's eldest.

Too well, according to Amanda. 'What do you think they're up to?' she asks Moppy as Jessica and Sam saunter off to the far beach for the morning.

'Nothing illegal, I'm sure. They're only twelve.'

'Old enough for some kids,' says Amanda. 'And Sam certainly seems very mature.'

'It comes from being the oldest in a broken family. Perhaps I lean on him too much.'

'So what are you doing about replacing Tim?'

'God, I don't want to replace Tim. Never, never, never. I just want a part-time lover. An intimate companion.'

'So what's Isaac?'

'The lover.'

'Isn't he a bit old for a stud?' Jill asks.

'I don't think so, going on the evidence so far. He's so into sex.'

'Tears before bedtime,' says Jill.

'Maybe, but you know me. I'm still curious to see what will happen. I think he really wants a ménage à trois.'

'Don't look at me,' says Jill.

'Any of us,' I say. 'Though I might get a poem out of it.'

Just then Jessica comes running up, tears streaming down her pale face.

'Sam nearly drowned,' she says. 'A man rescued him.'

Moppy is off and running. She's fitter than I thought. The three of us follow. By the time we get there Moppy is well into her interrogation.

'What were you doing?'

'Surfing. Pretty gnarly. A guy lent me a board.'

'What exactly happened?' I ask.

'Nothing.'

'Jessica said you had to be rescued.'

'She's just a girl. I was trying to stand up, right? And I got dumped. And a man pulled me up. That's all, okay?'

Moppy sighs. 'Now I'm an overprotective mother.'
'Anything but,' Jill says.
'I'm going back in.'
'Not too far,' says Moppy.
'Mum,' Sam says in an exasperated tone, running over to an older boy holding a surfboard. In the water he turns around to see if we are watching. On the next big wave he stands up for half a minute before falling off.
'That's it,' says Moppy, 'he's got the bug. I recognise the signs. Just like Dennis.'

That night Moppy borrows Ross's mobile phone.
'Who're you ringing?' he asks. 'Lover boy?'
'Mind your beeswax.'
I watch her climbing up the hill. Sitting at the top and surveying the land. I wish it was that easy for me. The simple dialling of numbers. As she runs back down, a turkey flies out in front of her.
'God, I've had enough frights for one day.'
'So what did the aging stud say?'
'He told me I was in his heart,' she says with flushed face. 'I told him about Sam and how I'm losing him. He said that was the nature of being a parent.'
'And he would know,' Jill says.
Sometimes she can be so dry my skin thirsts.
'That's right,' Moppy says. 'What the hell would he know? And where was he in my hour of need?'

~ a new tense ~

I'd just walked in the door, dying for a cup of tea and a hot shower, the first in a week, when Mati rang. I've no idea how he managed to get through. 'How was camping?' he asked.
'Okay. The weather was kind. I went swimming every day.'
'No,' he groaned. 'I can't bear the thought of the sea. I miss it so bad.'
'Are you all right? You sound a bit strange.'
'Yeah. I just wanted you to know I've been transferred to A block.'
'That's good.'
'Maybe, but it's pretty tense here. We've fucking had enough. Anyway I've got to go now. Just don't worry about me.'
The phone clicked in my ear before I had a chance to say goodbye.

An uneasy silence in my study. Now I know how mothers of teenagers must feel at 2 a.m., listening for every car in the street. At six o'clock I turn on the news. An unusual event these days. Mostly I prefer to read the paper.

The lead story, a riot in A block. The inmates are rampaging through the block, lighting fires in their cells. The cameras remain at a safe distance, focusing on the paddy wagons, ambulances, fire engines, and the prison wardens' families waiting at the gates. There's a distant glimpse of a fire at a window. A lone figure on the roof.

I'm uneasily certain that Mati's involved. He's a leader in there, one who is spontaneous but also articulate and charismatic.

All night I pace between the radio and the television. Finally on the ten o'clock news the riot is over. No one has been killed, but some wardens and inmates are injured. They show a van driving away with the ringleaders. I record it on video and play it over and over, eliminating the heavily tattooed faces. There is one face I cannot identify or dismiss.

After a sleepless night I wake early and hang around the letter box waiting for the paper. The front page is full of it. A visual feast of small fires at cell windows and, most prominently, an inmate giving the fingers through the iron bars of a police van. On the radio the experts line up. Their views are predictable, from the tight-lipped prime minister, 'The inmates won't be allowed to dictate to us,' to the prison reform spokesman, 'This indicates an extreme stress.' Surprisingly, some of the guards blame the riot on the new restrictions. Not so the prison's general manager. His opinions set into an uncompromising hardness.

I lie in bed hugging my feather pillow, wishing it was possible to revert to the halcyon days when I still believed in an uncomplicated love. When even the government approved of communes.

Moppy rings me. 'Have you seen the paper? Anyone you know?'
I start crying. It takes me by surprise. It's been a long time.
'God, what's wrong, Barb?'
'That guy on the front page, giving the fingers.'
'Yeah. Is he one of your pupils?'
'Worse than that. I'm involved with him.'
'What do you mean, involved?'
'We've been writing to one another. I really like him. In fact I probably love him.'
'Love him? How could you?'
'You can talk.'
'Well how come you didn't tell me? I'm your best friend. I tell you everything.'
'What's there to tell? It's not a public affair and I knew you'd disapprove. But these things happen.'
'But what're you going to do? What did he do?'
'It doesn't matter. I'm just so worried and angry. It's typical of him to get involved, though. He'll never get out at this rate.'

'Perhaps that's a good thing. You wouldn't really want him landing on your doorstep, would you?'

No answer to that one.

'So when are you going to see Isaac?'

'Don't think I haven't noticed you changing the subject. He's coming around this afternoon to take us out to dinner. I'm a bit anxious.'

~ the art of avoidance ~

'Now I see why you like coming to my place,' Isaac says.

'It's not that bad.'

'Well it is a little messy, darling. If I had the time I'd help you in the garden, but I haven't.'

'It doesn't matter, it's a cultivated mess.'

'And what's this, modern art?'

'That's my wall hanging. It's taken me five years to get it to this stage.'

'I think I'd prefer a nude self-portrait.'

'Hi, Mum.' The voice comes from the kitchen. Moppy jumps.

'Relax, I won't eat them.'

Sam walks into the lounge, followed by Thomas. Both are stuffing their mouths with large chocolate doughnuts. Isaac stands up and shakes their hands. Sam looks him over. Isaac is wearing tight black bike shorts and a sleeveless red T-shirt.

'Did you bike here?' Sam asks.

'No.'

'I've got to go, Mum, my mates are waiting. We're going to swim out to the raft.'

'You be careful. And be back soon, we're going out to dinner.'

'Handsome boy,' says Isaac. 'He looks like you, same shape of face, same eyes. Sexy. But I can't see any resemblance with Thomas.' He pats him on the head. 'You're the intelligent one, aren't you?'

'Say hello, Thomas.'

'Hello.' The word is mumbled. He runs off into his room and shuts the door.

Moppy turns to Isaac. 'What do you mean Sam is sexy? He's only twelve.'

'That can't be helped. He's got that look about him. Charismatic too, the way he looks you straight in the face. But I think you'll have your hands full. A difficult teenager, I would say.'

'You're not telling me anything new. Anyway, where are we going to dinner?'

Isaac clutches his head. 'Darling, I forgot. I'm the guest speaker at a Rotary meeting tomorrow and I have to go home and prepare my notes.'

'But you promised.'

'I know, but I forgot. I made this arrangement ages ago. There's no need to look like a little girl.'

'Well why can't you prepare the speech tomorrow? I've promised the kids.'

Isaac sighs. 'I've got so much to do, and I feel like I'm getting a cold so I need to have an early night. Anyway, darling, at my age I believe in respecting my own needs, and right now it's not to go to a restaurant full of screaming kids. But I'll make it up to you, I promise. Okay sweetheart?' He kisses her on the top of her head.

'I guess. What's your talk about anyway?'

'A terribly important topic. How sex keeps you young. They've done tests. Even if you've had a heart attack.'

Moppy takes the kids to the Pizza Hut herself. Knowing Ben is away on business, she persuades Jill to come. 'At least with you there I'll have some company. You can only take the conversation so far, with kids.'

'So what did you think of Isaac, then?' Moppy asks the boys.

'You've got terrible taste in men, Mum,' says Thomas. 'And Isaac's the worst so far.'

Moppy and Jill stare at one another with raised eyebrows. 'Out of the mouths of babes,' Jill says.

'And what do you think, Sam?' Moppy asks.

'Whatever,' Sam says. It's his standard response these days.

She waits until Thomas and Sam are off getting dessert. 'God, I can't believe what comes out of Thomas's mouth.'

Jill pats her stomach. 'I hope this one will be as acute.'

'So you agree with Thomas.'

'I'm afraid so.'

'I think I'll tell Isaac. That would be a challenge to him. He is rather full of himself.'

'Sometimes, Moppy, I think you deliberately set yourself up in these situations. Some complex game you're playing.'

'That's an idea, a board game, *Your perfect match*. No, *Your imperfect match*. Think of the possibilities, I could make money.'

'How? How would it work?'

'I don't know. But you could have personality combinations. The romantic with the cynic. The perfectionist with the neurotic. The bi-polar with the schizophrenic. And the results.'

'Murder, suicide, I should imagine.'

After the kids are in bed, Moppy gets a glass of wine and starts work. She assembles her photographs of naked bodies, dead hedgehogs and ants in the centre of frames encircled by scraps of poems, pictures of immigrants, prisons, moats, barbed wire, tongues, and dictionary definitions.

Her eye catches a note, previously unseen, in a basket of resources.

perhaps lapses of memory
are necessary
without them
we might never speak again

She walks into Sam's room.
'Sam, has Ted been over here?'
Sam is too busy to look up from his hand-held computer game.
'I didn't see him.'

~ lapses of courage and memory ~

Dear Barb,

I will persuade the nurse to post this. I guess you saw the paper. Good mug shot of me, eh? I couldn't help it, we had to protest to stop the bastards from grinding us down completely. It won't have done my chances of parole much good but I wasn't thinking of that at the time. It was a case of sticking together. Knowing who your mates are. Despite all the talk in the papers, it wasn't just the early lock-ups and the drug searches but the cutting back of classes. Word is that all visiting teachers will be stopped as well as the full-time teachers. The last straw for me, it's the only thing that makes life bearable. It looks like if you want to see me you'll have to visit me. We could get married. What do you think? I am hoping this won't affect us. I love you.

Love Mati

I also get another letter, coldly official, from AIT, explaining that their contract to supply education to the prison has not been renewed. My services are no longer required.

I'd been expecting this, steeling myself for it. Perhaps it's for the best. Time I moved on anyway. Sometimes the energy required to get through the morning in Parry is out of all proportion to the hourly rate. Just walking in, the overwhelming smell of stale air and tobacco. The doors clanging behind you. Of course, I also feel guilty and concerned. Guilty that I don't immediately ring up and offer my services voluntarily, concerned for the inmates, for the ignorance roaming the airwaves. Truth is, I will have to find another job. Poets are too poor to be volunteers. It comes down to me giving the time to my own writing or to theirs. It's not much of a competition.

Being a postie was once the favoured job for writers but talking to the postman I discover that these days they have goals to achieve and no time for blowing whistles or chatting with the lonely waiting at the letter box. As for stopping to jot down poetic observations gained along the way, NZ Post has ensured that the only thing going on in the postie's brain is the spreadsheet of performance comparisons. But I mustn't get started on the Roundtable Mafia. I look in the newspaper for part-time jobs for overweight scribes. There are none, nor any for ESL tutors since the Asian economic downturn.

I also have to decide whether to 'come out' in my relationship with Mati. Join the queue of prison wives holding back their sad or angry faces. A completely different prospect. My first proposal, and it's from a murderer. Unemployed. What would my mother say about that? I put Mati's letter under my pillow. As if it is a piece of wedding cake to sleep on for luck. Hoping for messages in my dreams. In the meantime I will keep my distance. Write something non-committal and obscure. This, after all, is something I am good at.

~ a sexual slut ~

I'm sitting at my desk contemplating my and the novel's future when Moppy bursts in crying *Barb* in an agonised tone.

'What's the matter? You look terrible.' But more angry than grief stricken.

'God you won't believe it. I even took him roses and a sketch of him. The bastard.'

'What's happened?'

'It's Isaac's birthday. So I paid him a surprise visit this morning.' She's almost screaming. 'I want to kill myself. It's Geoff all over again.'

'Calm down and tell me what happened.'

'As soon as I got there I had a strange feeling. You know? So strange I parked on the road and walked down. There was another car in my place. I didn't recognise it. I was going to go away again. Then I thought, why should I? He told me he loved me. So I knocked. No one answered. Then I heard voices coming from the back, so I walked around the balcony.' She shudders.

'And?'

'It was unbelievable. I heard Isaac saying, "Of course I'm a sexual slut. Once a year I advertise for women, then I invite the most lively one around for a finger fuck. But for you, ma cherie, I plan a slow seduction."'

'No.'

'Yes, the same fucking words. He was describing her aura. Purple, of course.'

I can't help it. I start laughing.

'Barb, that's not very helpful.'

'I know, I'm sorry. But it does have its funny side.'

'Not to me.'

'So, what did you do?'

'I crept back around the front and banged on the door again. There was no way I was going to embarrass myself in front of another woman.'

'God you're brave.'

'No, I was mad. Bloody, bloody mad. I thumped on the door and yelled, "Open up, Isaac, I know you're in there." After a while he came out, wearing nothing but a towel around his waist.'

'Go on.'

Moppy sighs. 'Do you have to have all the ghastly details? I don't want you using them.'

'Why not? It might be sweet revenge.'

'He just stood there saying, "I can't talk to you right now", over and over. And I held out the roses and the sketch and said in this pathetic voice, "I just wanted to give you these for your birthday." He made no move to take them, so I had no choice but to walk away. At the top of the driveway I bowled his dragons down and yelled, "You fucking bastard I hope you die of AIDS."'

'Did they break?'

'I didn't hang around to find out. I didn't know what to do. I went home and got into bed with the duvet over me. I just wanted to be invisible.'

'That's terrible. Really, I'm sorry for laughing. But I got the feeling when we were camping that you were having doubts anyway.'

'I was, but I didn't want it to end like this.' Moppy sucks in her breath. 'At least someone still loves me.' She hands me the familiar blue paper. 'Ironic, isn't it?'

for one moment
the world
so silent
no one
can be dying
or crying
anywhere

Then she starts laughing, a laugh verging on the hysterical, but a laugh.

'With any luck the dragons will have smashed into his ranchslider.'

'Not likely, knowing your bowling.'

'It's not funny, Barb. I feel totally gutted, as if I'll never trust another man again. What's the point? It always ends in disaster. What the hell is wrong with me?'

'Nothing, there's nothing wrong with you. Just that you're unlikely to meet the right person through the newspaper.'

'And you can talk.'

'The difference is Mati just happened. It wasn't as if he was waiting for a gullible woman.'

'I am, aren't I?'

'Well, in an *Alice In Wonderland* way. But there's worse things to be.'

'The worst thing is, I don't really know the full story. He's taken the phone off the hook.'

'The coward.'

'I'm not going to rest until I get an explanation. I just can't get the picture out of my mind. Him standing there shrugging his shoulders and saying, "I can't talk to you right now." It's like a recurring nightmare.'

~ the woman in this poem ~

lies on her bed curled up
she would like to replace the picture
in her head with something softer
a moment of tenderness perhaps
a man bending down to caress
but the other picture
is too insistent, too new

she is knocking on her lover's door
she hears the music being turned down
she knocks again loudly
he opens and closes the door behind him
he is wearing a towel around his waist
she looks at his chest and at the door
which has always been open
and at the strange car in the driveway

the woman is holding white roses
and a buff coloured envelope
she has written a poem for her lover's
birthday and printed it on recycled paper
she looks at his bare chest
at the car and closed door
and she tries to give him the roses
but his hands will not open

and the woman in this poem walks away
gets into her car and drives to work
where she jokes with her customers
and remembers how people often
laugh till they cry at funerals
after, she takes the roses home
admires the picture they make
on her varnished wooden table

and goes to bed late
but as soon as she lies down
the woman in this poem
is looking at his bare chest
the car, the closed door
and at his hands refusing
to take her

~ no easy answers ~

There's an electrical storm the following morning. Jill and Moppy arrive at my place with wet muddy shoes.

'I must be mad,' Jill says. 'Coming out in this weather when I'm seven months' pregnant. Ben will kill me.'

'You're not an invalid,' Moppy says. 'I'm the one who's in need of support right now.'

'You know perfectly well that by next week you'll be looking around for the next victim,' Jill says.

I'm not so sure. Moppy is moving slowly, none of the usual bounce in her step.

She waves a letter in the air. 'I've written out this ad. I was going mad last night. I tried to ring you both but there was no answer. From Isaac either, even at two in the morning.'

'Sorry. I was working on a poem. Surely you're not advertising again?' I ask.

'No, this time I really think I've learnt my lesson. And if tempted all I have to do is conjure up that scene. I promise. No, I thought of a garage sale ad.'

'What, sleazebag arsehole available to a bad home?'

'Not quite. I headed it, *Garage sale with a difference*. X-rated magazines, sex aids and toys. Owner no longer in business. And Isaac's address. Do you think I should send it?'

'It does have a ring of justice about it. But why ask us?' Jill says. 'You never listen to us. Still, if you want my opinion I don't think he's worth it.

Revenge only demeans the revenger.'

'So you regret the mussels?'

'Yeah, all I did was give Robert a story to dine out on. And make him seem bigger than he was. Actually I think dismissing them is more hurtful.'

'All very new age, Jill, but what about making Isaac think about his actions? Stopping him from trifling with emotions? Moppy doesn't deserve this.'

'No, I don't. But I keep thinking of Geoff and all the other disasters. Is it something I do? Tell me.'

'If we knew the answer to that one we could set up in business and make a fortune selling self-help books,' I say.

'You'll get over it, Moppy,' says Jill. 'You've got us and the kids.'

'And chocolate and Ted,' I say.

'Don't even mention another man. I'll stick to chocolate. It's safer.'

'And art,' I add, 'but that's dangerous too.'

'So have you heard from Mati?' Moppy asks after Jill goes home. There's no real interest in her voice but at least she's making an effort.

'No. From what I gather he's locked up in D block, incommunicado.'

I show her the paper. No ringleaders' names are mentioned but I'm sure Mati is among them. They are confined to their cells. Locked up for twenty-four hours with an occasional cold shower. The guards are not allowed to talk to them or refer to them by name. They are sub-humans. No language allowed. If they behave like animals, the prison manager said.

~ winging it ~

A week later Moppy says, 'Can I read you this?' She takes a deep ostentatious breath.

Dear Isaac,

You once said summer was the time for romance. That in winter you liked to hibernate. I think all the seasons have a place in love. But when I visualised winter I saw myself shivering beneath your satin sheets.

My mother always said, Go for the man who will mow your lawns. She is a practical woman, but I get waylaid by words. It was your voice I fell for. It dripped down my throat like treacle. But when I went to open my mouth I found I couldn't speak.

I've now extracted the treacle and discovered my own voice again. How sweet it sings.

Goodbye, Moppy

'Great,' I say. 'But don't send it. What's the point? Though I hate to admit it, Jill's right. You don't want to stir things up. And it's a fine womanly tradition writing letters never to be sent.'

'But I want him to regret losing me. Some satisfaction. I still can't sleep, you know.'

'You're not the only one.'

'So what is happening with Mati? Have you heard from him?'

'No, and I don't know what to do. I can't bear the thought of being another one to let him down. And what kind of state will he be in?'

'What do you mean?'

'Sensory deprivation can make even a sane person psychotic.'

'You've got to write to him, Barb, tell him you never meant to go so far. You want to be friends, not his wife.'

'Oh God, it's all so complicated.'

'Now you're sounding like me.'

'Well it would be simpler to go for the boy next door.'

'Ted?'

'Exactly.'

'Are you interested in him?'

'I might be if he wasn't so infatuated with you. You know how it is with lecturers and tutors. Listening to their minds is always a turn-on. Anyway, I'd squash him to death. Can you imagine his skinny body and mine? And he's a poet. Two poets don't make a right.'

'Hughes and Plath.'

'Exactly.'

'The Brownings.'

'The exception to the rule.'

On her back doorstep Moppy finds a poem twisted within two weeping willow stems.

notice how birds
rise above stalkers

and all unanswered
questions

flying is one way
or singing

winging it
word after word

part six

~ a white magnolia ~

One month later Moppy comes home to find a note wrapped around the stem of a white magnolia.

this flower
sweet scent
of innocence
stolen
for you
who, unawares
have stolen
my tongue

'Now he's being upfront,' Moppy says. Jill and I are round at her place for lunch. A week to go before the baby is due. 'Like you, Jill,' she adds. 'Remember my White Magnolia perfume?'

'No.'

'Don't you remember telling me it stank? Mind you, I had stuffed a cotton wool ball saturated in it down my bra.'

'What for?'

'I read it in one of Mum's magazines. A handy hint. Body heat was supposed to make the perfume last longer.'

'A bit much in a Morris Prefect crammed with six teenagers, though.'

'So you do remember.'

'Now that you've reminded me.'

'I never got rid of the smell, or the stain from my best bra, you know. Like my table.'

'What happened to it?' Jill asks, seeing the milky stain.

'It was those bloody roses I bought for Isaac. The vase was cracked. I should send him the bill.'

'Have you heard from him?'

'Yesterday. A letter.'

'What did he say?'

She takes it from a box she has decorated in bark, nuts, driftwood and shells. Reads in a scathing voice.

Darling Moppy,

I am in pain, sitting here reading your letters. Your words leaping off the page and grabbing me by the throat. What power you possess if you only knew it.

I wish you had not experienced the pain of knowing me. Wish that your happiness might have continued. That you had come to understand me better before our untimely end. Logic is not the language of love, my darling, and love for me is suffered in a selfish way. I have needs that are illogical perhaps, but I am reaching out to you. Willing to explore a possible future????

A sorrowful and wiser Isaac

'You're not going to reply are you?'
'No, rest assured, I have learnt something. But it is nice knowing he's sorry. It makes me feel better. Anyway, if I start to waver all I have to do is look at this stain.'
'That reminds me, have you had an AIDs test?' Jill asks.
'Oh God, come with me, Barb? I don't think I can bear to go by myself.'

~ blood and barbed wire ~

On the way to Family Planning, Moppy asks, 'What's up with Mati?'
'He's still there where I left him behind the barbed wire. I haven't had a reply to my letter yet, but I'm not surprised if he's still in D block.'
'So what did you say?'
'I said not marriage but friendship.'
'For ever?'
'All I know is I don't want to live with anyone. Blame my parents' marriage or whatever, I just don't think I can share my space.'

The young female doctor at Family Planning appears to take a dim view of Moppy. 'You should have thought of your children before taking risks,' she says.

Moppy looks sourly at her slim hips and unwrinkled skin. Even the nurse taking her blood seems to have little regard, ramming the needle in without the normal tenderness. She doesn't even put a plaster on the puncture hole. As we are walking back down the street, blood pours down Moppy's arm.

'I wonder if the same opprobrium is cast upon men,' I say.
'I don't think so. Things haven't changed much. It's still women who lose reputations. God knows what I'm going to do while I'm waiting for the results. Six months!'
'Forget about sex and concentrate on work.'
'I know. But it's difficult. Not so much the sex but thinking I'm only half a person without a man. I think I'm addicted to male approval.'

225

'Well you've always had it. Anyway, there's still Ted.'
'True. Jill tells me I should practise positive thinking. Visualise a letter telling me I've won the Visa Gold Award.'
'Jill lives in a fantasy world.'
'Well it works for her.'

We drive back to Moppy's. 'I've made lamingtons. We need to get there before the kids get home and scoff the lot,' she says.
In her letter box an official-type letter is waiting. Moppy has to sit down on the ground when she opens it. 'Read it,' she says, handing it to me.

Dear Margaret,

We are very pleased to inform you that your entry *Barbed Wire* has won the Visa Gold Award.

Moppy is rocking on the ground, her face in her hands, crying or laughing, 'I don't believe it. It's a trick. It's from Ted.'
'Of course it's not. Let's go over there now and tell him.'
'Okay, let's. He might open the door if you're with me.'
Pushing our way through the scraggly hedge, Moppy says, 'Surely it can't have been the power of positive thought. If that's the case, there's a real winner somewhere, someone I've deprived. It's the first time I've entered. It can't be that easy.'
'Don't be silly,' I say, though I too have my doubts. 'The judges said the work was emotionally powerful. Personal and immediate.'

~ at the heart of things ~

Ted's front door is open.
'Strange,' says Moppy. 'Ted, are you there?'
There's no reply. Moppy walks inside. I follow. 'Ted, it's me, Moppy.'
There are wall-to-wall books, paintings, a desk covered in papers, spider webs on the window sills and, in the corner facing the window and the sea view, a chair. Ted is sitting in it. His arm flopped over the side.
'Ted, are you asleep?' I whisper.
He doesn't turn around or move. Moppy runs over, grabs his hand.
'Oh God, I think he's dead,' she says.
His lips are blue. His eyes shut. His face sweating. 'No, no, he's still breathing.'
We pull him to the floor.
'On his side,' Moppy says.

I find the phone under a pile of papers. Mine.

'They're on their way. They said to loosen his clothing and keep him warm.'

Moppy keeps her fingers on his pulse. 'Ted, don't you dare die on us. Ted. Ted,' she calls in urgent voice as if her tone will drag him back from the tunnel. He opens his eyes briefly. Grimaces.

Within ten minutes, though it seems longer, the ambulance arrives. The driver places a oxygen mask over his face and wheels him out. Moppy and I follow to the hospital.

'I seem to be spending my life in hospitals lately,' Moppy says in the waiting room. 'It's not fair. I should be celebrating. But I can't now. What if he dies before we get a chance to really talk?'

'So you're sure now?'

'Absolutely. Even in all the drama I saw the blue notepaper on his desk.' She grabs my arm. 'Tell me he's going to be all right.'

'The ambulance guys didn't seem that worried.'

While Moppy is off phoning her kids, the doctor comes out. An impossibly young woman. 'Your friend should be okay. But we won't really know for a few days. He's had a mild heart attack.'

'Can we see him?'

'No, not today. He needs to rest. But he's a bit of a character, isn't he?'

'Is he?'

'Of course. He wrote a note.' She hands it to us.

Dear Moppy and Barb, it will be some time before I am able to resume normal correspondence. And would you mind securing my abode from alien invaders?

'Tell him message understood.'

By the time Moppy shakily drives us home, Sam and Thomas have eaten most of the lamingtons. 'We saved you some,' Sam says, giving Moppy a hug.

'There's good news and bad,' Moppy says. 'Ted's had a heart attack and I've won an art award.'

'How much?' asks Thomas.

'Is Ted okay?' asks Sam.

'I hope so, but we won't really know until tomorrow.'

'I'm going down to the beach,' Sam says. Thomas screws up his face. He walks past Sam, casually patting his arm.

'God, what a day.' Moppy collapses onto her sofa. 'I need a good howl but somehow I can't seem to summon one up these days. As if there's only a certain

amount of tears stored in the body, like eggs.' She sighs. 'I suppose I ought to go over to Ted's and clean up. He won't want to come home to a mess.'
'You stay there. I'll go over and check it out.'
'Okay, I'm not going to argue.'

If I was a nastier person I'd throw away the note I find on his desk.

there'll always
be visitors, enchanted
with your song

stay high in the branches
your white throat
honest and true

Moppy doesn't realise how lucky she is. I don't care what the ads say. Surely it is a matter of luck, meeting the right person? Like Jill and Ben. Mati is one of the few men I've met who has the ability to understand and accept me. Who hasn't wanted to melt me down, reshape me into his own narrow vision of beauty. But he's in prison, with no hope of parole for years now.

I gather my tentative beginnings of a novel. Ted has made notes in red on some of the pages. On one, *Point of View. Whose?* On another, *cliché, cliché.* And, *Is this believable? I don't think Moppy is as flighty as you make out. She's driven by curiosity more than anything else. She has a boundless imagination which regards everything as interesting.*

There's bound to be something I've missed. Some side of her I don't see.

Moppy clutches the poem I hand her.
'Perhaps we should put it back. We don't know it's meant for me.'
'You can ask him yourself tomorrow.'
'Maybe. Right now I've got to do something with my hair. The *Herald's* coming round to take a photo.'

Driving home in the dark from Moppy's, a news bulletin on the radio announces a prison breakout. Four men, armed and dangerous. Bank robbers and murderers. My blood runs cold. On the Upper Harbour Drive a police roadblock. A policeman walks over and shines a torch around the car interior.
'I know some inmates. Who are they?'
He looks at me without a great deal of curiosity. I thought that a prerequisite. 'No names at present. You just go straight home and lock your door.'

'I will.'

My ears stretch over the house. My eyes out on stalks. If it was Mati, would he come here? I check the back yard with a torch. Looking for the shape of a man, remembering how Mati said the first thing he would do on getting out is lie spreadeagled on the grass. Everything is as I left it this morning, though so much has happened I'm surprised the trees haven't grown another two feet.

For once I am relieved to see the answer phone is not blinking. I take some herbal insomnia pills and for good measure make myself a hot chocolate. What would I do if Mati showed up? I have no attic to stow a fugitive. Nor the desire, I now realise.

In the morning the newspaper does not throw up Mati's name, or any I recognise.

~ all the characters in dreams ~

According to Jung all the characters in dreams are manifestations of yourself. I wonder if it is the same in novels. Most would deny this of course. It suggests a lack of imagination. Sometimes there is an element of suppressed violence in my dreams. My ex de-facto, James, told me I was full of it. Why was I so flattered? Was it before or after the time I threw a belt across the bed? He was laughing, refusing to get out of bed and change his own child's nappies. The buckle clipped James on the cheek. There was blood but I wasn't sorry.

Last night, I dreamt a gunman was stalking Moppy's garden. There was no question the gun was aimed at Moppy and myself. Ted and Mati were also in the house. They told us to lie low. We spent the day hiding in Moppy's bedroom. No doubt the gunman was waiting for us to tire of crawling on floors. However, I noticed Ted and Mati were free to come and go as they pleased. Laughing and talking. Moppy and I were not at all sure what to do about the gunman in her garden. I suggested we offer him breakfast. It had been a long night without any sustenance. And he would have to lay down his gun to eat. Moppy suggested taking a photograph. 'He's quite handsome, after all,' she said.

Writing in my journal I come to the conclusion she's a modern Moll Flanders, except not quite as clever because she wheedles only excitement, not money, from her lovers. Then again, the swiftness of her neck suggests she's unlikely to lose her head at the gallows. In the paper this morning there's a photo of Moppy beside her collages. The headline reads, *Artist cuts through barbed wire with black humour*.

~ regaining fluency ~

'How are you?' Moppy asks Ted the next day. He is sitting up in bed drinking a cup of tea, looking pale and embarrassed. On his bedside table, the newspaper, Moppy grinning.

'Okay.'

She leans towards him to hand him a bunch of Dutch irises and takes the opportunity to peck him on the cheek. This is the difference between us. I could never take that sort of initiative with Ted. A matter of place. Ted is senior to me. He blushes and takes the flowers, looking bemused. 'Th th th th thank you.'

'Don't be silly. It's the least I could do. After all,' she says, 'what about everything you've given me?'

'W W W What do you mean?'

'The notes, the vegetables, the shells. I used some of the notes on my collages. Copies only on brown paper. They seemed apt. So I owe some of my success to you.'

He looks at me. 'D d d did you tell her?'

'No, I saw the paper at your place,' Moppy says.

'I'm s s s sorry. I just c c c c couldn't st st st stop myself. Once I started. And I c c couldn't talk to you. Writing is the only way I c c can communicate with people I don't know.'

'But you do know me. Better than I know myself, I think.'

'You r r r remind me of my wife. She was a d d dancer.'

'I wanted to be a dancer,' says Moppy, 'but my father told me I had the wrong shaped legs.'

'He did you a favour then,' I say.

'Why?'

'You wouldn't have been an artist.'

'My f f f father,' Ted takes a breath, 'wanted me to be an accountant. He was a lawyer but he knew I w w wouldn't be able to speak at the bar.'

'My father wanted me to be a wife and mother.'

'My father had conflicting ideas: on the one hand a nurse, on the other a princess,' Moppy says.

'Should have been Princess Di,' I say, getting up. 'Ted, can I do anything for you? Bring anything?'

'Some books would be nice. Anything. I'll be here for a week.'

'All right. Moppy, I'll wait for you outside.'

Now it's her turn to blush.

Ted winks. 'F f f friends?'

'Yes,' says Moppy. 'I'd like that very much. And who knows?' She smiles. 'Should we seal it with a hug?'

'Please.'

She's shocked at his thinness.

'Well it's not obesity that gave you a heart attack.'

Ted laughs. 'Coronary thrombosis. They s s say with exercise I could live for years yet. I've got to anyway. I've got too much to do. I'm writing a new book.'

'You've stopped stuttering.'

'My tongue regains its facility with friends.'

'I'm flattered.'

'Don't be. Flattery has no place among friends.'

'You mean you won't tell me nice things?'

'Only if they're true.'

'What about lovers?'

'Pardon?'

'Has flattery a place among lovers?'

'Lovers, if they are true, always believe what they are saying to each other, at the time anyway.'

~ stone hearts and the real thing ~

In the middle of the night Ben rings. He apologises to Moppy for waking her. She was awake already. Staring out her uncurtained window at the stars. Jill has had her baby. A girl. A caesarean birth on account of foetal distress. 'But the baby is fine. The most beautiful girl in the world,' says Ben, 'even the nurses said so. Apparently caesarean babies are less wrinkled.' Moppy can only just remember Sam, his squashed button nose, his intense dark eyes, his smooth skin. 'I'm writing up the beginning of her life in her diary now. She's got soft dark hair.'

'They all have,' says Moppy.

She's not sure if she is jealous or not. A girl. Thomas was supposed to be a girl. But no way would she replace him now. Anyway, it is not the baby she wants to hear about but Jill.

'She's fine, a little upset about the caesar, and tired naturally, but thrilled.'

After the phone call, though it's only 5.30 a.m., Moppy gets up and looks through the boys' baby photo albums. The photos look like anyone's. Standard naked in the bath. Nothing to point to an artistic mother. I must have been distracted or too busy, she thinks. And now it's too late. Lost opportunities. The kids automatically poke their tongues out if she focuses a lens on them.

The sun is rising from the sea. Moppy stands on her back steps watching the sky, listening for waves. On the floor of the porch she finds a small flat grey stone tinged in red. A natural heart shape. Not quite perfect. She goes back to bed clutching the stone.

'Funny I didn't notice it before,' Moppy tells me on the way to visit Jill. 'Oh God, I wonder if Ted put it there just before his heart attack.'

'Who can tell?'

The baby lies in Moppy's arms and grasps her finger. As if she knows that being here is enough. Jill is pale and stunned and not really with us.

'I'm glad Tiffany's a girl, I couldn't see myself as a mother of a boy. And she'll look gorgeous in smocked dresses.'

'She may have other ideas,' I say, for in the brief moment I get to hold her I perceive this is not a pretty dress-wearing child but someone altogether different.

~ how to frame ~

The secret of good wine, they tell me, is observation. The exact moment for picking the grapes, recognising the particular bloom on the skin and then, years later, opening the bottle when it has declared itself to be ready. If only virgins would apply the same principles. So many vinegary after-tastes avoided.

The experts have it down pat, but for me nothing is certain or permanent. Sometimes it is necessary to pick the grapes the moment they ripen. Sometimes to let them develop a faint overbloom of mould. I go home promising a poem for the baby, only to find I have no wisdom to pass on.

I go outside, lie on the ground and write a poem for Mati instead.

how to frame it

the inmate said
the first thing

he'll do when
he gets out

is lie
on the grass

eyes facing up
raining or not

in my back yard
spring buds

and the sky
deepest blue

I lay beneath
the melia tree

looking for
an angle

the earth smells
of rain and fat worms

I get
the picture

Moppy rings to tell me she is going to be on *Holmes* tonight. 'I've borrowed Jill's purple Wallace Rose top.'

'Isn't it more important what you say?'

'Of course, but I'm not going out to the nation looking like a scruffy no-hope artist. Bugger the stereotypes.'

~ it ain't over till the thin lady sings ~

I should have known Moppy would end up winning nearly everything. Do I need to spell it out? Fame and fortune, even love in a funny kind of way. When Ted comes home after a week she has a small party to celebrate. Ted shuffles in, smiling shyly. I notice he's wearing a new green jumper. Reflecting the colour of his eyes and of mine. Sean is invited but declines on the grounds that he is currently inspired. 'Whatever that means,' says Moppy, rolling her eyes. Ben and Jill arrive with Tiffany who's sporting a pink bow around her bald head and is asleep, thankfully. Jill wants to see Moppy's interview with Holmes. Moppy half-heartedly protests, 'This is not about me,' before inserting the video. 'Oh God, I look so fat,' she says, expecting us to contradict her. We do.

She comes across as charmingly naive. Holmes is leaning forward as if he's really interested.

'I see you surround your photographs with letters, feathers, driftwood, poems. Where do you get your inspiration, Moppy?'

'By being observant and willing to use what comes my way.'

'Ah ha, and does a lot come your way?'

Moppy laughs. 'You could say that I have a talent for attracting material. You know, things happen to me.'

'I do know.' Holmes raises his eyebrows with a sideways glance off camera. 'You're a solo mother with a part-time job and two kids, is it, is it hard to find the time for art?'

'Yes, though it's even more difficult claiming space.'

'Claiming space? You mean a studio?'

'No, I mean believing in yourself, in your right to be an artist. Coming from a working-class background I've found it a struggle. Friends help. One of my oldest friends is the poet Barb Ballard. She's always believed being an artist was possible. Such faith is infectious.'

'Already you've attracted negative comments on your work. How do you deal with that? With the tall poppy syndrome.' Again he passes a sideways, I should know look.

'It's not easy. I don't really fit into any category. Neither painter, photographer or sculptor. Some people accuse me of being too personal, of tearing up pieces of my life. As if I'd achieved the whole effect with a glue gun and sleight of hand. As if I'm not capable of thinking.' She laughs, edgily.

'And what are you trying to say?'

'I don't believe it's my job to interpret my work. I will say my mother has a Depression mentality. She never wastes anything. And she taught me to appreciate the things around me. Natural things. I've always been a collector of flotsam.'

'A woman after my own heart. And those were our people today,' says Holmes.

'You might have mentioned me,' says Jill.

'Oh Jill,' says Moppy, giving her a hug, 'don't be mad. You know I love you. Anyway I was distracted. Thinking, was Holmes going to make a move?'

'C can understand that. You are an enchantress, after all,' says Ted. 'But are you a collector of jetsam as well?'

'What's the difference?' asks Moppy.

Ted takes a breath and it's as if he is taking a tutorial again, disciples at his feet. 'Jetsam are goods deliberately thrown overboard to lighten a load maybe. They may sink or float. Whereas flotsam comes from a wreckage and floats.'

'I was really talking about driftwood and shells, but it's an interesting distinction.'

'Especially if you use it as a metaphor,' I say.

'What for?'

'Think about it. In personal relationships. Jetsam: deliberate, unwanted, may sink.'

'I get it,' says Moppy. 'With flotsam you only pick up what comes your way accidentally.'

'Exactly.'

'Does that include poems?' Ted blushes.

'Of course.'

'Well from now on I'm sticking to flotsam only. I promise.'

~ sorry Moppy but I get the last word ~

Trust Moppy to insinuate herself into the last page. I was saving it for myself. A subtle subversion. But though the story is hers, in the end I am the writer, owning the last word. Unlike the art salesman at the bar whose story I began with and never finished.

'Western women talk too much', he said, telling us about his trip to Japan. Geishas are taught how to listen. Make-up caked on so thick, clients can relax, knowing the real person's face is deep beneath and impenetrable. Only the mouth opening enough to permit a small, agreeable smile.

The salesman was curious to know the fate of the tigers. Like Jozef, he maintained he was once tricked into marriage. In other words, he didn't get what he'd bargained for.

He ordered a Virgin Caesar for himself and asked Moppy and I if we wanted a Screaming Orgasm.

Moppy nodded.

'No,' I said, anxious to leave before I gave too much away, before my tongue shrank to fit.